The Master of Geneva

Books by Gladys H. Barr

Monk in Armour

The Master of Geneva

For Children

The Tinker's Armor

The Master of Geneva

A Novel Based on the Life of John Calvin

By Gladys H. Barr

Holt, Rinehart and Winston / New York

Library of Congress Catalog Card Number: 61-13077

Designer: Ernst Reichl

80814-0111

Printed in the United States of America

For Ruth

with deep affection

Acknowledgments

A book is the product of the efforts of many people. This one could not have been written without the encouragement, advice, and shared knowledge of the late Dr. J. M. Batten, former Professor of Church History at the Divinity School, Vanderbilt University, Nashville, Tennessee; John Tiffany Elliott; Miss Ruth M. Elmquist; Mrs. Denise Lemoge, former secretary to Dr. Clayton Williams of the American Church of Paris; Dr. Paul Conord, Executive Secretary of the Reformed Church of France and compiler of *Images du Passé Protestant Français;* Mme. Conord and Mlle. Suzanne Conord; Mlle. I. L. Teillas, Calvin historian and guide at the Cathedral of St. Peter's, Geneva; Dr. Paul Freeland, Secretary of Overseas and Interchurch Aid for the Board of World Missions of the Presbyterian Church in the United States and recent chairman of overseas secretaries for the World Council of Churches; Dr. Bard Thompson, currently Professor of Church History at the Divinity School of Vanderbilt and author of *The Emblems of Our Tradition* and *Reformed Liturgies in Translation;* Dr. Ernest Trice Thompson, author, Professor of Church History at the Union Theological Seminary, Richmond, Virginia, and recent Moderator of the Presbyterian Church in the United States; my very dear friend and critic, the late Raymond Goldman, and Mrs. P. M. Davis, both of Watkins Institute, Nashville, Tennessee; Dr. George A. Buttrick, whose helpful literary criticism was invaluable; Dr. Harry W. Hastings, former Professor of Creative Writing at the University of the State of New York, Albany; J. Edward Lantz, an executive secretary of the National Council of Churches; and my husband, Thomas Calhoun Barr, theological consultant, adviser, critic, and companion on the journeys through France and Switzerland on the trail of John Calvin.

G.H.B.

Nashville, Tennessee

Preface

This book is the result of sixteen years of research and writing. I have explored libraries in this country and in many parts of Europe for material that would help me to depict the real John Calvin, who has been buried under the dust of the centuries, the errors of his biographers (Protestant, Catholic, and others), the misconceptions of those who claim his theology today, the ignorance of the many, and the misunderstanding of those who have not delved thoroughly into history and contemporary records.

Although this book is fiction, it is written within the historical framework of the Reformation period, for the Master of Geneva can best be understood from his many writings, including portions of his commentaries, the prefaces to all of them, his sermons, his prayers, and his letters; from the letters of his friends and acquaintances; from the records of Geneva and Bern, including the *Livre des Anglais,* and, most important of all, from the definitive edition of *The Institutes of the Christian Religion.* Many other memoirs, documents, histories, articles, and papers were studied in the original, and I myself translated a number of them.

John Calvin needs no defense. But in the process of completing this work I came to agree with the late Dr. J. M. Batten that Calvin is the most misunderstood figure in the history of the Christian

Church. Any informed, thinking person would concede his genius, his great contribution to civilization and religion. But how deluded we have been about his warmth and humor. No one could read his letters without being warmed by the radiance of his personality, for his devotion to God and to his friends, his love of companionship, his great faith, his selflessness, the breadth of his intellect, his humor, all shine forth. Let any who doubt Calvin's humor read his *Antidote against the Articles of the Sorbonne*.

An example of the many errors made by his critics is found in the accusation that Calvin was responsible for the "burning" of Michael Servetus. Probably Servetus himself died believing this.

Having been trained as a lawyer, and having, therefore, a knowledge of the rules of evidence, I have examined the facts and they do not support this contention. On the contrary, *according to the records*, John Calvin interceded with the councilmen, begging mercy for this scoundrel. Although a product of that era in believing it better to destroy a blasphemer than to allow his diseased conception to be passed on at the expense of souls, Calvin was opposed to the stake. Further, in the case of Servetus, it is clear that the sentence was pronounced by Calvin's enemies, the Libertines, who were in the majority on the Council. William Farel, who was instrumental in bringing about the Reformation in Geneva, states in a letter to Calvin his feeling that it was magnanimous of him to plead for mercy for such a man. It should be pointed out that previously, in Vienna, the Roman Catholics had sentenced Servetus to the stake and that he had escaped. In fairness, it should also be said that Servetus—although a troublemaker, condemned by all the churchmen of the day for stirring constant dissension—was a brilliant man.

The drama of Calvin's life seems incredible, but the facts are on record. He walked between drawn swords, offering his life as a sacrifice. The story of his journey to Ferrara and his visit to Renée of France has a basis in history. Some may ask if it actually took him a decade to leave the Church of his youth. Again the facts are plain: he had grown up in a family devoted to the Church of Rome, and he never ceased to long for unity *among all Christians* with Christ as the cornerstone.

Calvin's love of the inheritance from Judaism and his joy in the belief that Christians are the spiritual children of Abraham, direct descendants by the Spirit, were also abiding.

In our own country today we hear—and will continue to hear—much of the doctrine of the separation of Church and State. Calvin's insistence on the distinction between a religious and civil society was at the root of much of his struggle. He speaks of the Christian State and the Christian Church upholding each other and at the same time independent of each other. The State must protect the Church, but has no right to dictate to it. At the same time, the field of politics is an important concern for the Christian.

The dialogue in this book is based on Calvin's beliefs and includes, as far as possible, statements in his own words, taken from his writings.

Mention should be made of two quotations from his contemporaries. The first is from the *Life of John Calvin* by Theodore de Beza, his co-worker in Geneva: "The thing to be wondered at is that a single man, as if he had been a kind of Christian Hercules, should have been able to subdue so many monsters, and this by that mightiest of all clubs, the Word of God." The other judgment was made by Pope Pius IV when he learned of the reformer's death: "The strength of that heretic consisted in this, that money never had the slightest charm for him. If I had such servants, my kingdom would extend from sea to sea."

For those who would like to read more about the Master of Geneva, I suggest Theodore de Beza's *Life of John Calvin*. There is also a modern scholar who has shed new light on this reformer and his life—Dr. John T. McNeil, a former professor at Union Theological Seminary in New York. Anyone who is interested in Calvin's attitude toward politics should read Dr. McNeil's *John Calvin on God and Political Duty*. I have never met Dr. McNeil, but he is a scholar to applaud!

G.H.B.
Nashville, Tennessee

The Master of Geneva

Christmas Day, 1559

The people came through the melting snow from every part of Geneva—from the isle, St. Gervais, and the city proper—crossing the new stone bridge, pressing forward to St. Peter's Church with the tall wooden spire that pointed to the clear blue sky. Soon hundreds were assembled in the old church—boys, girls, young men, young ladies, women noticeably without unseemly jewelry; men from all walks of life—syndics or magistrates, councilmen or senators, ministers, educators, prominent citizens, and the humble who worked with their hands. No seats had been reserved for the influential. In St. Peter's the rich and the poor were treated alike.

It was Christmas Day in the year the first Synod of the Reformed Church met in France and the year the Academy at Geneva was founded. In the high tower where John Calvin, the Master of Geneva, had worked, meditated, wept, and prayed, the ancient bells, the *Clemence* and the *Bellerive,* rang forth. An eminent personage was to be honored by the gathering, and the bells were honoring him, too.

Below, in St. Peter's Square, a herald, in blue velvet with epaulets

15

of gold, motioned to the people to make an aisle. There was a stir as a thin man of fifty, dressed in a black vestment, a heavy cloak, and a small velvet hat, walked quietly toward the church. His eyes in their sunken sockets were diamond-bright. His frame was bent, but he walked proudly, slowly, through the crowd toward the large stone church. For an instant there was silence; then a cheer sounded, and another, until the air trembled with shouts for this man who was to be made a citizen of Geneva this wintry morning.

Inside there was a turning of heads, a whispering as of dried leaves stirred by the winter wind, a flutter as the man made his way past the city guard, in neat blue uniforms, with breeches that were not slashed or otherwise unseemly. "There goes the Master of Geneva." "Master Calvin, God bless him!"

As he became aware of the excitement his appearance aroused, tears came unbidden. He moved quietly to his accustomed place behind the communion table and turned compelling black eyes to survey tenderly all the love-filled faces. His spiritual children!

His enemies, the enemies of the Gospel, had accused him of political ambitions, but he had never asked to be made a citizen or burgher, though actually he had ached to belong, to be a Genevan. Now he would no longer be a foreigner, "that Frenchman" as he had often been called in derision. He would never again be pelted with stones or filth from their chamber pots. Dogs would no longer be named "Calvin," except perhaps a favorite or beloved pet. This was triumph indeed! The plotting against God and against him as God's servant had stopped. After twenty-three years of agonizing struggle he belonged, for today the people were voluntarily making him a citizen.

How grateful he was! God still worked miracles. The stone which Geneva's builders had rejected—the Son of God—had become the chief cornerstone. These spiritual children would grow in grace, in the knowledge that their Saviour, the Schoolmaster, the Lord Jesus Christ, had led them and their city out of a labyrinth of darkness into the light. How satisfying to come to such a day!

Memories of years gone by crowded upon him. He could see the woman he had loved smiling warmly, her deep devotion shining from her clear brown eyes. She knew what was happening on this

Christmas Day. She, too, was proud and happy that he had won God's battle. From Geneva the word of God was spreading into many parts of the world. From the newly founded Academy, begun as a dream in his mind, pure Christianity would permeate the nations of the world, as its students, nourished in Christian Truth, returned to their native lands.

Beside John sat Theodore de Beza, his most beloved disciple, who had been reclaimed by the Gospel and would one day, perhaps not far distant, succeed Calvin and carry on God's work. On the front bench sat François Bonivard, who had served a prison sentence at Chillon for his faith, and through whose generosity the Academy had been built. John could not help comparing such men with the Libertines, or patriots, whose covetousness and hard hearts had brought havoc to the city. The prisoner of Chillon would long be remembered. Theodore would grow great in his service to God. Future generations, reading the Minutes of the Council of Geneva, learning of the evil deeds of the Favres, Ami Perrin, the Camaret brothers, young Philibert Berthelier, and Pierre Ameaux, might well ask: Why do men created in God's own image stumble through the darkness when they have eternal life within their reach?

John sighed as he listened to the voices lauding God's work which he had helped God accomplish. The years rolled back. I did my best, he thought. I tried to seek God's will and do it. Poorly sometimes, but I tried. God led. I followed. Obedience. . . . If only men would make that the key to their lives.

"Dear God"—John's lips moved silently—"what an ignorant superstitious fool I was!" In his mind a phrase repeated itself: After darkness, light. That was what the sign over the entrance to the Academy read. After darkness, light. "Light for thy city, God. I knew thou wert sovereign. Yet at times the way was so difficult. But I never prayed for an easy task, only that I might be thy faithful servant."

17

1

April, 1521
Noyon, France

"John! Wake up! The bishop has come to see you!"

John opened his eyes to see his nine-year-old sister, Mary, standing in the high-arched doorway. He caught his breath in surprise. "The bishop has come to see me?"

He sprang out of bed and washed his face hurriedly with cold water from the blue bowl on the table, rubbing away the chill with the linen strip hanging on a peg above him. He combed his long, black hair and slipped into his clothes. Then, tiptoeing past six-year-old Anthony, who was still asleep, John closed the door quietly behind him and ran down the stairs.

Bishop de Hangest, a corpulent man with earnest blue eyes and something no other bishop had—a rich, curling beard—sat on a sturdy chair at the big round table in the family room. A smile of kindness lighted his square face.

"John, sit here beside me," he said. "I want to talk to you."

John drew up a chair.

"You may know why I have come, John. You are a bright boy. You could be a valuable servant of the Church when you grow up.

I have discussed the matter at length with your father. You are almost twelve years old. Have you thought about becoming a priest like your brother Charles?"

John found it difficult to answer because of the lump in his throat. Had he thought about it? It was an obsession.

"Oh, your Grace," he said exultantly, "I have dreamed of nothing else! There is only one thing . . ." He drew his brows together in a troubled frown.

"What is that, my son? If you are worried about the cost of your education, you will be given a small benefice to defray that."

"That's not it, your Grace. I am timid. A priest has to help people. Perhaps I would make too poor a priest. Maybe I should do something else."

"Nonsense! As far as I can determine, there's only one thing wrong with you. You're as thin as a lathe. You study too much. You must get out and play. And I suggest that you receive the tonsure next month on the day of Corpus Christi."

"There is nothing I would rather do, your Grace."

"Then it is settled." The bishop rose and placed a reassuring hand on John's head. "If you will trust God, he will give you courage, my son."

He smiled so warmly that John lost all of his doubts. If the bishop said God would help him, there was nothing to worry about. Joy flooded through him.

"Oh, your Grace! I will study hard. I will do everything to help people be good Christians. And I'll always remember that you had faith in me!"

Three of the bishop's nephews, who were of the noble family of Mommor, lived near Noyon. The two youngest, Joachim and Ives, had large blue eyes set widely apart in a square face, like their uncle's. But the eldest, Claude, at fourteen, had an aquiline nose, narrow green eyes, and prominent cheekbones. He was tall for his age, with broad shoulders, a narrow waist, and a large frame. He enjoyed sports—falconry, fencing, fishing, and hunting—but he was not a good student. Nor did he have any inclination to enter the priesthood. The bishop deplored both attitudes.

That afternoon, after Bishop de Hangest's visit to the son of his

Apostolic Notary and secretary, he announced to Claude that John Calvin was to receive the tonsure.

"Let John study with Joachim, Ives, and me!" Claude pleaded, his green eyes alight. "Why not hire one teacher for us all?"

"I was considering that. Later when you go to the College of the Capettes, the high school, and the colleges in Paris, he could accompany you. He has such good common sense that I would feel better having him with you in a city like Paris."

"Then it is settled? I may go and tell John?"

"Yes. Tell him to arrange to stay at the castle with you during the week."

Claude ran to the stables and ordered his horse saddled. Vaulting onto the animal's back, he headed at a swift gallop toward the city and the grain-market square where John lived with his father, two brothers, and two sisters.

A sudden commotion caught Claude's attention as he slid to the cobbles. In front of the inn next door, a group of boys circled a small figure—John Calvin.

"Little Bird," a big bully taunted. "So you want to play Leap-over-the-Frog? You couldn't even jump over a broomstick!"

Anthony, John's little brother, spoke. "He could, too! My brother can do anything!"

"All right. We'll see if he can fight. Put up your fists, Little Bird."

John flushed. "Do we have to fight about nothing?"

The boys guffawed loudly. "No," said one with a face like a weasel. "If we were the size of a bird, we wouldn't want to fight either!"

Backed against the iron fence, John faced his antagonist, distressed and silent. The bully opened his mouth and spit. As the saliva found its mark on John's face, his black eyes began to glitter, his jaw tightened, his lips thinned. He lifted his fists and somehow he suddenly looked taller.

The bully's fist caught John on the side of the head and sent him reeling, but he sprang forward and with lowered head struck his tormentor in the midriff. The bully let out a roar as he landed on the cobbles. Cursing, he scrambled to his feet and edged toward John like a tiger stalking a small woods animal.

Claude shoved between them. He was a head taller than the bully. "Why not fight somebody nearer your own size?" he challenged.

The bully bit his lip. "I have nothing against you, Claude," he managed in a small voice.

"Well, I have against you. I hate cowards. Put up your fists!"

With an oath the bully began to dance about, striking the air as Claude sidestepped his blows. When the bully began to pant and puff, Claude knocked him down, and standing over him, said, "If I ever hear of you heckling John Calvin again, I vow I'll knock your crown off. Maybe he is small. Maybe he can't fight a boy twice his size. It was a magnificent try!"

"I—I was just having a little fun, Claude. I have nothing against John Calvin."

"Well, he has some qualities you'll never have. He has a loyalty to everything good. Get up and get out of my sight before I mop the cobbles with you!"

Claude smiled to himself as the bully scrambled to his feet and ran off, head bent, shoulders drooping. The other boys followed with solemn faces. Claude turned to John and their eyes met. There was no need of words. John couldn't speak anyway. His full lips quivered and he was close to tears, but the squeeze of his hand was warm as the two walked together to his house.

The May sunshine was streaming through the door which opened onto an oblong balcony outside John's bedchamber. Birds, perched on the slanting roof of the inn next door, were singing. A single robin flew down to sit on the wooden railing. From the tall towers of Notre Dame of Noyon, on the hill above, bells were pealing. John's heart swelled with their melody, the song of the birds, and the joy within him. This was the day of Corpus Christi when he would give himself in service to God and to the Church!

There was a knock on the door and a young man with shoulder-length brown hair peered around the paneling. He had a thoughtful face with great, dark eyes, large nose, and rounded jaw.

"Peter Robert!" John threw himself into the arms of his favorite cousin.

21

Peter hugged the lad against his dusty doublet, touching a whiskered cheek to first one side of the bright young face and then the other.

"I had to come for the rite, little John. My best wishes for a life of service!"

"The cassock is big"—John pulled out its loose folds and laughed —"but I shall grow." He grabbed Peter by the hand and led him to the bed. They sat on the edge of it facing each other. "We have an hour before the procession starts. Tell me about Paris, Peter Robert. I shall go there one day!"

Peter Robert described the walled city with its dark crenelated turrets, its gardens heavy with growth; the great churches of St. Chapelle, St. Étienne du Mont, St. Gervais, St. Mathurin, St. Germain, Notre Dame; the Louvre, which was the Palace of King Francis; the Inn of the Pelican, where the students spent their evenings; the musty college buildings. He told, too, of the immorality, the brutality, and all the new ideas circulating there.

"With so many churches men should be good!" John said.

Peter Robert shook his head. "Brute strength and success are men's gods today. If a man stands in another's way, he is cut down."

"I can see why a man would want to fight for God, a good woman, or for his country."

"Today men fight for the sake of fighting. They are not only bloodthirsty but foolhardy. In Paris you will see sights you must turn away from. Human life is cheap."

"There are good Christians in Paris?"

"Oh, yes, many of them. But they find life very hard."

"Have you ever known any heretics, Cousin Peter?"

Peter Robert smiled. "One of my professors, Dr. James Le Fèvre, is considered by some the most dangerous heretic in all France. But he loves the Church with his whole heart. He vows he will never leave it as the Lutherans do."

"What does he teach?"

"That Christians ought to obey God rather than man. That they should study the Word of God in the Holy Bible, which tells them not to bow down to images or pray for the intercession of saints, but to look only to God for their salvation."

"Dr. Le Fèvre must be a wicked heretic."

"I am wondering if he could be right. 'Tis true your father defines heresy as anything against the Church of Rome. But freedom's foundation is the right to disagree. If people are worshiping the Church today instead of Jesus Christ, that is usurping God's power."

"Peter Robert, a man could lose his soul listening to a professor like that!"

"At least Dr. Le Fèvre knows what he believes, and why. He will never surrender the authority of his mind. A heretic these days seems to be anyone who has opinions of his own."

When John followed Peter Robert downstairs, he saw his father standing in the family room surrounded by some of the canons. He could tell at a glance that his father was angry, for Gerard Calvin's heavy black brows were drawn together above eyes that sparked.

"We will continue our discussion in the morning," a short priest with protruding ears said stiffly.

John's father nodded wearily. "In the morning."

The canons filed out, shaking their heads.

"Is something wrong, Papa?"

"The canons threaten to appeal to Rome unless the bishop gets rid of his beard. There is no end to the silly wrangling."

"With our Gallic temper, if Picards are not fighting about one thing, it will be another," Peter Robert said with a twinkle. "But why won't the bishop shave?"

There was a tiredness about Gerard Calvin's mouth and eyes and his large body slumped visibly. "It's a matter of principle with him. His beard has become a symbol of mental freedom. After all, what does a beard have to do with man's salvation?"

"Is the bishop a Humanist?" John asked later, as he walked across the grain-market square beside his cousin.

"No, I wouldn't say so. He has a mind of his own. He chastises any priest who fails to live like a Christian."

"I hope I can live up to his faith in me," John said, "even though

23

the world seems to be in the midst of a great revolution. Where do the Humanists seek converts?"

"Everywhere. Many believe in God, yet call everything into question, including the fundamental beliefs of the Church. These disciples of the New Learning vie with each other to convince people that they are right."

The procession was moving toward the cathedral as John and Peter Robert reached the top of the hill. Crimson and gold banners were flying in the wind. The smoke from the censers rolled upward as the Sacred Host approached, borne by four lackeys in uniforms of gold-cloth. Happy children skipped behind it, trailing wreaths of ivy. Four horses in scarlet blankets drew the carriage of the bishop and the visiting cardinal. Boys robed in white lifted sweet voices in a litany.

Peter Robert nudged John. "Look at Anthony. Your little brother may be dressed in choir white with a proper black bow under his dimpled chin, but the Devil still peeps from his eyes."

John smiled. Anthony's sweet, clear voice could be heard above the others and his expression was that of a saint. But in truth he was all boy, as their housekeeper often complained.

The stately parade trailed on: wardens, monks, and priests in their fiddle-shaped garments, followed by portly citizens in fine doublets, breeches, cloaks, and elaborate hats; nobles in velvet, fur, and brocade; the common people in somber-hued clothes.

"The relics today have magical powers to protect us from demons, witches, and other evil spirits," John whispered, as he stood in line with Peter Robert, waiting to see them.

"What are they?"

"Two nails from the cross and the original crown of thorns!"

"How happy your mother would have been to see them if she had lived, and how proud when you are shorn this afternoon!"

John reflected that her piety was one reason for his wanting to enter the service of the Church. Although he had been very young when she died, he could remember her sweet face as she bowed in prayer. She had often taken him on pilgrimages and he had watched as she wept over the bleeding wounds of an image, or kissed the piece of wood from the "true" Cross, some hairs from the head of John the Baptist, or a tooth of Our Lord. He had a sudden feeling now that her spirit was hovering over him, and he knew she was happy because he had decided to become a priest.

As John took his place on the bench at the front of the chapel, golden sunshine, streaming through the cloister windows, seemed to give warm promise of good to come. The smell of incense mingled with the musty odors of the high-ceilinged room. In the flickering candlelight, the bright threads of the embroidered sleeve of his surplice glistened as he sat quietly, the holy silence broken only by the pealing of the bells, the shuffling of feet on the decorated stone squares, and soft whispers of those assembled for the solemn rite of tonsure.

An excited, fluttery feeling spread through him. There had been occasional doubts, but ever since he could remember he had felt that whatever value his life might have would lie in the priesthood. Now, with the peace of the chapel enfolding him, he reflected that being a priest in such a world as Peter Robert described was not going to be easy. There would be pitfalls, but Bishop de Hangest said that a man's duty was to seek God's will and do it.

The bishop came through the cloister door, moving majestically, his face almost hidden by the rich, brown beard. He was clothed in canonical robe and wore a miter on his head, and he carried a pair of long, shiny scissors.

As the boys' choir came in, two by two, moving to chairs at one side of the altar, Anthony's round, bright eyes met John's as if to say: I know what this means to you.

And suddenly in the high-arched chapel the only sound was the deep voice of the bishop. The moment had come!

John could see his family sitting near the front. His father's massive figure was leaning forward. His little sisters, Mary and Tina, stared wide-eyed. His older brother, Charles, was sitting up very straight.

John's knees were shaking and he turned for an instant to look directly at Peter Robert, who smiled his approval.

Then the bishop was saying, "What is your wish, John Calvin?"

"To serve God and His Church."

"Kneel."

John obeyed, and the bishop, placing a huge hand on the boy's head, began to pray: "May the Lord guide you . . ." Then he read from the Holy Writ those verses in which Jesus said it was the duty of his followers to love the Lord their God with their whole heart and their neighbors as themselves.

"May God guide you to be his good servant," intoned the choir.

When the chant died away, the bishop sat on a high-backed chair and, one by one, slowly clipped five pieces of John's shoulder-length hair, signifying his separation from the world of the five senses.

"What is your inheritance?"

"The Lord is my inheritance!" John's voice was a bare whisper.

In that instant he felt as if he could reach out and touch His garments. He hoped it would always be that way. Then he would never be afraid, not even of strange people.

He bowed his head and breathed a prayer: "I give Thee my life, Lord. It's not much, but I will try to seek Thy will and do it. May I do all for the glory and honor of Thy blessed name. And for the glory of Thy great Church! Amen! Amen!"

The bishop raised his hand in blessing. "My son, you are now a chaplain in God's Church. Serve Him well!"

John's heart was racing faster and faster, and he ran his hand proudly over his shorn head.

2

April 6, 1523

Standing on the steps of the Cathedral of Notre Dame, in the Island City of Paris late on a spring afternoon, young John looked about him at the houses with their overhanging upper stories and square chimneys, at the domes and spires visible in all directions under the cloudy sky. Gray and white pigeons, strutting on the cobbles, filled the air with their gentle chatter as people crossed the great square from all directions, converging on the church. A lop-eared dog scratched fleas in the middle of the Grève beneath a dangling gallows, and some tattered mendicants, palms outstretched, sat near the wide cathedral doors. High in the stone towers the bells were pealing, calling the faithful to worship.

It was John's first day in the city, and in all his fourteen years he had never seen so many elegantly attired people. There were gentlemen in velvet, silk, or brocaded doublets and fine hose; students in bright colors; ladies with jewels and a bold display of bosom, their silk and velvet gowns rustling under beautiful cloaks; most of them clung to the arms of noblemen in furred coats and feathered hats. But there were poor citizens, too, wearing drab garments, even rags;

their features were pinched, their eyes tired. Coquettes passed, eying John with knowing glances. When one sidled close, he quickly looked the other way. Peter Robert had been right when he said that material possessions, brute strength, and success were men's gods, for many who passed appeared to have their minds on everything and anything except God. With a sigh John turned and entered the cathedral.

At one end a window of many-colored glass let the sunlight through like the radiance of God's love. Tall tapers burned before the saints in their niches. Crossing himself, John moved to an altar where he knelt to recite the litany to the Blessed Virgin. The image was a thing of beauty, gowned in soft azure and hooded with a white wimple below which clear blue eyes looked down from an oval face of great purity.

Nicholas Cop, the eighteen-year-old son of the First Physician to King Francis and former physician to Louis XII, kneeling behind John, noticed the young chaplain's concentration, the earnestness with which he moved his lips, his great reverence as he bowed his shorn head. When he rose and began to walk, his determined stride was that of one of great purpose. His angular face was arresting. Large black eyes beneath slightly arched brows had an expression of wisdom unusual for one so young. The nose was straight, the sensitive mouth full-lipped. Nicholas, following him out into the square, felt that there was an appealing quality about him, a fresh earnestness that seemed touching.

At the fountain across the Grève, some citizens were exchanging news of the war. Rumors had spread, filling the city with awe. When John paused to listen, Nicholas paused, too. The King, one rough citizen was announcing, had sent twenty-five thousand men toward the Alps and he would follow to take command. It was feared that Pope Adrian VI, having been the Emperor's tutor, would be as powerful an ally against France as was Henry VIII across the channel.

"A united France must defeat her foes!" "The day of the old dukes is gone!" "We are now a French nation!" "Death to all enemies, be they dukes or peasants!" "*Vive la France!* Down with her enemies!" the voices shouted, and hands waved two-edged daggers.

28

"Death!" "Death!" "Death!" "Down with the King of England! Up with the salamander!"

Nicholas remembered that the salamander was on the standard of Francis I. Apparently these citizens were loyal subjects. He wished the King could hear them.

There was a sharp clatter of hoofs as a troop of gendarmes descended upon the square. Waving swords and halberds, the soldiers charged at the citizens.

"Disperse! To your homes, rabble!" the captain shouted. "Out of the way!"

A little boy was directly in the path of the thundering hoofs, and there was a sharp cry as the child dodged this way and that.

"Run, you ugly whelp," one of the men shouted. He made straight for the child, and flying hoofs struck him, knocking him to the stones. The gendarme did not even pause as he charged after the fleeing citizens.

By the time Nicholas reached the limp body, the young chaplain was bending over the child. Gently he lifted him and carried him to a grassy spot at the edge of the square where he laid him down.

The boy opened his eyes, felt the welt on the side of his head, and rubbed one of his unusually prominent ears. For an instant he looked dazed. Then he cried, "The gendarme! He——" The child broke off, choking back a sob.

"The gendarmes are beasts. Somebody ought to report them. The King should be told of the outrage. I shall speak to the rector of the Collège de la Marche. He will know what to do!"

The boy sat up, his grimy face streaked with tears. He pulled frantically on the chaplain's doublet. "Not Rector Beda. Pray do not tell him. He will flog me!"

"Rector Beda? Do you know him?"

"I work at the school for my food. They call me Nerien. Promise, oh, promise you won't tell the rector!"

"Has he ever flogged you?" The young chaplain was frowning. His fists were clenched tightly, and his eyes seemed to shoot sparks.

"He flogs me almost every day." The boy pulled down his ragged shirt to show the ugly welts that striped his back. "He says I am lazy!"

The young chaplain gritted his teeth. "He has no right to be so cruel! I am a student at the school. Maybe I can do something."

The child threw his arms around the older boy. "I have another friend, Master Cordier, who teaches Latin. I have never had two friends!"

"You have now, Nerien."

Nicholas Cop was sure these two were people he wanted to know. He turned to the chaplain. "My name is Nicholas Cop," he said. "I am a student at the Collège de Montaigu. I will help you carry the boy."

Every time John said his prayers, in the weeks that followed, he gave thanks that he did not have to live in the school. Nerien had not exaggerated. The Collège de la Marche comprised two filthy old houses on a dingy courtyard; in one languages were taught; in the other, literature. Too often the pupils appeared with bruises on their bodies and welts striping their backs. The rector said openly that he welcomed an excuse to flog a boy, since his leather-thonged whip made young Christians. The boys, who slept in crowded bedchambers, scratched and squirmed during classes as lice and bedbugs grew fat upon their undernourished bodies. Their meager food, they whispered, often had long brown roaches in it, but to complain was to receive a flogging. So they were silent.

In John's large, airy room at his uncle Richard's near the Louvre, he studied long hours and then slept soundly. As at Noyon, he was awakened by silver-toned bells, for his window opened toward the Church of St. Germain. He watched the royal processions pass and wondered what it would be like to journey with a long retinue to the King's country château. He ate his aunt's good food and grew a little. The bishop's nephews had rooms nearby in the Rue St. Jacques, where John studied with them twice a week. Peter Robert lived with another uncle. On Sundays they all had dinner together at the home of one relative or the other, and sometimes John's aunts let him invite Nicholas Cop.

One Friday in May, as John sat at his table with his quill poised, he could hear through the open window the noise of the traffic on the streets below, and the loud pounding from his uncle's blacksmith shop downstairs. Master Cordier had told him that morning that he had had only one other pupil who so excelled in Latin, a nobleman named Berquin. He had divulged, too, that Joachim, Ives, and Claude were improving their skill in translating and writing Latin. How pleased the bishop would be to learn of such progress!

"John!" The shrill voice of his aunt broke into his thoughts, and he rose and went to the door. "You have a small visitor, John. Such a one!"

Up the stairs came Nerien, his face wet with tears. "Oh, *mon ami!* Something terrible has happened!"

John put his arm around the small boy and led him to the bed. "Sit down, Nerien, and tell me about it."

The little face quivered. "The rector says I must leave the school, but I have nowhere to go!"

"What happened?"

"I dropped a heavy tureen, broke it, and spilled the soup. The rector beat me until the blood came," the child sobbed. "Please ask him to let me stay. I will do anything!"

"Can you sweep?"

The boy stopped crying. His blue eyes brightened, and he nodded eagerly.

"Can you scrub?"

Again he nodded.

"Do you like horses?"

"Oh, I do!"

"Then, come. We shall go to Messire La Farge, who runs the Inn of the Pelican. Perhaps he will give you work."

"Would he let me sleep with the horses? I would like sleeping near something alive."

"I have heard he is a kind man. He feeds poor students."

Nerien smiled, and lifted his chin. "Then let us go to Messire La Farge!"

"First we must wash your face and comb your hair. I have a fresh shirt and some hose that will be too large, but they will do. Then we shall present ourselves to the good innkeeper and say, 'Here is Nerien, a bright lad with a clean face. You are lucky, Messire La Farge. He will do your work. He has come to stay. What a lucky man you are, Messire. Congratulations!' "

As they walked hand in hand to the inn in the Rue St. Martin, John prayed that the innkeeper would help the foundling. "What if he will not?" he asked himself. "Master Cordier might know what to do, but it is late, and he goes to bed early."

The noise coming from the tavern was deafening. A group of irate citizens stood outside the wineshop, talking and gesticulating.

"What is the trouble?" John asked.

"The students!" a citizen with a rotunda of stomach answered. "They are creating a dreadful disturbance. They won't go home. Nobody can sleep. I fear I must go for the gendarmes."

John peered through the small-paned windows. A throng of students glutted with wine were seated at the long tables, the three Mommors among them. Claude, like his companions, was banging his mug on the wood and singing loudly. And John had promised the bishop he would look after the others!

"I just can't interfere," John told himself, as the little man with the protruding stomach scuttled off. "I will talk to the boys tomorrow." But then he remembered how much the bishop wanted Claude to be a priest. If the gendarmes arrested him, it might prevent his getting a proper start in the Church.

"Wait here," John told Nerien. "There is something I must do."

Fighting down a desire to run, he moved slowly into the tavern. The only light came from a bronze lamp hanging from the beamed ceiling. John's knees felt as if they would buckle, but he gritted his teeth and crossed the hard-packed mud floor toward the table where the boys from Noyon sat.

"Joachim, Ives, Claude. All of you——"

The room was bedlam, with the thumping of mugs and the shouting of voices. The din was so great nobody heard John's voice. Reaching out, he grabbed the mug from Claude's hand and sent it crashing down on the table with such force that the wine splashed all over before the container bounced to the floor. The students paused in their merrymaking, and stared with widened eyes and lifted eyebrows. For an instant there was only stillness. Then John's voice trumpeted through the raftered room.

"I had to do that. We are scholars and gentlemen. We have no right to drink so much and annoy everybody in the neighborhood. Come Claude, Joachim, Ives. I will help you back to your rooms."

Nobody moved. Again the stillness was awful. The next minute a Spanish student with a dark Latin face pointed a finger in ridicule. John recognized him. His name was Michael Servetus. There was something about him that repelled people. Perhaps it was his eyes; they reminded John of putrid pools.

"'We are scholars and gentlemen.'" He mimicked John's voice. "'We have no right to drink so much and annoy everybody in the neighborhood. . . .' Who wants to go to his room? Go along, little cabbage. Preach your sermons elsewhere. And take those eyes away. I can't stand them!"

For an instant John stood frozen. He wanted to back away, run to his uncle Richard's, and hide his head under the coverlet. Instead he took a deep breath, and said, "Claude, you listen. *Please.* Come quickly. There is no time to lose. A citizen has gone for the police. If you are found here like this and the rector hears of it, you will be flogged. Use your head!"

"Who has a head?" Michael hiccuped, with a look of indescribable hate.

John ducked as Michael's empty mug flew at him.

A young man a little older than the others rose on unsteady feet. He stood arms akimbo, square shoulders swaying. His large brown eyes were bloodshot, but there was an impish set to his happy mouth and his brows drew together in a whimsical frown.

"Clement Marot, young sir," he said thickly, "song maker, at your service. I should immortalize you!" He took off his feathered tam with a flourish and bowed so low that he almost fell. "Valet in the household of Marguerite of Valois, the sister of the King of France! We meant no harm, little chaplain, but we thank you for wanting to save us." He waved his arms in a wide arc. "To our beds in haste lest morning find us lying in the dungeon!"

The students mumbled and muttered, especially the young Servetus, but one by one they stumbled toward the door.

The song maker patted John on the shoulder. "Don't look so glum. We're going. I understand. You have a duty. You do it. Too many of us are cowards. More of us should be men."

"Hear ye, fellows! The accusative case," Claude said goodnaturedly as he staggered toward the street door. "We stand condemned for our merrymaking. The little chaplain of Noyon speaks."

33

He, too, bowed low in mock homage. "On your feet, men. Before the accusative case. It's time, anyway, as the poet says, that we were in our beds."

Étienne de la Farge was getting ready to lock the door for the night when John and Nerien returned after leading the Mommors home. A well-built man of forty with a brown beard, wavy brown hair, hazel eyes, he smiled amiably.

"By the time the gendarmes arrived, everything was so peaceful that they thought our citizen friend was a bit touched. The boys got out of hand tonight. Thank you!"

"I have a favor to ask, Messire. This is Nerien. He is a foundling, and he needs work. Will you let him be your stableboy?"

The hosteler stared down at the bony child, and Nerien's sad blue eyes gazed solemnly back. Short yellow hair fuzzed around his pointed face, making him look like a little duck. His body tensed, his fingers clutched John's hand.

"Messire, I would be very good to have around. I can sweep, scrub, rub the horses, and give them oats. If you will let me stay, I will eat only scraps. I like scraps. I will do the work of two. You will never be sorry, Messire!"

Messire La Farge stared at the child, and John saw him swallow before he said, "Then you are just what we need at the Pelican. I have a shop, too. I need a good boy. You are hired."

"Will you let me sleep with the horses?"

"I have a better idea. You can serve in the wineshop. There is a little room on the third floor across from mine. That will be yours, Nerien, but you must keep it clean."

The child's face was ecstatic. "My room? I have never had a room of my own. Oh, Messire, I will keep it so clean that it will shine. And I will sweep and scrub your room, too. You will never be sorry!"

"Messire," John said, "would you object if I come one evening a week to teach Nerien to read and write? Every boy should be able to do that, and I think Nerien is bright."

"That is agreed. We will have a scholar here before we know it."

Nerien's small mouth fell open. "You mean I will learn to read and write as some gentlemen do?"

"If you will work hard and listen carefully."

The boy's blue eyes kindled like lighted tapers. "One day I shall be of great use. How I would like to be a teacher like Master Cordier! Then I could help little boys who have no homes. They need friends, Messire. You don't know how they need them!"

"I see you are kind, as well as willing," said the innkeeper. "You are the very boy for me!"

3

1524-1525

The next year when John was promoted to the Collège de Montaigu, Claude was promoted, too. It was another bug-haunted place, where the students wore hooded uniforms and the boarders were beaten and half starved, for Rector Beda now headed the Faculty of Theology and the rigorous schedule was in effect at the Collège de Montaigu, too. John stayed out of the way except when his superior paired him in a classroom disputation with a student toying with the new ideas. John's arguments seemed to please the rector, especially when he said that to speak of freedom of conscience apart from the Church was impious.

As John was leaving the college one afternoon just before Easter, a student ran after him to say that he was wanted in the rector's office. He wondered what he had done to displease his superior and if he would be flogged. His heart was thudding as he knocked on the heavy door.

"Come in," the rector's clipped voice said.

He was a tall, large-boned man with thin lips set in a bitter curve

36

below a pinched, bony nose. His narrow eyes were eager-bright like those of a hawk about to spring.

His study smelled of dust and stale air. A large crucifix hung on the wall. On the polished table before him were quill pens in a marble holder, a pile of parchment, an inkhorn, and a sand flask. There were three hard chairs. With a nod he indicated that John should take the nearest one.

"Sit, my son. I have much to say to you." John sat down. "I want to commend you on your excellence in the ancient languages, in theology, and philosophy. But even more for your zeal in defending Mother Church."

"In a few years I will take my final vows and become a priest. I am a servant of the Church, Dr. Beda."

"I wish we had no heretics to worry about. John, is there anyone you suspect of heresy?"

"Students ask questions. They seek truth. Should they be afraid of it? If God is Truth, is it wicked to seek Him?"

"That depends. It is our duty here to discover in these dangerous times who might betray the Church as Martin Luther did in Germany. The King's soldiers patrol the highways, arresting those we suspect. There are those who, unknown, patrol the colleges."

John forced a weak laugh. "The spies won't find heretics in our college!"

The rector's next words almost destroyed his equanimity. "What I really sent for you for is to question you about a kinsman of yours, Peter Robert, known as 'Olivétan' because he burns so much olive oil studying and writing. John, you know your cousin pretty well. What is he writing?"

John could feel the rector's eyes burning into him. Instinct told him to be cautious and say little.

"Peter is seven years older than I. We grew up in Noyon. He was reared a devout Christian. He hasn't told me he was writing anything."

"Don't be afraid to tell me. I only want to help him."

Could Peter Robert be a heretic? The thought was a dagger thrust. Peter always advocated integrity of mind. He continued to laud his former professor, Dr. James Le Fèvre, who had been forced to flee Paris.

37

"Peter Robert asks questions as I do sometimes. Is that being a heretic?"

"No, not if he comes to the right conclusions. Your cousin was a student of Dr. James Le Fèvre whose books attack the Church, claiming that a Christian is to look only to Christ for salvation! They denounce the authority of the Church!"

"Has he ever retracted these beliefs?"

"No. We can thank the King's sister, Marguerite, for that. She persuaded the King to refuse to allow a scaffold to be built. We could have tortured the heretic!" The rector's eyes blazed with fury. "We did torment him until he fled Paris. He is now at Meaux."

"I have heard about the disturbances there."

"One of these days we will deal with Bishop Briconnet, who encourages the Gospelers. We are watching any here, such as your cousin, who might have been influenced."

"I don't think you have to worry about Peter Robert."

The rector's narrow eyes held John's for a long moment, making him feel like an eel over a hot spit, and he was grateful for a knock at the door.

The man who entered looked like a greyhound. He had a thin body, slender face, a long nose, and gray eyes. A spotted gray cloak covered him. He paused uncertainly when he saw John.

The rector waved a heavy hand. "This is John Calvin, a chaplain of the Church. What is the news Meheste?"

"I bring word of heresy," the man exclaimed. " 'Tis whispered in the streets that a group of Gospelers meet somewhere near the colleges, and that one of them is translating a Bible into French from Dr. Le Fèvre's Hebrew text."

Beda turned purple. "They wouldn't dare!"

"It is common knowledge that the heretics are under the protection of the King's sister. She encourages them."

"Do you know who they are?"

The spy shook his head. "I will find out. One is said to be a doctor."

Meheste backed out, closing the door quietly behind him.

John leaned forward. "Surely if this is true, the students would know of it."

"These Gospelers can be very clever. If we find them, they shall have their tongues torn out!"

"Shouldn't the Church strive by every means to help such poor wretches back to its bosom? Shouldn't they be given every chance?"

"Yes. The chance to retract their errors—publicly!"

"Is there anything I can do, Dr. Beda?"

"Yes. Yes there is. Keep your eyes open. Watch for heresy. And let me know if you discover that your cousin, Peter Robert, is mixed up in this. A chaplain's first duty is to his Church."

The next day John was out strolling with Nicholas Cop. They passed the market where the vendors cried their wares, the stone-towered buildings with balconies and iron tracery, and some gabled houses with red-tiled roofs and square chimneys. At last they reached the woods of Livry.

As they walked in the cool shade, an odd bent-shouldered figure approached through the twilight. The man had long, white locks, corn-flower blue eyes, and skin which was furrowed like the fields. His feet were bare and his toes looked like the gnarled roots of old trees.

He blocked their path, staring intently at them. "Have you heard, young gentlemen, that Christ's great gift is free?" he demanded in an earnest voice.

How like one of the gargoyles on Notre Dame he is, John thought. But his eyes are not like stone. They are warm and kind.

"What gift are you talking about?" Nicholas asked.

"Salvation. I live nearby in the woods of Livry, but I have just come from Meaux where the true Gospel is preached. Cease paying for Masses and prayers, and receive the true pardon of Christ!"

"You have been influenced by Dr. Le Fèvre, Bishop Briconnet, and William Farel!" Nicholas said sternly. "Don't you know that they are heretics?"

The old man shook his head. "That is what their enemies and the enemies of the Gospel say. But these men preach after the manner of Paul, Augustine, Pthinius, Iraneous, and the early disciples. They say we should make Christ the center of worship, as the Christians did in the early church, and cease worshiping the Blessed Virgin and her images."

"You are confused and tired," Nicholas said gently, taking a coin from his purse. "Here. Buy yourself some bread and cheese. You have had a long journey."

The old man drew himself erect. For an instant there was something magnificent about him. "I have something far more precious than silver. Men think of worldly treasure with one part of their mind and try to worship the Eternal with another. Love of money is truly the root of evil. I have no need for money."

"Won't you accept the gift of a loving heart?" John pressed.

"You don't understand. I have the true treasure. A man is justified only through God's Grace; merits devised by an earthly church will never save him."

John felt his temper rising. "You sound like a heretic!" he said gruffly. "You are disloyal to the Church!"

"All I know is that Christ is mine. I am His. I have repented. By his Grace he has forgiven my sins. And I am happy."

"It is getting dark. You should be safe at home."

"Don't you know that a man is safe anywhere when he is Christ's? I must seek others and tell them, too. I must hurry. I haven't much time, you know." As he disappeared in the warm, spring night, his voice drifted back. "I must tell others."

"I fear for that man." Nicholas frowned. "When Noel Beda discovers he is telling people that pardon is free, he will be thrown into prison, tortured, and perhaps burned. And he is so earnest."

"Surely the authorities wouldn't harm that old hermit!"

"He is teaching heresy."

John sighed. "I'll be glad when I have more knowledge of the Holy Writ, so that I'll be able to have an answer for men like that."

"More and more men will ask questions. 'Tis whispered Messire La Farge harbors Gospelers. Perhaps he can explain their beliefs."

"Messire La Farge? I don't believe it. If I found out it was true, I would have to tell the rector. And I couldn't stand it if Messire were arrested. Then what would happen to Nerien?"

John tossed that night, unable to sleep, the hermit's words burning in his mind. At dawn, when the bells of St. Germain tolled for Mass, he rose, dressed, and walked to the church.

As he came out after the service, Nicholas Cop joined him. "You know, John," he said with a frown, "I could hardly sleep for thinking about that old man. His life is in danger."

"But nothing can silence him. He is on fire with his beliefs. He feels the limitations of time, Nicholas. He must speak."

"That's the way with these Gospelers. They are so sure they are right that they are willing to die."

"Could penance, the observances, confession, the rules of the Church be of men and not God?" John asked in a terrible whisper.

Nicholas' gently inquiring eyes clouded, his long face was solemn. "The King's sister thinks so. Beda cannot silence her, because her brother adores her. There is so much talk about the New Religion, which seems a part of the New Learning. The more I read the more confused I get."

"You mean you read the Lutheran books?"

"Yes, I read them."

"That is wrong," John snapped. "Why get confused? I have questions. But Master Cordier has suggested I start studying the Latin Vulgate, the Bible of the Church, for my advance Latin work. I should find answers there."

"Jerome made the translation from the ancient Latin?"

"Yes, improving it, and also from the Septuagint. He used the Hebrew, too, for part of it. It is a composite of several versions. Cousin Peter claims it has errors, but since the seventh century it has been the official Bible."

Nicholas sighed as they began the long climb to the college. "When you study the Vulgate, I predict you will be troubled. Have a care. Too often where the Scriptures are studied, revolt breaks out against the Church. You are one of its chaplains."

That August morning all Paris was in commotion. The bells in the church towers pealed in mournful strokes to summon the citizens. Clouds hung low in a stormy sky, and a heavy wind swung the sign and rattled the wooden shutters of the Inn of the Pelican, ruffled the feathers of the pigeons high on the eaves above Notre Dame's ugly gargoyles, and blew grit into the eyes of the crowds flocking through the narrow crooked streets and muddy lanes to the Grève.

The square was soon filled, and the noise was deafening. The boorish citizens and bands of students from the high schools and colleges were the most vocal. The burghers, the nobility, and the clergy lent a little dignity as they stood on the steps of the old cathedral watching the scaffold sharply etched against the gloomy sky.

The bells began to toll faster as John was leaving the Collège de Montaigu with Claude. They, too, hurried to the Grève to see what was happening. When they saw the buckets of water and the high pile of bunched faggots, they knew. A verdict was to be carried out: death by slow fire.

It was common report that the Emperor Charles was holding King Francis in an attempt to force him to sign a treaty ceding Burgundy and giving up all claims to Naples, Genoa, Artois, and Milan. The rector is taking advantage of the King's absence, John thought. But he did not speak his thoughts aloud. Meheste, the spy with the long nose, might be listening.

Claude was more reckless. "I wager the heretic-hunters of the Sorbonne have been at work," he blurted in a loud voice. "Some confused soul is about to fry."

John looked around uneasily. His spine tingled when a voice asked, "Do you believe, young man, that heresy should be condoned?"

A tall monk in the garb of the Dominicans stood right behind them, his black eyes glittering in his dark, swarthy face. John tugged at Claude's doublet and frowned a warning.

"I may be wrong, my brother," Claude said mildly, "but I think perhaps hatred consumes some of our professors. What of the love of Christ for the sinner?"

"Is it better to burn heretics or to allow them to pass on their diseased beliefs?" the Dominican persisted truculently.

Before Claude could reply, another voice sounded. "That all depends on whether or not the beliefs really are diseased," it said glibly.

Facing the Dominican, was Clement Marot. He was accompanied by a young woman with blue eyes and golden hair. His new wife, John thought, for Nerien had told him the poet had wed.

"Could it be that you have Lutheran tendencies, Poet?" The monk's voice crackled.

"Oh my, no!" the poet said quickly, rolling his brown eyes piously. "I believe in the sanctity of Mother Church."

There was a stir just then as the lieutenant of the gendarmerie appeared, shoving the people aside to make room for the soldiers who led the prisoner. John stared, and the hair on the back of his neck stood up. The "dangerous" prisoner in heavy chains was the hermit of Livry! John wanted to cry out, to protest that this old man was harmless. He longed to rush forward, throw his arms around the bent shoulders, and tell the soldiers to loosen the chains!

The prisoner stood quietly while the executioner draped him in a black cloak painted with a bright red cross. The wind blew his white locks around his shriveled face. He moved willingly as the soldiers led him near the scaffold, where he stood looking around quietly. The lieutenant waved a white-gloved hand to the bishop on the cathedral steps. An austere man with an apoplectic face, he reminded John of Bishop de Hangest, for his eyes were not hate-filled like the rector's, but warm and compassionate.

"Old man," the bishop began in a voice that wavered, "you are charged with fouling the city and its environs with the doctrines of the arch-heretics of Meaux, James Le Fèvre and William Farel. You have taught that Christ's salvation is free. You have declared it a sin to pray for the intercession of the Holy Virgin, Queen of Heaven. Surely, old man, you do not believe these things!"

The clear blue eyes looked at the black-masked executioner, who stood beside the piled faggots, holding a flaming torch, then looked back at the bishop. The old man's furrowed face glowed at if a candle had been lighted in his soul.

"It is my glory, your Grace, to be called a heretic by those whose lives and beliefs are opposed to Jesus Christ."

The Rector Beda, in velvet tam and black robe, stepped forward. His eyes in his pinched, bony face had their customary hawk-brightness. As he pointed an accusing finger, some of the people shrank back, but the hermit did not flinch.

"The flames will be hotter than Purgatory when the torch is set to the pile," the rector threatened.

"I rejoice that I am called to die for Christ's Truth. Our Blessed Church seems to have forgotten His Cross. He himself told us that a man must lose his life to find it. And to lose my life for His Glory is glory indeed."

Beda shouted, his face livid, "Old man, will you recant your lies, or burn?"

"Good sir, Christ's salvation *is* free. A man is justified only through God's Grace and not by merits devised by an earthly church. If every man, woman, and child gathered here to see me burn could have the Holy Scriptures in French and be able to read them, His Holy Spirit would light their minds and hearts. That, my friends, is my prayer!"

"Gospeler lies! We shall see how the heretic prays when the torch is set to the faggots!"

The doctors of the Sorbonne surged forward to urge the heretic to deny his errors.

Shaking his head gently, the old man lifted a bony hand for silence. "You are learned men. Search for truth, I pray you. It is your only hope when man lies to man to keep him in subjection to an institution, the Church of Rome!"

The bishop tried again. "Old man, in the name of God, come to your senses. Nobody wants to burn you!"

"All your work will never earn your salvation, your Grace. Christ alone gives it. And God is sovereign!"

"Let us close our ears to the blasphemy of the heretic!" Rector Beda thundered. "Tie him to the stake. Light the faggots. We shall soon hear him cry for mercy."

John's heart was pounding crazily as he tried to elbow his way through the crowd toward the scaffold. It was hard work. Bodies were wedged tightly together. But he had to get through, he had to do something to help the old man. He didn't understand what the hermit was talking about, but he recognized in him the integrity of mind for which Peter Robert argued.

When John finally reached the steps, a strikingly tall man, with wavy hair and a shovel-shaped beard the color of walnuts, blocked the path. He was dressed in a green velvet doublet and gold hose, and he faced the rector, feet spread apart, arms akimbo.

"Release the old man to me!" he pleaded.

"You dare interfere, Berquin?"

"I simply want to prevent an outrage, one the King will abhor. Release the prisoner until the King's return. I will be responsible."

John remembered that Berquin was the excellent Latin scholar of whom Master Cordier was so proud.

Beda did not deign to answer. He cast a scathing look at Berquin, then signaled the lieutenant, who gave a sharp command. As two gendarmes flanked the young nobleman and led him away, struggling, two others advanced toward the hermit.

John shot forward. "Dr. Beda! Please remember that a heretic should be given every chance. Let me talk to this man. Perhaps I can make him understand!"

"You, John Calvin? What business is this of yours?" The rector's eyes were cold now, his pinched nose lifted. With a gesture of impatience he turned away, his mouth set in its downward curve. "Tie the criminal securely. Touch the torch!"

The executioner, a man of tremendous proportions, did not move. "Do we have to burn this old man?" he whispered hoarsely, his eyes mere oval slits filled with agony.

The rector's face turned purple. "Enough of that, Michael Sept. We are carrying out a sentence of the court!"

Sept moved with dragging feet toward the piled faggots. Reluctantly he touched the torch. The flames licked upward, consuming the kindling gathered from the forests whence the old man had emerged to tell others of his faith. The bishop turned his face away. The executioner vomited into the flames. John felt sick, too. He wanted to leave, but he could not drag his eyes from the scaffold.

"Now will you recant, you old fool?" the rector shouted. "The fire will grow hotter. Tell the people you lied and you will be spared."

"No. God calls me to obey Him." The voice was loud and clear. "Our beloved France must be dug out from under idolatry, superstition, and corruption. Oh, my dear countrymen, accept the new life in Christ which He has earned for you. For the Glory of God, the greatness of France, and the salvation of your immortal souls!"

The gendarmes, obeying the rector, poured water on the fire. The hermit of Livry writhed, but he did not cry for mercy. Instead, in a voice charged with triumph, he began to sing:

"A mighty fortress is our God,
A bulwark never failing;
Our helper He, amid the flood
Of mortal ills prevailing:
For still our ancient foe
Doth seek to work us woe;
His craft and power are great,
And armed with cruel hate,
On earth is not his equal!"

"Cease, old man, cease," the rector shrieked. "Are you a thing inhuman? A witch? A demon? Don't you feel pain?"

But the hermit's hymn rolled on like a wave man cannot stop:

"The body they may kill:
God's truth abideth still.
His kingdom is forever!"

Beda, in a frenzy, shook his fists and danced up and down. "You dare sing that devil Luther's Battle Hymn here on the Grève as you prepare to enter Purgatory!"

The executioner moved aside and retched again. The bishop left, shoving his way through the people. He did not look back.

As John watched, the light on the old man's face grew brighter than the flames licking upward. "I won't enter Purgatory," he whispered, shaking his head, "I am going to Heaven!"

"What ideas are these that a man will suffer such torture to witness them?" an ancient crone beside John wheezed in wonderment.

The crowd began to turn away, too. It was no longer a laughing, shouting crowd. There was no joy on the faces. And on top of the battlements of the ancient church the ugly gargoyles, placed there to frighten evil spirits away, sat on their smoke-black haunches, smiling gleefully at the wickedness and cruelty of men.

An old man was burned, but life had to go on. There were lessons to prepare and after supper John sat down as usual at his table. But he kept seeing the hermit; he could not blot the scaffold from his mind. He could smell the smoke and the terrible odor of roasting flesh. And he was afraid! Would he receive a summons to Dr. Beda's study and a lecture on how a young chaplain should behave at an execution?

A rapping at the door made him jump. The door burst open and Peter Robert rushed in. His face, framed by long, wavy hair, was ashen, and in his hands he held a large bundle wrapped in monk's cloth.

"John, I am in grave danger," he cried. "I need your help."

"My help?"

"Yes. I have just learned that Louis de Berquin and Clement Marot were arrested after the execution today. They are charged with heresy."

"But why are you in danger?" John held his breath.

"I fear they will be tortured in an effort to make them divulge the name of a man who is translating a Bible into French from the Hebrew."

"I still don't see—— Peter Robert, surely you are not that man!"

Peter sat on the edge of the bed, leaning forward earnestly. "How can I expect you to understand, John? You are young. You are a chaplain in the Church. I should not confide in you."

John frowned. "Confide what, Peter Robert? I don't understand."

"If you were at the execution this morning, you heard what the hermit said, that everyone should have a Bible. I have been preparing a French Bible in secret. Dr. Beda has heard rumors about it, and he arrested Clement, thinking he may have learned something at the palace. I may be arrested next!"

John's mind was in a turmoil. Peter Robert a heretic! One of the worst. How could he? Peter Robert a heretic . . . a heretic. Again John saw the scaffold rising before him. But the old man was not on it. Peter Robert was! The flames licked upward, and Peter's rich voice was singing the hermit's song:

> "The body they may kill
>   God's truth abideth still.
> His kingdom is forever!"

John felt as if he were suffocating. If anything happened to Peter Robert, he couldn't stand it! Terror lifted him to his feet and he faced his cousin.

"How could you turn against God by disobeying the authorities? You may well be next. It's not worth the price, even if the old man was right!"

"Following Christ is worth any price, John; even the scaffold."

"I know, Peter Robert. I didn't mean that."

"False religion was invented by man—the Mass, ceremonies, and observances. These things separate souls from God."

"But why are *you* doing this, Peter Robert?"

"Why? Because I am convinced it is God's will that I translate a Bible the people can read. I believe He wants me to live to complete this task. That is why I have come to you." Peter Robert thrust the bundle at his cousin. "This contains the finished sheets of the French Bible. Whatever happens they must not fall into Beda's hands!"

"But I can't keep them here!"

"Wait until eleven o'clock tonight. Secrete them under your cloak and take them to Messire La Farge at the Inn of the Pelican. He will be expecting you."

"Peter Robert, you forget that I am a servant of the Church!"

"If you are, you will do as I ask. Only as the pure light of Christ shines from these pages will France, her people, and the Church be truly great!"

"That's what the hermit said. But the people are forbidden to read the Bible without the help of the priests. Many cannot read at all."

"You err in thinking men are forbidden to read it. As far as I can determine, the Church has never forbidden its reading. The Bibles are chained in the monasteries, churches, and libraries to prevent thieves from making off with them. The people need the truth. *John, please!*"

John paced back and forth, considering. How could he be a party to such intrigue? The priests did not want ignorant men to study the Bible. How could the unlettered understand?

He shook his head firmly. "Peter Robert, I can never tell you how dear you are to me, but I cannot and will not do this. Not even for you. It's wicked."

"Wicked? To help poor, stumbling man find a guide to walk tall by? To bring him out of the darkness into the light? To give him

48

Truth and Christ, as revealed by the Holy Spirit to each man's heart? Oh, John, in such delusion lies the power of the Roman Church."

John clenched his fists. Peter Robert really was a heretic! "The Holy Father is God's representative on earth," he blurted. "Have you no loyalty to your church?"

"Calm yourself, John. If you will do as I ask tonight, I will make you a promise."

"And what will you promise?"

"Read the book of Romans in the Vulgate. That is what wrought such a change in our Saxon monk, Martin Luther. Open your mind and face its statements. And I promise you that if, by the end of the year, you have not discovered that Lutheranism is Christianity in its purest form, I will never publish the French Bible."

John did not hesitate. "In that case I will take your manuscript to Messire La Farge. You are wrong."

Peter Robert shook his head. His dark eyes gleamed. "God has spoken loudly time and time again. I am counting on Him and on that excellent mind of yours. You always said you were not afraid of truth."

John looked behind him so frequently on his way through the dark, twisting streets that he felt as if he were walking backward. Dim lamps blinked over doorways. There were the usual odors of slop and filth. But there came no fall of feet. There was no heavily cloaked figure darting in and out of the mud streets, and no sign that anyone was following.

Nerien was serving one of the guests as John entered the tavern. Hurriedly depositing a tall flagon before the customer, the boy ran to John and threw his arms around him. John stooped and, French fashion, they touched cheeks.

"Messire told me to watch for you and tell you to be careful. One of the Sorbonne's spies is in the corner by the fire. Follow me, and the minute we are through the door leading to the cookhouse, give me the bundle. Then block the door so nobody can pass!"

John managed to smile serenely. There were only a few hangers-on at the tables. The gigantic executioner, Michael Sept, was having a late supper with some cronies, already in their cups.

49

Nearby Claude and Nicholas were eating together. John glanced toward the fireplace corner and his heart thumped against his ribs. The chief spy, Meheste, sat staring at him with cold, gray eyes.

Nerien was trotting toward the cookhouse door. Affecting an air of nonchalance, John sauntered behind him. The instant they were outside John passed Nerien the bundle, and the boy dashed for the exit leading to the stables.

The door slammed into John's back. He broke into a cold sweat, but he held his position. Again the door struck him. He moved back so that it could open, blocking the center with his body, moving to the left, to the right and then to the left, like one confused. Meheste stood there. A curse exploded from his pale lips. His gray eyes were no longer cold but fiery like a mad dog's eyes.

"Monsieur Meheste!" John bowed, still blocking the doorway. "I met you at the rector's when I first came to Paris. How do you do?"

"Where is that serving boy? I would order another pudding. Quickly. Where is he?"

"Ah, my good customer Monsieur Meheste!" a hearty voice boomed from the common room. The hosteler held out both hands. "Did I hear you say you wanted a pudding? Here, boy!" He clapped his hands for service. "A black pudding for the gentleman!"

To John's relief, Nerien appeared at his elbow and his hands were empty. Meheste scowlingly started back to his corner. Messire La Farge looked at John, a spark of deviltry in his brown eyes.

John strolled to the table where Claude and Nicholas sat, and took a chair between them. When Nerien came to ask what he wished, he ordered a cherry cobbler. Then he scissored his thin legs and heaved a sigh. He had had a narrow escape. Without intending to, he was now allied with those the Church considered its worst enemies. How could he find God in that?

Messire came over and leaned down to whisper, "The Duchess of Alençon, Marguerite, secured the release of Berquin and the Poet Marot. Lucky for Peter Robert."

John nodded fervently. "I would hate to see anything happen to him!"

Later, threading his way home through the empty streets, John tried to collect his thoughts. He succeeded only in feeling the unreality that comes to one emerging from a room where someone has died. Peter Robert and Messire La Farge were heretics. Little Nerien was being infected. And he, John Calvin, God's chaplain, had helped preserve the manuscript of a French Bible intended for distribution to the common people for their interpretation without the aid of the Church whose priest he would be.

A scene from Noyon flashed through his mind: The bishop, high in the stone pulpit, was speaking of the way God guided men. "Man's greatest duty is to seek God's will and do it," he said. The boy, John Calvin, listened intently. *Obedience. Obedience. Obedience to God.* . . . The words echoed and re-echoed.

Later he had gone up to Bishop de Hangest to say, "Your Grace, how does one know God's will?"

The bishop had smiled gently as he placed a huge hand on John's head. "John, there are times in every man's life when he is not sure what God wills. He must listen for the Voice. It will come, perhaps not as he expects it to come, but it will sound for the servant who longs to hear it. Be certain that God is in all events, leading, shoving, pushing his servants into the right paths of service."

Leading . . . shoving . . . pushing . . . he thought now. Perhaps God wanted me to prevent Peter Robert and Messire La Farge from saving the Bible. But how can I inform on them? "Surely, God, Thou dost not want that. I vow I will search the pages of Holy Writ to see how the Gospelers can get so mixed up!"

4

1526 -1528

As fall passed into winter and the weather grew colder, it seemed to John that his soul was withering with the leaves, shrubs, and flowers. Gloom wrapped around him like a heavy cloak. In the classrooms, the students discussed and debated the beliefs of the Gospelers. Not even Beda's worst threats silenced the questions that tumbled from their lips. Many of the Lutheran books were secretly circulated, but John would not read any of them.

He worked very hard at the translation of the Latin Vulgate, attended Mass daily, prayed, confessed his sins, and did penance. Yet the turmoil in his mind grew greater. Even after penance, the restlessness churned within him, plaguing him until he wondered if the legions of Hell had been sent to try him.

The news on the political front distressed him, too. In February, word reached Paris that the King had been released from his imprisonment at Pavia. But not until Charles had succeeded in forcing him to renounce all claims to Milan, Genoa, Naples, Artois, and Flanders, and to cede Burgundy, return his land to the duke there, and agree to marry the Emperor's sister, the dowager Queen of Portugal.

Instead of clearing, John's intellectual confusion increased as he studied the Gospels. He hungered to seek answers from a scholar. To whom could he go? Claude, when consulted, pointed out that John was young. With maturity would come understanding. Claude confided that he had made his own choice. He would enter the priesthood. He was not, however, going to question anything. He was determined to live in subjection to his brethren in the Lord.

Nicholas suggested consulting Peter Robert. While John feared his cousin's heresy, he respected his intelligence. Every Thursday night after Nerien's lessons, John had supper with Nicholas and Peter Robert. To be sure their discussions were not overheard, they went up to Messire La Farge's third-floor bedchamber where he kept a copy of Dr. Le Fèvre's Bible hidden in a secret panel in the wall. They read that, debating and praying. When Peter Robert expounded salvation by Christ alone as a free gift, and John tried argument, Peter Robert quoted from the Scriptures passages to which John had no answers.

The debate grew heated one night when Peter Robert insisted that the Apostle Peter had had a wife, mentioned four times in the original texts. John couldn't believe it. The first Vicar of Christ to whom He had given the Keys to the Kingdom had a wife? Like a mere man?

Then one Thursday evening Peter Robert came into the inn frowning. During supper he appeared distraught, and kept drumming his fingers on the table.

"What's wrong, Peter Robert?" John asked at length. "I know you well enough to know something's amiss."

Peter Robert looked around carefully. "Somebody searched my rooms last night. Everything was in disorder. Tonight I was followed here."

"Did they get any of your manuscript?"

"Fortunately I had brought the additional sheets to Messire two days ago. They found nothing."

"That was lucky," Nicholas said.

"That was God. He will preserve me until I complete His work. Some inner sense warned me to get those sheets out of my rooms."

"Don't you think it wise, Peter Robert, to stop meeting here? The persecution is heightening against all who advocate a return to the religion of the early apostles. It is dangerous to defy authority!"

Peter Robert agreed solemnly.

"Pope Clement VII has sent Parliament a letter!" Nicholas announced one June night at the inn after John had come downstairs from Nerien's room. "I heard at the Louvre that it was read today. He informed the Parliament that he has sent men to Paris charged with punishing those who seek to destroy the old religion and commands Parliament to help these men."

"That will increase persecution!"

"I fear for Clement Marot. He has a way of making fun of people and seeing that they like it. But he has the Catholic Court singing psalms of Protestant beliefs. The Dauphin is so enthusiastic he sings them everywhere. Clement will be arrested again!"

In the spring of 1526 news spread through Paris: "The poet attached to the household of the Duchess of Alençon, the King's sister, Marguerite, has been arrested again, charged with writing a dozen songs with Protestant sympathies. His sponsor is out of the city!"

"The poet tells everyone who visits him in the gaol that he is neither Anabaptist nor Roman Catholic nor Protestant, that he tries to be a Christian," the tongues wagged. "The Duchess of Alençon will get him freed." "Wait until the King's sister returns to Paris. Her poet will be released."

On January 24, 1527, Marguerite married again and became the Queen of Navarre. When she returned to the Louvre and found Clement missing, she had him released. To make amends for what Clement insisted was an unjust imprisonment, she used her influence to have him made the King's Valet de Chambre and Court Poet! Once again the immoral court delighted in his tunes, hymns, and humor, even at the expense of their Catholic faith.

"Let him be taken!
  He ate the bacon,"

referring to the heretics who ate meat on Friday was sung with smiles everywhere. And in a more serious vein:

54

"The gold and silver whence all pleasures flow
Cause griefs which greater than all pleasures grow."

"I want to leave the world a little better in some way than I found
it," the poet told John one night at the Pelican. "I am going to set
some more psalms to tunes."

That July of 1527, Nicholas came to John's room one Sunday
afternoon and asked him to take a walk. "Duprat has been made a
cardinal," Nicholas confided. "He is waiting for some excuse to have
the poet arrested again."

"Does Clement know this?"

Nicholas nodded. "The cardinal is also watching Clement's
friend, Triboulet, the Court Fool, who has been chanting his
rhymes."

"Are they heretics?"

"I don't think so. They worship the Queen of Navarre. Her approach to religion is an intellectual one, and they follow her."

Just then a voice began to sing. It was that of Clement, sitting
under a big oak beside the Seine. They paused to listen:

"Then since it hath not pleased thee to allow
That my vile flesh be burned to ashes now,
    Make me to bring, while I still write for men,
    Thine honor in the service of my pen.
And if predestined this my body be
One day in hot fire to die, by thy decree,
    Not for a foolish cause be this, O Lord
    My God, but for thy glory and for thy word,
And may the agony, God, I entreat
Not wring my soul with torture so complete
    That from its memory the pain should thrust
    Thee in whom stays all my trust;
So that I may when the long sleep draws nigh,
Call upon thee with the last sound I sigh."

"That's beautiful, Clement," John said, moving up to him. "You
are a good poet and you have a quality of reverence François Villon
lacked. You are rightly named after one of the good saints."

55

The poet smiled faintly. "Saint Clement was the patron saint of sailors. My mother thought that in dedicating me to him she would save me from death by water. But"—he shuddered—"I am in more danger of death by fire."

"Are you a Lutheran?"

He shook his head quickly. "I want to live like a Christian, but I need courage. My wife keeps begging me for the sake of our little son, Michael, to be careful."

Nicholas shook his head. "You know Cardinal Duprat hates you because your verses have denounced his abuse of justice. The King's mother, Louisa of Savoy, shares his dislike. Why do you persist in antagonizing them?"

"People laugh at what I write, but they understand. I fear for France. Ever since Duprat was made a chancellor in 1515, he has conspired with others to rule France! *And I love France.* One day I want to see the little Dauphin became king. By planting suspicion in the minds of the court, I can hold the cardinal in check."

"Have a care," Nicholas pleaded. "'He is a conniving man!"

As John continued his translation of Jerome's Latin Vulgate, he sometimes felt as if the new ideas were closing in on him. He would rush to Notre Dame or St. Germain and there, in the vast emptiness, pray that he would always think first of Christ's Church. Still the upsetting questions tumbled through his brain. Was he to confess his sins to Jesus Christ instead of the priest? Should he cease praying for the intercession of the saints, viewing relics, attending the sacrifice of the Mass? What of images? Could they be idolatrous? Could it possibly be true that reformers such as Le Fèvre, Farel, Luther, Melanchthon, Zwingli, and Peter Robert were led of God? Wouldn't works and observances save a man? Should he learn Greek so that he could study the translation of the Bible prepared by the most famous of the Humanists, Desiderius Erasmus?

And the voice of the hermit of Livry rang again and again in his heart: "Have you heard, young gentlemen, that Christ's salvation *is* free. . . . A man is justified only through God's Grace; merits devised by an earthly church will never save him. . . . Oh, my dear countrymen, accept the new life in Christ which He has earned for you. For the Glory of God, the greatness of France, and

56

the salvation of your immortal souls!" The martyr's song pounded in his ears:

> The body they may kill,
> God's Truth abideth still
> His Kingdom is forever!

But what is Truth? How can I know? John prayed, "Dear Father in Heaven, show me thy light!"

It was the last Sunday in October, 1528. John attended early Mass at Notre Dame, and was coming out when Nerien came racing across the Grève. The twelve-year-old was almost as tall as John, who was now nineteen. Nerien's big ears stuck out through the yellow shoulder-length hair which sparkled in the morning sunlight. The blue eyes were wide.

"John, Messire sent me to find you. The Court Poet discovered that your cousin was to be arrested today. Peter Robert plans to flee Paris, and he wants to say good-by."

"Where is he?"

"In Messire's bedchamber. In case the soldiers come before he escapes, there is a secret passage to the stables. If the inn is watched, the Gospelers leave that way. A horse is saddled and waiting."

John thought quickly. A secret passage from Messire's bedchamber! That explains the talk that the Gospelers meet near the colleges. Nobody has confided in me before. Now that I know, what is my duty?

"John, we of the New Faith have been hoping you would join us," Nerien said as they strode along. "Anyway, Messire said you would never betray your friends. Some have felt you would be better off if you did not know. You are so conscientious. But I am trusting you."

Who are the others? John cudgeled his mind as he moved through the winding streets to the Pelican. The sign with its weathered bird was swinging back and forth in the whistling wind as they entered the inn. At that early hour the large common room was empty.

Upstairs in Messire La Farge's raftered bedchamber, a figure in a

57

monk's black cowl and white habit stood at the latticed window. It was Peter Robert. His powerful shoulders were bent, he had lost weight, and his eyes were as dull as pewter. In his arms was a large bundle.

"John!" he cried. "At Orléans I will finish the translation. There is a little inn near the Porte Jacques where I will live disguised like this and using the name of Louis Sandre."

What if I never see him again? John thought, and the lump in his throat felt like a great cloak button. Why I love Peter Robert more than anyone in Paris! And he is going away!

"Peter Robert," he managed to say after an interval, "somehow I hope you preserve your Bible. I sympathize with such a great faith. I know now about the secret stairs. Nerien told me this is the meeting place of the Gospelers. But I could never report any of you!"

"The light will break for you, too, John. Perhaps not all at once, but with your keen mind, it will surely come."

Tears streamed from John's eyes as he bent to touch his cheek to Peter Robert's, which was wet, too. "In the meantime, I will pray to God to keep you safe!" John whispered.

He watched Peter Robert shove back a wide panel in the wall on the side toward the stables, revealing a narrow stairway. With a wave of his hand he vanished and his manuscript with him.

As John climbed the hill toward the college on the mountain, again a feeling of guilt bit at him. The Holy Father was the Vicar of Christ on earth. His authority extended to cardinals, bishops, all canons, priests, monks, and chaplains. And he, John Calvin, was a chaplain. A chaplain who was in league with Gospelers, the scourge of the Church. He knew their meeting place, but he wasn't going to report his knowledge to Rector Beda and his heretic-hunting Sorbonne. Wasn't he as guilty as the Gospelers?

When he returned to his uncle's that night, he found a letter addressed in his father's familiar scrawl. He read it with varying emotions, disappointment predominating. The letter ordered him to pack at once and go to Orléans where arrangements had been made for him to study law and to board with Nicholas Duchemin, a former resident of Noyon. Lawyers, his father pointed out, were men of influence. An ordinary career in the Church these days was heartbreaking, and Charles, John's brother, was already in difficulty with the canons because he raised questions.

John felt hollow inside. He did not want to be a lawyer; he wanted to be a priest. Once he found answers to his questions, he knew he could be a useful priest. And he didn't want to leave Paris. He had looked forward to attending one of the secret meetings of the Gospelers and confronting them with some arguments. But Holy Writ commanded that a son must obey his father.

As he packed, the sudden conviction came that God was in this summons. He didn't know why. But if God was leading him to Orléans, he would wait and see where His will was pointing. And as he threw his books into the leather box on top of his clothes, he remembered that the famous Melchior Wolmar taught theology there as well as Greek. Dr. Wolmar, a man of remarkable physical ugliness, but of brilliant mind, was said to be a great Bible scholar. Perhaps at his feet one might learn the truth.

In Orléans, the first thing John did after unpacking was to walk to the inn to find Peter Robert. The innkeeper directed him to the room "Louis Sandre" occupied. When John knocked on the heavy door, there was no answer. He tried the handle. The door was bolted from the inside.

He rattled the knob, saying, "It is I, John. Let me in."

Then the bolt slid back, and Peter Robert stood there, smiling welcome. "John! Never have I been so surprised. Come in."

John noted the tired tone of his voice, his sagging shoulders. "Tell me, Peter Robert, why you bolt your door. I thought you would be safe in Orléans."

"Dr. Wolmar believes word was sent from Paris that I might come here. He has heard rumors. Every new arrival is scrutinized. I go out only after dark."

"Then there is trouble here, too?"

"A group of the canons persecute Dr. Wolmar, but he goes on teaching his beliefs. They threaten him with arrest unless he stops declaring the doctrines of salvation by faith and God's sovereignty."

They chatted on for a while about the continuing unrest within the Church and without.

59

As John rose to leave, he asked, "Can I buy you any supplies? Is there anything I can do for you, Peter Robert?"

His cousin's strong face brightened. "Yes, John. Will you write a preface for the French Bible?"

"Me? Why?"

"You made a reputation for yourself as a student in Paris. You write with clarity. Too, you are my favorite cousin. It would mean a great deal to me, John."

How can I refuse? John thought. Yet to do such a thing will be like chaining myself to the stake.

"If you don't feel that you can——"

John cut him short. "But I do. Since the Church has never officially forbidden the common man to read the Bible, I am not going against its authority. I have come to believe in your work. I want to have a part in it."

Professor l'Etoile was expounding some of the writings of the Dutch scholar, Desiderius Erasmus, one morning. Dr. Erasmus blamed the corruption in the Church on the rule of celibacy. John remembered that the original Scriptures said that the Apostle Peter had a wife. He raised his hand.

"Professor, if the Apostle Peter had a wife, why cannot the Holy Father marry?"

There was a silence, during which nobody moved. The professor's mouth dropped open, and he looked down his beaked nose, frowning.

"Thieves can steal your purses," he roared, "but heretics your Heaven. You, Monsieur Calvin, have evidently been associating with heretics! When you speak of the Holy Father, remember that he is Christ's representative upon earth!"

"I'm sorry," John gulped. "I thought you commended the use of the mind."

"I commend the use of the mind, young man! But beware lest you use it in such a way as to injure the Church!"

After supper that night at Duchemin's, Jodocus, John's roommate, who had formerly been a gray friar, John, and another roomer, Francis Daniel, continued to sit around the table. Their talk turned to the favorite subject of students everywhere, the so-called New Religion versus the old. John told them how disturbed Professor l'Etoile had been over his question.

"A Christian's first duty is to obey God," Jodocus said. "To do that today he must first disobey the Roman Church."

"Doesn't it all boil down to the question of authority? God's or the Holy Father's?" Francis asked thoughtfully.

John could feel his temper rising. "Do they necessarily conflict?"

Jodocus was upset. "There is nothing in the Holy Scriptures which says that a man must look to one man or any organization for his salvation. It comes as a free gift from God, not because of anything man merits but because of His Grace!"

"But God created the Church before the Bible and gave Peter the keys to the Kingdom," John said.

"The keys to the Kingdom belong to all Christians, not just one!" Jodocus insisted. "The popes have progressively assumed authority never given them by God!"

Francis Daniel came to John's aid. "As God's Holy Vicars, the popes rule by divine right."

Jodocus gasped. "Do I have to sit here and listen to you make such an assinine assertion. You are supposed to be an intelligent man!"

John rose and faced Jodocus with fists clenched. "I will not sit here and listen to your blasphemy! You are a disgrace, Jodocus! A disgrace to the name of Christ!"

"To the name of Christ or to the name of the Vicar of Christ? There is a difference."

"Enough of this," Francis said placatingly. "Make your protests somewhere else. John and I are in agreement that we will respect the position of the head of the Church. Do you have to be so violent?"

"What are you both so afraid of? Using your minds? What about the time there were *two* popes? Were they *both* ruling by divine right?"

John turned on his heel and left the room. . . .

He was studying when Jodocus came upstairs and said humbly, "Forgive me, John. Ever since the Diet of Spires, those who believe in the simple Gospel of Christ, as set forth in the Scriptures, have

61

felt obliged to protest abuses in the Church. That is where we got the name Protest-ant. I didn't want to wound you. I was just stating what I believe the Bible says."

"That's all right," John said gruffly.

The next night before they left the table Francis Daniel started the discussion all over again. "I've been thinking about our conversation last night. My sister is about to take her final vows, and it's all so simple when one is told what to believe. There is no mental struggle. Authority can be a good thing."

John was about to agree when a messenger strode in with a note for him from Dr. Wolmar. John ripped it open.

"Bad news?" Francis asked.

"The worst. Dr. Wolmar has a cold and has to stay in bed. He wants me to teach his classes!"

"What an honor!" Jodocus was impressed. "Of course you will do it."

"I don't know. I'm making progress with my Greek. But theology! I have to compare the beliefs of the two great theologians, Augustine and Thomas Aquinas! Then I am to compare their beliefs with Paul's theology in the Book of Romans! As it is, I am up half the night studying for my law classes."

"That is an assignment!" Jodocus whistled.

"You can do that," Francis encouraged.

"No. No. I cannot."

Francis nodded in understanding. "It seems to be dangerous to teach Paul's theology today because of the Protestant emphasis on it."

Man's greatest duty is to seek God's will and do it . . . He must listen for the Voice. . . . It will sound for the servant who longs to hear it, for be certain that God is in all events leading, shoving, pushing his servants into the right paths of service. The beloved bishop had told John that long ago.

He turned to Jodocus. "I will try. If Dr. Wolmar has that much faith in me, I can try. But I am so ignorant!"

"There's hope in that," Jodocus said with a chuckle. "I didn't think you knew it."

Ever since the motherless nine-year-old Theodore de Beza had come with his Greek teacher, Dr. Melchior Wolmar, to Orléans, he had heard the doctor talk incessantly about a brilliant young scholar, John Calvin. Theodore idolized Dr. Wolmar with whom he lived, and he liked to know the doctor's friends.

As the days passed Theodore heard others speak of John Calvin, who was well known by the time he had been in Orléans seven months. Some said he was on the road to becoming a dangerous heretic like Dr. Le Fèvre or William Farel, and that the spies of the Sorbonne were watching him. There were those who declared he was called of God to purge the Church that it might return to the true Gospel preached by the early apostles. Theodore, as curious as most youngsters, longed to see this man who was at once so hated and so admired.

One cloudy April morning, as he was playing near the city gate, a gaunt man above medium height strode across the Rue des Arenes. He was a purposeful figure in his flapping black robe and flat velvet cap, and quite handsome, although a trifle thin.

"There goes that heretic, Calvin," Theodore heard one monk whisper to another as they went through the gate.

A band of students approached, greeting Calvin respectfully. Some traders drew their wagon to a halt, and one asked if Calvin would come to his home the next night to teach the Scriptures. Two women on horseback stared at him.

At the Porte de Jacques Coeur, where Theodore was playing, Calvin paused and his bright eyes fastened on the motto written large on the gates: "To the valiant heart, nothing is impossible."

Theodore ran to him to tug on his black sleeve. "Do you have a valiant heart, Messire, or are you a heretic?"

The young man's face came alive like that of a man waking up. Theodore felt the black eyes burning into him, and made a bobbing bow. The smile that crinkled the corners of Calvin's full-lipped mouth seemed to light up the whole street. There was kindness in those eyes, and honesty and goodness on that face. This was no wicked man. He couldn't be.

When Monsieur Calvin spoke, his voice was melodious and very deep, a wonderful voice, warm and kind like his eyes. He put a hand on Theodore's shoulder.

63

"I try to have a valiant heart, little boy. But I'll tell you a secret. Sometimes I am afraid."

"Of what are you afraid, Messire?"

"Strange students. I find teaching difficult." He pointed toward the motto on the gates. "When I read that, I add something: 'To the valiant heart,' *which seeks and does God's will,* 'nothing is impossible.' I repeat that over and over. I pray. Then I can do anything."

"You looked scared a few minutes ago."

"Did I?" He drew a deep breath. "I am all right now. I have to lecture again this morning in Dr. Wolmar's place. An hour ago I would rather have been tied to the whipping post."

"Why do you do what you do not want to do?"

"Because I am a Christian. I have vowed to seek God's will and obey him. Obedience, my son, is the key to a successful life, because a man can never be truly successful apart from God. Now run along. You should be in school. Obedience begins with duty."

As Monsieur Calvin stalked into the Rue du Dieu d'Armour where the heretics were burned, Theodore said a prayer of intercession to the Virgin to protect him. The last the boy saw of Monsieur Calvin, he was vanishing around the corner of the rusty cage where King Louis XI used to imprison his enemies.

When I grow up, Theodore thought, I want to be like him. He looked up at the motto again: "To the valiant heart nothing is impossible." Then he read it aloud, inserting Monsier Calvin's clause: "To the valiant heart, which seeks and does God's will, nothing is impossible!" So that is the key to a successful life. I must remember it.

"You may have to take my classes permanently," Dr. Wolmar told John one day in May. "Attempts have been made time and time again to silence me on Scriptural theology. Your cousin, Peter Robert, thinks that both he and I should flee."

"I'd hate to see you go, and I'm sure the university would never ask me to take your place."

"The opposition to truth has never come from the authorities there. You have made remarkable progress in all your studies. People are begging for your instruction in the Holy Scriptures. You are the only one who can carry on my work."

"Teaching languages is not such a strain, but you must have sensed how difficult I find the teaching of the Scriptures. I manage only by trying to think of myself as a lawyer pleading God's cause."

"You are an excellent teacher, and I have appreciated your help."

"If this is good-by, I wish you well."

"Pray for me, John. I shall be needing it."

That evening after supper, Peter Robert appeared at John's room at Duchemin's. Jodocus was at the library, so they were alone.

"Dr. Wolmar and I are to leave tonight," Peter Robert announced. "He is going to Bourges. I expect to have the Bible printed in Neufchâtel or Strasbourg. It will be a relief to leave Orléans. I tremble every time I hear a footstep at my door. I cannot sleep. My appetite is gone. And I haven't completed my translation yet."

"Have a care, Peter Robert!"

"God will take care of me. Once the translation is finished, whether I live or die matters little. But I will spend whatever remains of my life teaching others about salvation."

"It took a long time for me to figure out that you were behind Dr. Wolmar's request that I teach his classes. You knew I would study hard and discover the truth for myself!"

Peter Robert laughed, dispelling the tired lines around his mouth. "I had to win you to our cause, John. The Reformation had to have you."

"Peter Robert," said John, after a moment of thoughtful silence, "I never want to leave our Church. Don't you see that I should work to glorify it, and by so doing glorify Jesus Christ? Don't you understand, Peter Robert? I do not want to be a Gospeler. What I long to do is to bring the religion of Paul and the apostles back to my Church!"

Three weeks later John sat in the Duchemin garden one afternoon reading the little Book of James. Since Peter Robert and Dr. Wolmar had left the city, certain hotheads had persisted in denouncing the faked miracles of four or five priests, attacking the Church because of them. John, trying to help Professor l'Etoile

65

quiet the disturbance, had remonstrated with the troublemakers, but to no avail. He thought the admonitions about the tongue, presented in a forceful manner, might have some effect. So he was preparing a pointed lesson for the next day.

He looked up to watch a white cat stalking a robin. The little bird lifted its wings and flew to an apple tree out of reach of the sharp teeth and sharper claws. Cats! Claws! Cats had no business in gardens! There were cats in God's garden, too, waiting to pounce, but the birds were careful. He said a spontaneous prayer for Dr. Wolmar and Peter Robert.

Soon the unbelievable greenness all about him began to give him a sense of peace. The unease within him lifted, and closing his eyes, he dozed, the sun warm upon him.

"John!" The excited voice of Nicholas Duchemin aroused him. "This letter just came from Noyon for you by special messenger."

John took the letter and broke the seal. It was from Charles. Their father was very ill. He was receiving the best of care. He had recently remarried and his wife was devoted. But if John wanted to see him alive again, he had better come now.

5

June 29, 1529

As the twenty-two-year-old John rode into Noyon, memories pressed down upon him. . . . He was a small boy again, moving forward, with his hand in that of his pretty mother, to kiss the thorn from Christ's crown. Blood spurted from the wounds of the crucified. Tall tapers beside the gold reliquary shed their golden radiance into the gloom, and incense filled the air as he knelt, vowing allegiance for all eternity. . . . It brought an odd ache to view this self of earlier years. Is my allegiance the same? he thought. Or have I changed? What would my mother think of her son today? He sighed as he rode down the hill to the grain-market square. It looks just the same, but time changes many things.

He tied his horse to the iron hitching-post, and went inside his old home. For an instant he felt as if he had dreamed the years of his absence. The sailing ship his father had made for him so long ago was on the wide window ledge. Every picture was in its familiar place. In one—his favorite—St. Francis still fed the cowled larks. At the table, circling a blue bowl filled with spraying lilies, sat the clerics. Everything was just as he remembered it. The clerics looked up, frowning at first. As recognition came, they bowed stiffly.

"John Calvin," one with grizzled eyebrows greeted. "Welcome home. You return our distinguished son. We hear you are a noted scholar. Nicholas Duchemin has written us of your efforts to quell the disturbance against the priests. Your loyalty is to be commended."

John thanked them, and asked, "How is my father?"

There was a slow shaking of heads, and voices said, "He is a very sick man." "He is waiting for you upstairs." "He is too sick to receive our complaints today." "We are going to the chapel now to light candles for him and say our prayers."

They rose in a body and filed toward the door. One with a sharp, swarthy face paused, scowling, and John held his breath. Have any of them heard that I've been teaching the theology of Augustine and Paul? he thought.

"Before you leave," the sharp-faced canon said, "we want to hear about your plans for the future, specifically if you plan to take your vows."

As the canons filed out, Varnessa Calvin came down the stairs and found herself facing an erect young man with narrow black beard and the blackest, most penetrating eyes she had ever seen. In wonder she looked at her stepson: John Calvin, the scholar people talked about, had come home. She hoped he would approve of her. She wanted all Gerard's children to like her. But she quailed before this one; there was something forbidding in his dignity.

"I am glad you have come," she ventured.

John moved one foot and then the other like a nervous colt. At last he spoke in a small voice: "How do you do?"

"I am fine, John. I hope we will be friends. I could never be a substitute for your mother. I wouldn't try. But I hope to have a place of my own in your heart."

Suddenly the friendliness on his face transfigured it. "I am grateful for all you are doing for Father. Mother would be, too." Impulsively he put his arms around her.

"Come, John, your father is waiting. Let us go to him together," she said.

As they entered the quiet room, John felt that he was in the presence of a dying man. His father's face was flushed, his limbs emaciated. The tired eyes in their sunken sockets had been fixed on the ceiling, but now they turned toward him.

"John, my son," Gerard Calvin whispered, "I am glad they sent for you. This is the end."

John leaned over the bed. "With such a wife to care for you, you may get well."

The sick man looked doubtful. "A tumor. I don't see how I can last many months." It was difficult for him to speak, but he seemed to want to tell his son something more and John waited quietly. "The bishop has retired, and a relative has succeeded him. The canons have complained time and time again that I ordered you to study law. John, are you unhappy at the prospect of becoming a lawyer?"

"I have never ceased longing to be a priest."

"Then perhaps you should take your final vows and aim for a high place in Rome."

"I wouldn't want that."

"Why not? A man owes it to God and to himself to make the most of his life."

"I would rather write and teach."

The older man was quiet for a moment. "In your teaching, have you been able to keep your faith?"

"In Christ? Yes. It is stronger than ever. But I am convinced that our Church needs to return to the simple Gospel of the New Testament."

Gerard Calvin sighed. "Sometimes I think the Church needs purifying. But never underestimate the work of the good priests and canons who live like Christians. Youth has the idea that it can change everything overnight."

"And perhaps age is too tired to fight for the right."

"I am tired."

"I didn't mean you would compromise with evil. But every servant of Christ must have His ideals before him and strive to hold them."

"You haven't been taken in by this tenet your brother Charles proclaims, that only faith can save a man?"

John leaned forward. "Father, that was the Apostle Paul's great theme. St. Augustine emphasized it. Man has lost sight of it. But

69

it's true; Christ has earned our salvation. The gift is given only through His Grace. The Pope cannot give it. The institution of the Church cannot give it. Only Jesus Christ!"

"Oh, my son, those are the Protestant beliefs!"

"They are Scriptural. I have vowed to do everything possible to help the Church return to the authority of the Bible."

"What is the matter with you and Charles? I have spent my life trying to keep heresy out of the Church. First Charles became infected"—his voice broke—"and now you! Your mother's greatest hope."

"God is leading me."

"Be careful, Son. Be certain it is really God's voice you hear. Do not make decisions rashly."

"Can you imagine me doing anything without good reason?"

"No, John. You usually think through your problems."

The younger man swallowed the lump in his throat. "Then do not grieve, dear Father. When the time comes to take my vows, I will know what I am doing."

"Can you take the vow of obedience?"

"That is the key to my life—obedience to God's will as revealed in His Word."

Gerard Calvin frowned, gritting his teeth. "That settles it. You are confused by the new ideas circulating at Orléans. You are to continue the study of law. You shall go to Bourges!"

As John went downstairs a few minutes later, he asked himself if it was God's will that he go to Bourges, or his father's. His father was too ill to argue the matter, and he had always obeyed him. He decided not to rebel.

The next morning as he closed the door of his home on the grain-market square behind him, his heart was heavy. He rode away thinking that he would never see his father again. And the question burned in his mind: "Can you take the vow of obedience?"

In Bourges, John studied under the famous Italian, Professor Andrew Alciati, whom King Francis had invited to France. The professor applied philology in a manner that delighted John, to whom the science of words had always been fascinating.

There, too, he was reunited with Dr. Wolmar, and they often

70

walked together, discussing theology, the battle going on in the Church, and the political situation. The city, with a Protestant sympathizer, Queen Marguerite, ruling it, was free from persecution.

Ambling beside Dr. Wolmar along the banks of the Auron late one Saturday afternoon, John suddenly felt that God was trying to speak to him, that He was there at his side, within him—but the voice was muffled. He turned to look at the man strolling beside him. God leads me to men who can guide my thoughts, he meditated. Why not consult Dr. Wolmar about taking my vows?

Before he could phrase his question, Dr. Wolmar said, "John, God led you to Bourges just as he led you to Orléans."

"I was just thinking that."

"Do you feel that He is calling you to face persecution for the Gospel's sake?"

"I am certain He wants me to teach the Bible."

"Yet you are torn between the truth and the authority you must obey."

"I shall never forget the day I was shorn. I felt as if I could not wait to take my final vows. Now everything is so complicated. My father has ordered me to become a lawyer."

"And you want to be a priest?"

John nodded. "Yet—something is holding me back."

"I understand. With a knowledge of the Scriptures a problem has arisen."

John answered slowly, reflectively, "My first duty is to obey God. The Church is God's instrument. Surely He has delegated His authority to the Church in the person of the Vicar of Christ. Yet——"

Dr. Wolmar cut him short. "Yet you feel that you cannot obey the authority of the Church at Rome and God at the same time."

"Yes. Someone said that to begin to obey God today a Christian first had to disobey the Church of Rome."

"Had you stopped to realize, John, that there is the visible church and the *invisible?*"

As the days mounted into weeks and months, John pondered time and time again Dr. Wolmar's question: "Had you stopped to realize, John, that there is the visible church and the invisible?"

71

He began reading the Lutheran books which were freely circulated in Bourges. He continued delving into the Scriptures. He wrote the preface for Peter Robert's Bible and sent it to him. As at Orléans, he taught some of Dr. Wolmar's classes. John was content except for one problem—whether or not he should take his vows. His father wanted him to be a lawyer, and a son was commanded to obey his father. The command of the Father in Heaven, however, was above that of an earthly father. If God wants me to become a priest, he thought, I will obey God. But how can I be sure?

In September of 1531, when Louisa of Savoy died, people everywhere were discussing the mounting persecutions in Paris. Michael d'Armande, the Queen of Navarre's confessor, was seized and sent to the stake. Louis de Berquin interceded with the Queen for those arrested for heresy, and she in turn interceded with her brother, the King. His paramour, Madame d'Étampes, used her influence to help the Lutherans, too. But Cardinal Duprat, scheming with some of the professors of the Sorbonne, also had the King's ear. Actually the King, who worshiped art in all forms, seemed to care little for any religion.

One night, unable to sleep, John rose from his bed, lit a candle, and opened the Bible. Turning to the book of Romans, as he so often did, he read: "The Spirit also helps our infirmity, for we do not know how to pray as we should; but the Spirit himself makes intercession for us with groanings that cannot be uttered. . . ." *If the Spirit intercedes for us, why do we need saints?* he thought. *Isn't the Spirit of God all-sufficient?* He continued to read:

And he that searches hearts knows what is in the mind of the Spirit because he makes intercession for the saints according to God. And we *know* that all things work together for good for those who love God, to those who are called according to his purpose. For whom he did foreknow, he also did predestinate to be conformed to the image of His Son, that he might be the first-born among numerous brethren. Moreover whom he did predestinate, them he also called, and whom he called, them he also justified. And whom he justified, them he also glorified.

"I shall be glorified," the hermit of Livry had said. John read on, his heart beating faster and faster. "What then shall we say of these things? *If God be for us who can be against us?*"

And in that instant came a revelation. The Scriptures, God's Word, plainly said that a man can never *earn* his salvation, *for every man is a corrupt sinner*. That is why he needs salvation! But God, the merciful judge, says: "I will forgive. Come unto me through faith. Repent. You will be born again. Born to a life where you will seek my will and by doing it glorify me."

These are the things I will have to teach, John thought in dismay. Man is nothing. I know now. God is all. The great church is the Church Invisible!

When the Lord of Signiéres asked him to preach in the parish church the next week, his heart felt like water. How could he accept the invitation? After supper the day he received it he went to see Dr. Wolmar.

"I know now the Church Invisible is the great church," he confessed, "but I do not want to stir up dissension."

"You seek truth, do you not?"

"Yes. But good men differ as to what that is. Surely it would be wrong to go into the pulpit of the Church of Rome and preach in a manner that would make for disunity among Christians!"

"Then you believe in peace at any price? At the price of truth?"

In soul-searching agony, John asked himself: Is God commanding me to go into the parish church and tell the people about salvation? If the New Testament is the rule of faith and the people are confused, isn't it my duty? He had to find an answer.

He left Dr. Wolmar and walked swiftly along the narrow street to the Cathedral of St. Étienne. Inside the cool darkness enveloped him. A solitary candle lit the gloom. Nothing stirred in the beautiful sanctuary; not even the priests were about. John moved toward the altar and stretched full length on the cold stones. "If it is thy will, O God, make me ready to speak freely at all times and face death itself for the Gospel's sake. . . ."

As he prayed and meditated, he seemed to see the world as a dark maze. Man was stumbling about in the labyrinth, lost without a light or a map. Then Christ, the Schoolmaster, appeared in the darkness and gave lost man the Bible, the guide to life. John stared in awe at the painted image of the Christ, certain in this moment that God was calling him to hammer His Truth into the hearts of men.

The next Sunday, as he began to preach, bright sunlight, streaming through the stained-glass windows, suffused the figure on the Cross with a jewel-like glow. Again knowledge flowed through him in a swift surge of joy. God had never intended His Word to be chained. Peter Robert had been right; he had been right about so many things. When God's light shines, the darkness is dispelled.

John spoke with confidence, explaining election, grace, God's sovereignty, man's salvation, and the priesthood of every believer. He was so intent on his message that he did not see the monks' hands tighten on the edges of the benches, or their lips freeze in displeasure.

Later, as he led in the Pater Noster, he suggested, in a flash of inspiration, that it be ended without the usual "Hail Mary!" A startled ripple went through the congregation, and as the service ended, he was surrounded by disapproving eyes and forbidding faces.

"Dear Brother John," an Augustinian with eyes the color of warm earth began, "we always follow the Pater Noster with a 'Hail Mary!' Surely you do not intend to belittle the power of the Mother of God!"

The monk's distress was pathetic.

But John, mindful that Christians were one in Christ, did not want to quarrel. Some words flashed into his mind, the words of his Lord: "Who is my mother? And who are my brethren? Behold my mother and my brethren. For whosoever shall do the will of my Father who is in Heaven, the same is my brother, and sister, *and mother*."

Slowly he repeated the words aloud, and the monks winced.

"Cease such blasphemy!" a fat canon said. " 'Tis offensive!"

"Is it blasphemy against Christ to give Him the place He deserves at the *center* of our worship?" John inquired gently.

"What of the blessed saints?"

"Is it honor to the saints to rob God of his honor and transfer

74

it to them, that they be worshiped promiscuously with God? If this be true, a block of wood could be our Father in Heaven!"

The monks murmured in unison. One with glacial eyes protested, "Watch out, Brother John. That sort of talk leads to the stake!"

"We warn you as friends," the fat one said, folding his pudgy hands piously over his plump middle.

"Wait until the archbishop hears of this!" a jaundiced man whispered, his face contorted in horror.

"Perhaps you are bewitched," the moon-faced monk said brightly. "There is a woman in Paris who can exorcise demons."

Once again the winter snows melted and green shoots showed in the fertile land. John had not been asked to preach since he had horrified the clergy, but he continued to teach, even at the Augustinian monastery, since he was expounding rhetoric and not theology. Sometimes a monk came up to question him about the new ideas; they seemed to be conscious of the fact that it was one of their order, Martin Luther, who had set in motion the machinery of the Reformation.

Early in July, a messenger from Noyon brought a summons from Charles. Their father was unconscious and sinking fast. John packed, hired a horse, and set out once more for his old home. As he rode down the familiar hill, he saw the long, black ribbons on the door and knew he was too late.

Charles and Anthony met him at the steps. Charles's vestment hung on his large-boned body, for he had lost flesh. His face had acquired the austerity of their late father's. Anthony, now twenty-one, had a well-developed body, a strong face with deep black eyes, and a pronounced cleft in his chin. They greeted John with swift embrace. Mary and Tina, his sisters, appeared from the cookhouse.

Again John had the feeling that he had dreamed the years he had been away. The five of them sat down about the oak table where the clerics so often wrangled. The sailing ship stood on the window sill. St. Francis fed the larks. Outside there were the usual sounds of pigeons cooing and children at play on the cobbles. In a few minutes Varnessa joined them, her eyes red from weeping.

"Have you told John?" she asked, as she drew up a chair.

Anthony looked at his brother. John had the appearance of a scholar, the pallor of skin, the slight frown between his arched brows. With his ear-length black hair, large arresting eyes, and neatly clipped black beard, he was a young man people would turn to look at. It was a relief that he had come, for there was strength in him. And strength was needed now.

Charles turned toward him. "Before father got sick, John, the Chapter accused him of misappropriating an account, the one for your benefice at La Gesine Chapel."

John clenched his fists, and his eyes sparked. "Why wasn't I told of this?"

"Father thought he could straighten it out before you resigned your benefices and became a lawyer. He didn't want to worry you."

"But why was he accused of a breach that damnable?"

"I think it was to silence me," Charles said, "about some frauds I had discovered. Some money the Chapter controlled disappeared mysteriously once before. There is a thief among the canons. By accusing father, they thought they could divert my attention."

John leaped to his feet. "These are the clerics supposed to reveal God to the people!" His fist pounded the table until the flower bowl rattled and the water splashed to the floor. "Why didn't the bishop conduct an investigation?"

"He's not here. The new bishop grew a beard, too, wider and longer than the one Bishop de Hangest had. The quarrel over his beard grew so heated that he took off for Rome, ordering Father to be responsible only to him in the matter of accounts. Now the canons have usurped the authority of the absent bishop and refuse to allow Father to be buried in hallowed ground."

Again John's fist pounded and again the flower bowl rattled. "There must be someone to whom we can appeal!"

"Your old friend and classmate, Claude, is now the Abbot of St. Eloi."

"Claude! Of course. I shall go to him at once."

As John left, slamming the door behind him, Anthony felt as if a weight had fallen from his shoulders. John would turn Rome itself upside down when he was in a rage. Then people forgot how slim he was and quailed before him.

In less than two hours John was back, his face grim. "Proceed with the arrangements," he said. "Father's funeral will be at ten in the morning and the internment will be in the churchyard!"

On the Sunday following the funeral, John was preaching in the gray stone church at Pont l'Évêque, a second parish the bishop had assigned to him since he had not yet resigned his benefices. Again he was making salvation his theme, telling the friends of his childhood in Augustine's own words: "He who created you without you will not save you without you." His mind was suddenly jarred from his sermon, and he started as if a whip had flayed his back. A familiar face stood out in the crowd, a face with cold gray eyes and a long nose; Meheste's. The Sorbonne's chief spy!

Icy terror gripped him. Meheste! In Pont l'Évêque! John felt stone walls closing in, suffocating him. He murmured a prayer, and in a few seconds regained his self-control. His mind cleared, and he finished his message.

Immediately after the service Meheste approached him. He came so close that John could smell his putrid breath and unwashed body.

"I must speak to you in privacy," Meheste said sternly. "Come."

John followed Beda's informer to the little room behind the altar.

"We have been trying to trace your cousin, Peter Robert, known as 'Olivétan,' " said the spy. "Where is he?"

"He was in Orléans briefly. I don't know exactly where he is now."

"We have reason to believe he is in Picardy. I am staying at the inn on the road to Noyon. Notify me if he shows up."

Could Peter Robert be in Picardy? Had his Bible been published? Was that why the Sorbonne sought him? So alarmed that it sent its most important bloodhound to trace him? Or had they learned that he, John, was teaching so-called Protestant theology? Was this man here to spy on him, pretending it was Peter Robert he sought?

"Well, Monsieur Calvin, speak up! You are willing to help Mother Church? You will notify me?"

For an instant John saw an unholy light in those gray eyes. Meheste enjoys hunting men, he thought. He is like a wild dog sniffing blood.

"If there is anything I should tell you, I will come to you. But as far as I know my cousin is in Germany somewhere."

That night John stayed up late talking to his brothers. Although it was almost midnight when he went to his room, he lay sleepless on the curtained bed. If he were the target, how would the heretic-hunters proceed?

The clock downstairs chimed two. Somewhere a cat cried. After an interval an owl screeched. Then John thought he heard someone calling his name and wondered if he had dreamed it.

"John! John!" Someone *was* calling him.

He jumped out of bed, padded across the cold floor in his bare feet and stepped out on the balcony. A tall, black-cloaked figure stood below.

"In the name of God, John, let me in quickly."

John's hand was shaking so that he could hardly light the candle. If Meheste were hiding in the shadows over by the grain-market stalls, it would go ill with any who sheltered a heretic. John ran down the stairs and drew back the bolt. Peter Robert darted in, his shadow reflected on the ceiling by the quivering candlelight.

"Did you see anyone out there?"

"No, John. Why?"

John told him quickly about Meheste and his questions. He blew out the candle and they sat down in the dark to talk. "What are you doing here?" John asked.

Peter Robert sighed. "Life has not been easy since I left Orléans. Disguised, I have just been to Paris to consult the Protestants about smuggling in the new Bibles which will be ready within the year. Clement warned me not to tarry. I had had a letter from Uncle Gerard telling me how ill he was, and I circled around hoping for a last visit with him. I had no idea I would be followed from Paris."

"You knew Father died?"

He nodded. "I met a servingman near the Mommor castle who told me Uncle Gerard was being buried, but I dared not come out of the woods to attend the funeral."

"I fear he died thinking I was a heretic," John said solemnly.

"He knows better now. I guess there are surprises in store for all of us the other side of the grave."

"Yes." John was silent for a moment. "And what of Paris? What is going on there?"

"Nicholas Cop is distinguishing himself as a professor in the College of St. Barbe. The Court Poet still manages to keep in the good graces of the King by promising him immortality."

"Does he continue to write good poetry?"

"He is an excellent poet. After all, his father was one of the last precise rhymers, a purebred Norman from the neighborhood of Cahors. Clement has the passion of our countrymen for struggling, so he opposes the Papists, but only in secret!"

They both laughed.

"Then the persecution continues?"

Peter Robert shook his head. "It mounts. Berquin was imprisoned for the third time last month. The King was at his chateau and the Papists took the opportunity to put Berquin to death. Within an hour he was sentenced for heresy and tied to the stake!"

"He was one of the brave!"

"What worries me now is that the Protestants may do something rash. The hate-mongers among them are inflamed over Berquin's death. Somebody should try to keep them in check."

"I think I will go back to Paris. I have my own decisions to make now. I have had three years of law, and I am giving it up. Ideas spread all over the world from Paris, like spokes of a wagon wheel."

"Do not underestimate the danger."

"I will be prudent."

"As for me, I think I will start traveling before dawn. When the Bible is ready for distribution, I plan to follow William Farel to Geneva. You can write me there."

"Again we part. You go to publish and distribute your Bibles. I go back, perhaps to confess Christ under Beda's nose. And, Peter Robert, if you hear the echoes in Geneva, say a prayer for me. I shall be needing it!"

6

1530-1533

When John reached Paris in April, he took a small, secluded room on the third floor of the Collège de Fortret in the Rue Sept Voies opposite the Collège de Montaigu. Its only window looked out toward the Convent of the Bernardines. The furnishings were simple: a plain bed, a square table, one chair, and a small armoire. As soon as he had unpacked, he enrolled in a Greek class taught by Peter Dane, and in a Hebrew course with Paul Paradis.

Early dark was falling as he walked toward the Pelican. Lights were coming on and a damp wind was blowing up from the Seine. John was bursting with excitement at the thought of seeing Nerien, Nicholas, and Messire La Farge after such a long separation. As he pushed open the ponderous door, he was greeted by the delicious smell of beef browning on the spit above the huge hearth. There was the odor, too, of brewed posset. A buzz of conversation arose from students and guests at their evening meal, but his friends were not there.

A boy with buck teeth appeared to ask for his order, but John told him he would have his supper later and inquired about Nerien,

Nicholas, and Messire. The innkeeper had gone to St. Denis, Dr. Cop had not been there all day, and Nerien was upstairs studying.

John ascended the familiar steps two at a time, and as he knocked at Nerien's door, his memory conjured up the picture of a grimy child with tear-streaked face, so pained, so unhappy, so deprived of love.

"Come in," a deep voice called.

The smells of tallow and flowers mingled as John entered. A large candle and a bowl of apple blossoms were on the plank table beside several stacks of books. One volume was propped open, and the young man reading it was so intent that he did not look up.

"That must be interesting," John said quietly.

"It is." Nerien lifted his blue eyes.

What a contrast he was to that boy of ten years ago. This neatly dressed youth, in yellow doublet with full green sleeves, was an educated gentleman. His face was still solemn, but as recognition came, his eyes brightened. He shoved the chair back, and moving swiftly from the table, threw his arms around his friend, hugging him as he had when he was a small boy.

"Master John! I wrote you a letter only last night. How are you? What are you doing in Paris? Are you well?"

John smiled. "First, Nerien, let me sit down. Then I'll tell you everything you wish to know."

Nerien offered him an armchair, and took his own seat again, leaning forward eagerly while John answered all his questions.

"The situation is worse than ever here," Nerien said at last. "The awful fact is that Beda has become a syndic, a magistrate, and is even more powerful than before!"

"I am glad you are safe. God is in this Reformation, but at times we all tremble!"

"The Protestants pray together. We are holding a meeting tomorrow night. Will you come?"

A secret meeting! John's heart beat swiftly. He had thought about these meetings and wished he could attend. How helpful it would be to pray and worship with those who shared his beliefs!

"What time? Where?" John was actually trembling with excitement.

"Midnight. Here at the Pelican. In Messire's bedchamber."

"Do I just walk in the front door?"

"No. Enter the stables as the clock on Notre Dame strikes the hour. You know the secret stairs leading up from the left rear corner. Shove the panels aside. But be alert. Listen for the warning."

"The warning?"

"Men will be posted to watch for spies. If you hear a man who seems to be a drunken reveler singing the poet Marot's 'Ballad of a Friar,' under no circumstances enter the inn yard."

"But I do not know the 'Ballad of a Friar.' "

"In it Friar Lubin represents an evil priest, and the ballad made the monks hate him. The refrain goes like this:

"At kind deeds few and evils many
Friar Lubin is as skilled as any.
And when there's mercy to be at
Friar Lubin can ne'er do that."

"If that is intended as an insult to the priests, I resent it. Many of them sacrifice everything for our faith!"

"But Master John, I did not mean to offend. I have no hatred for anyone."

John frowned. "Forgive me, Nerien. I'm touchy these days. Above all else I long for unity among Christians!"

"We should all strive for love of our fellow men, but sometimes I find it difficult."

"Sin has a way of coating us, if we allow it to."

"Master John, I was reading Niccolo Machiavelli's *The Prince* when you walked in just now. The author's ideal, Cesare Borgia, lacks the beliefs of Jesus and his disciples. Listen to this: 'A Prince in order to preserve his Princedom must act against good faith, charity, human rights, and religion . . . !' Such a one is a Prince of Darkness, while you, my very dear friend"—there was a catch in his voice—"you are a Prince of Light. Who else would have taken time to come week after week to teach a foundling to read and write so that he could become a useful citizen?"

John gulped. "Serve God, Nerien, and you will be a useful citizen."

"I have vowed to serve him. I want to be like you."

The next night at five minutes before midnight, John was striding along the crooked street toward the Inn of the Pelican, excitement churning within him. At last he was going to a secret meeting
of Protestants! He glanced over his shoulder, noting with relief that
nobody was in sight. Then, lost in thought, he forgot for a time to
look around again until an uneasy consciousness of danger coursed
through him. He turned quickly, but the street was empty.

Just ahead in the blackness was the Pelican, its leaded windows
dark, so that it seemed to be closed for the night. A gust of wind rattled the shutters and the tower clock struck twelve.

John was about to turn into the inn yard, when a man staggered
along the street and began to sing with the slightly thick tongue of
one under the influence of strong drink:

"Some ten or twenty times a day,
 To bustle to the town with speed,
 To dabble in what dirt he may,
 The Friar Lubin's the man you need!
 But any decent life to lead
 Upon an exemplary plan,
 Requires a Christian indeed,
 The Friar Lubin is *not* the man!"

John recognized that tenor voice. It belonged to the Court Poet!
Certainly this was the signal of danger. A chill ran through him,
and he did not turn into the inn yard but walked on, circling back
to his room. Disappointment gnawed at him. He had looked forward
to meeting others who shared his faith.

The next afternoon he noticed two straws protruding from the
slats of the shutter nearest the heavy door which led into the Pelican.
Nerien had sent a message that this was the signal for a meeting
that night, provided it was safe.

Again just before midnight John reached the entrance to the inn
yard. This time no drunken reveler staggered by. There was no
moon, and darkness like a shroud covered him as he trod softly across
the cobbles to the stable. While he was feeling his way slowly along
the rough walls, his hand touched something warm and alive, and
he barely stifled the cry that rose to his lips.

83

"S-h-h-h, Master John. It is I, Nerien. Come."

There was the scraping sound of a board being pushed back and then another, revealing a stairway where a small candle flickered.

"Take this," Nerien commanded, handing him the light. "When you reach the top, knock three times. Someone will let you in."

The steps leading up through the stuffy hole seemed countless. Up and up he went until he reached a small platform the size of a pillow. The sound of his knuckles on the heavy panel reverberated in the small closed space. Then the wood panel was shoved back and John stooped to go through the low opening.

About three dozen men and women were kneeling in prayer. Heads bowed, hands clasped, they recited the Pater Noster, the Lord's Prayer. John knelt, too, joining his voice with theirs.

As soon as everyone had resumed his seat on the plank benches or on the floor, Clement Marot stood up and quietly led them in the singing of a psalm:

> "How blest the man who ne'er consents to walk
> In sinner's ways, where men profanely talk;
> But who doth keep the law of God full truly
> Praising him mightily, worshiping right duly.
> Like a tree by pleasant waterside,
> Bearing sweet fruit in his own time and tide."

Then a man John had never seen before read from the Scriptures: " 'Blessed are the poor in spirit; for theirs is the kingdom of heaven. . . .' "

A prayer for guidance and protection concluded the brief service. Afterward they all discussed how best they might spread the truths they professed.

"Is there no way in which we can unite with the Church?" John had to ask. "If the Church can be reformed, what more can we ask?"

"Efforts are being made to that end," a lame man said hopefully.

"The political situation is more promising," Messire La Farge said. "Ever since the war ended, the King has devoted himself to the ideal of peace. He is making overtures to the German Protestants who have banded together against the Emperor. An alliance with them should help us."

84

"But be not fooled that our King is a man to whom religion is of importance," Clement Marot warned. "He observes the ritual, but where political interests are threatened by religious ones, he will sacrifice the religious. The more the pity!"

"If only in some way we could convert the King!" Messire frowned.

"He is very wroth that Syndic Beda should so malign Queen Marguerite. I heard him say that perhaps the scaffolds should rise for other than heretics. A controversy is raging at the Sorbonne over the Queen's book, *The Mirror of a Sinful Soul*, which makes no mention of saints or Purgatory." Clement shrugged.

Then John noticed, standing in a corner, a man he had not seen before. Matthew Cordier, his Latin professor! His eyes swept the others, and surprise almost took his breath away. There on the last row sat Nicholas Cop! Nicholas, too? The public executioner, Michael Sept, leaned against the paneling.

"With the King making overtures to other Protestants and Syndic Beda attacking a book written by a member of the royal family, we should have our day!" Cordier said happily.

Early in May a letter arrived from Peter Robert, who was in Geneva:

William Farel is trying to take the city for the faith of the New Testament. For years the people suffered under the Savoy yoke. The duke and the bishop fight to keep the New Faith out. But I am convinced the hand of God is moving here.

The prior of the Abbey of St. Victor outside the city proper has a nephew, Bonivard, who succeeded him. With two other patriots, Benzanson Hughes and Philibert Berthelier, Bonivard waged a fight for liberty. Berthelier was executed within sight of the people as a warning. When the duke and his bride, Beatrice of Portugal, who is the Emperor's sister-in-law, arrived in Geneva and had an heir, Hughes produced a mystery play upholding the infallibility of the Bible. That was the beginning of reform. The Protestants, or Huguenots, as many have called them since Hughes' mystery play, increase. Hughes had to flee for his life. The duke ruled with a horde of halberdiers, and the people pretended to submit.

But when Benzanson Hughes returned, the citizens forced the

duke to leave, annulling his decrees and claiming duress. With the alliance of Bern and Freiburg, the Genevans formed a state like the other Swiss cantons. It is said that Abe Holpen, one of Bern's early deputies, brought the true faith here the year the Emperor sacked Rome.

My life is satisfying. Bonivard has been raising money to help cover the cost of my Bibles. If the Gospel spreads from Geneva, which may soon be the Rome of Protestantism, it will go like a parched fire in a dry woods. Bonivard has been imprisoned again. There is the rumor he will soon be denied visitors. But I confer with him at the Castle of Chillon.

The seed is laid. The soil is fertile. God must have great plans for making Geneva His City. Wise leaders are needed. In His good time He will supply them.

Ever your faithful cousin,
Peter Robert

John replied, saying that he wanted a copy of the Bible as soon as one could be sent to him. He told Peter Robert, too, about the secret meetings he attended, and how much he hoped the Church would be reformed.

One day during the following October, as John started for a late afternoon walk, he met Nicholas Cop coming into the College of Fortret. Nicholas enjoyed his teaching at the school of medicine. In fact he took his responsibility so seriously that John did not see him very often, for Nicholas spent most of his time in his rooms preparing his lectures.

"John! Some of the students of the College of Navarre are to present a play this evening. I came by to see if you would like to go. Clement Marot thinks they are to caricature Queen Marguerite."

"They wouldn't dare!"

"Wouldn't they? If Beda is instigating it, that is in character. The man is a devil straight from Hell!"

"Maybe a lot of these rumors originate with the Protestants. Surely Beda would fear the King's wrath."

"The immorality at Court is no rumor. Filthy stories are told to while away the hours, and for years Claudette, Queen of France, has had to hold her head high and sit in the same room with her husband's light-o'-loves. I know. My father is the King's physician."

"If only the Court would turn to the reading of the Bible!"

"Not likely!"

"Perhaps there is some way——"

"The King is turning his special attention to literature these days. If you could write a popular book, he would read it."

A book! Suppose I wrote a manual setting forth the beliefs of the New Testament, John thought, the truth about salvation! God could bring the harvest according to His will. What if He is speaking through Nicholas? Books can penetrate where I cannot—even to the palace of the King, into the homes of those who shut their ears to Paul's theology, into the hovels of the humble and the castles of the noble. If it be God's will, such a book might endure through time, speaking to the hearts of men of an omnipotent God who offers a great gift, who draws them by His irresistible Grace to Himself with the words of the unerring, infallible Bible, the sole authority of His Truth!

"John. John!" Nicholas Cop was pulling on his sleeve. "What's the matter? Are you ill?"

Like one awaking from a dream, John turned and looked into his friend's eyes. "No, Nicholas. God just spoke to me through you. I believe he wants me to write down His plan to bring men to Him."

"Then let me order the first copy, John. Such a book will be read and talked about. That is certain. But about tonight—do you want to go?"

"Indeed I do. I have always heard that the Queen of Navarre is good and kind. Certainly she must not be ridiculed!"

"The play will be presented in the courtyard. We had better meet at the entrance an hour beforehand, about seven o'clock."

Several hundred people filed into the courtyard of the College of Navarre that night. They came from all walks of life—students, professors, clergymen, noblemen, burghers, and common citizens. The rumor that the King's sister, the Queen of Navarre, would be attacked had gone out through the city. John and Nicholas, on a plank bench against the high stone wall opposite the crudely built stage, sat chatting until the curtain was drawn.

On the stage sat a beautiful woman with a crown on her head. She was working with a distaff and a long needle. A man with matted red hair and the wild eyes of a maniac burst upon the scene waving a torch. The lady screamed as he flung the torch and her filmy gown flamed. Throwing it off, she knelt at his feet in homage. Above her he lifted his arms and the voluminous sleeves of his vestment spread like a bat's wings. Then, with rolling eyes and an evil grin, he drew forth a book labeled The Gospel, and presented it to her. Eagerly she opened the volume, but as she scanned it, her lovely features changed to the ugly, repulsive ones of a witch.

"The Queen has been bewitched by the Evil One," a hollow voice off stage proclaimed. "No longer can she commune with the saints or offer up her prayers for their holy intercession. She does not believe in the Purgatory where she will burn. Ah, woe is me! The Queen has betrayed the Holy Church. Her mind is no more, for she has become a Gospeler!"

A rumble of laughter floated over the courtyard as the curtains were pulled.

John felt his temper flaring. The play was an outrage. Somebody ought to do something about it.

He leaped up and climbed onto the bench. "Damnable lies!" he shouted, shaking his fist.

Par Dieu!" Nicholas whispered, pulling on John's doublet. "John! Have you lost your mind?"

"Long live the King!" John's voice was vibrant. "Long live the King's sister, the fair Christian, Marguerite!"

"Long live the King!" "Long live Queen Marguerite of Navarre!" "To the scaffold with the traitors who sully her name!" "Long live the royal family of Valois!" The crowd took up the chant, which was broken by the thundering of hoofs as the King's soldiers charged into the courtyard. Their helmets gleamed like gold in the torchlight and their red coats blazed as they rode through the aisle to the stage, where they began rounding up the players. Bedlam followed, with women screaming, men cursing, people scurrying, shoving, and struggling toward the street.

"John Calvin," Nicholas said after they had escaped from the confused masses and were walking up the hill toward the colleges, "you are about as big an idiot as ever I saw!"

"But somebody had to do something, Nicholas. You know I am not by nature rash. It wasn't only Queen Marguerite who was being ridiculed. It was the Gospel of Jesus Christ. As His servants, we cannot allow Him to be attacked."

"There is virtue in discretion, too. If the King's men had not shown up, you might have been stabbed!"

"Now, Nicholas, a Christian has to attack evil where he finds it. I only wish that I had protested in the midst of that scene."

Nicholas did not speak again for a few minutes. Then, his tone once more even, he said, "You gave me a fright, John. If I sounded harsh, forgive me. You have great courage."

"There is a difference between discretion and taking an opportunity to witness. As for danger, can anyone who truly lives like a Christian get away from that? Didn't Christ himself say He came not to bring peace but a sword?"

The next day some startling news blasted Paris. Beda had been banished. The King was very angry that the syndic had dared insult a member of the royal family with such a play.

When John passed the Pelican late that afternoon, he again saw two straws protruding from the shutters, signaling another Protestant gathering.

All was quiet when at midnight he entered the courtyard, crawled through the opening, and climbed the narrow stairs.

The room was full. Dr. Poitent, who had read the Sermon on the Mount at the last meeting, again read from the Bible:

"The fool hath said in his heart, There is no God. Corrupt are they, and have done abominable iniquity; there is none that doeth good. God looked down from heaven upon the children of men to see if there were any that did understand, that did seek God. . . ."

As John listened, he thought that if Beda ever returned to power, Dr. Poitent would probably be one of the first to burn, for he urged moderation in the rule of celibacy for the priesthood, saying publicly that a change would decrease unnatural acts, sexual immorality, and the number of fatherless children.

As the meeting ended, Nicholas Cop crawled through the opening. There was on his lean, brown face an expression that John had never seen before. He looked as complacent as a cat with a mouse under its paw.

"I called the four faculties together—the arts, medicine, philosophy, and divinity—to insist that they offer their apologies to Queen Marguerite and her court chaplain, Gerald Roussel. The apology is forthcoming!"

There was a murmur of approval.

"There is further news." Still that complacent look. "They elected a new rector in Beda's place."

"Whom did they elect?" Dr. Poitent looked anxious.

"Me," said Nicholas. "As long as I have authority, there will be no more persecution. Untold harm has been done the Kingdom of God."

John's mind worked quickly. The new rector would have to deliver an Inaugural.

"Nicholas!" he exploded, leaping to his feet. "You are called of God for this hour. He has given us an opportunity to make an attack on those who blaspheme His Name, and appointed you to lead it."

Nicholas paled visibly. His gently inquiring look changed to a puzzled stare. "John Calvin, what is in that rapierlike mind of yours?"

"Don't you see, Nicholas? You have the greatest opportunity a Christian has had since the Reform began to sweep Paris! You can give your Inaugural in French and embody Christian truths!"

"Oh, come now, John. You are a careful student, but when it comes to religion, you want me to do something like this that will endanger my life!"

"Can't you imagine the sensation you will cause when you get up before the four faculties, the students, and other educated people of Paris and present in French a plea for salvation?"

"But the Inaugural has always been in Latin. Anything else would be absurd!"

John felt excitement rushing through his body. "Nicholas, how fortunate you are! You can give a speech that will echo like Martin

Luther's hammer blows on the door of the Wittenberg Church, pounding truth into the hearts of men!"

"But I am no theologian!"

Messire La Farge came to John's aid. "John is a theologian. Let him write the speech. All you will have to do is deliver it."

"All I will have to do!"

Dr. Poitent was enthusiastic, too. "Cop, it is the chance we have been waiting for. You must do it."

"Yes, indeed!" Master Cordier agreed. "Nicholas, you have no choice."

"Would that I had such a chance," the public executioner, Michael Sept, murmured sadly. "It would wash some of the blood from my hands."

Nicholas seemed to droop. He had a frightened look, but he tried once more. "I come here and worship. I read the Bible for myself. I believe in grace, repentance, salvation by faith. But I have no great knowledge of the Scriptures."

John moved toward his friend of the years. "I know the Scriptures. Don't worry, Nicholas. Leave everything to me."

When Nicholas appeared at John's room the next night to go to work, John greeted him excitedly.

"Nicholas, I have it! We will call your address 'Christian Philosophy.' That title will confound the monks. Come, now. Sit here at the table. Tell me: what have you decided to say?"

Nicholas groaned. "John, I thought you were my friend. Now, I'm not so sure. You said to leave everything to you!"

John grabbed the quill. "Salvation is a free gift of God. We must emphasize that. Priests cannot grant it, nor can the bishops. The cardinals and even the Holy Father himself are powerless to do so."

"You want me to say that?"

"Do you realize we have an anniversary to celebrate? Sixteen years ago to the day of your Inaugural, Martin Luther stated these truths in Germany. The blaze we start will warm the whole of France!"

"All hell will break loose!"

"Fine. Then the speech will truly commemorate a day in man's spiritual development!"

"It won't be any fun for me!" Nicholas gave a rueful smile.

John opened Dr. Le Fèvre's Hebrew Bible, translating aloud into French:

"For whom he did foreknow, he also did predestinate to be conformed to the image of His Son, that he might be the first-born among numerous brethren. Moreover whom he did predestinate, them he also called, and whom he called, them he also justified. And whom he justified, them he also glorified!"

John grabbed a piece of parchment, and began to write, his intoxication mounting. His brain raced and his fingers tried to keep up with it: "Christian Philosophy is the revealed will of God, the plan of salvation by Jesus Christ. *And only Jesus Christ.* The Grace of God alone remits sins! All Christians possess the Holy Spirit. I repeat, there is only one who can save you, Jesus Christ himself. Mary was a good woman, but she cannot save you. . . ."

He wrote on, pausing every few paragraphs to read what he had written. He inserted additions Nicholas suggested, and as the first gray dawn crept through the tower window, they finished. Breakfasting together while the church bells tolled for Mass, they went over the Inaugural again, and Nicholas took it with him when he left.

Exhausted, John stretched out on his narrow bed, but he couldn't sleep. Words kept rolling around in his mind. He imagined the looks of amazement and horror on the faces in Mathurin's Church on All Saint's morning. The monks wouldn't be more surprised if Dr. Erasmus, the great Dutch scholar and Dr. Luther's critic, arose and sang his Battle Hymn, "A Tower of Strength."

The rest of the month passed in a round of work for John. He continued his study of Greek, Latin, and Hebrew, and his mind began to revolve around an outline for the manual he intended to publish. As he worked, he became more and more determined to plead God's cause before His people. In the manner of a legal brief setting forth its points, he proved the beliefs propounded by the Bible, his sole authority. And about this time his first book was published, a little volume confuting the view of some of the Anabaptists that the soul slept from death until the time of final reckoning; *Pschopannychia* (Sleep of the Soul) was its title.

Messire La Farge sent Nerien to John the Friday before All Saint's Day to ask him to teach the Scriptures at a meeting the Protestants would hold that night.

Word had come also that the King had pardoned Syndic Beda, and his return would surely bring a renewal of persecution.

John's heart sank. He still felt he could work within the Church. To begin such teaching as Messire requested would be to set himself against the Church and align himself with its enemies, for these people had declared themselves against much that it stood for; on the other hand he shared their beliefs.

Nerien was watching him closely. The lad would never understand. He could not know how John broke into a cold sweat every time he thought of cutting himself off from the visible church. What was it Nerien had said? "You are a Prince of Light. . . . I want to be like you."

John felt tears scalding his eyes. These people who were sacrificing everything for their faith needed him. Finally he answered in a low voice, "Tell Messire La Farge I will come tonight and we will worship together."

About thirty Protestants had gathered in Messire's bedchamber. When John began to read from the leather-bound Bible, his voice quavered, but it grew stronger as he read on:

"Who shall separate us from the love of Christ? Shall trouble, or sorrow, or persecution, or famine, or nakedness, or peril, or sword? As it is written, for my sake we are killed all the day long; we are accounted as sheep for the slaughter. Nay, in all those things we are more than conquerors through him that loved us.

"For I am persuaded, that neither death, nor life, nor angels, nor principalities, nor powers, nor things present, nor things in the future, nor height, nor depth, nor any other creature, shall be able to separate us from the love of God——"

The sound of the secret panel sliding back interrupted the reading. Nerien burst into the crowded room, his eyes wide with terror, a warning finger at his lips. "The King's men!" he whispered.

Halberds could be heard striking wood in the stables below. There was the tread of heavy feet going this way and that. One of the

93

horses whinnied. In the meeting room the only sound was that of breathing, as the Protestants waited to see if the secret passage would be discovered.

John was very frightened. His hands were clammy, and he was panting so he felt he would choke. As he looked at the group that circled him, he saw eyes dilated in alarm, fingers clutched together, lips trembling or moving silently in prayer. There was fear. Of course there was fear! But there was trust, too, and determination to stand on a faith that was not an easy one. But stand they would!

It seemed an eternity before the noises below died away and the sound of steel-shod hoofs ceased. Men and women relaxed, some sighing, some smiling in relief, all grateful that they had been spared. And John was certain that most of those present would continue to carry on God's work.

He voiced their thoughts in the words of the Scriptures, his tone as triumphant as the bells of Notre Dame on a Festival Day: " 'If God be for us, who can be against us?' "

7

1533-1534

It was All Saint's Day and the appointed hour for the rector's Inaugural. The spired Church of the Mathurins was full. The members of the four faculties sat together on the front rows. Behind them were students, scholars, noblemen and citizens, all looking bored in anticipation of the traditional Latin oration on the saints.

Nicholas Cop, in a doctor's flat cap and a red wool gown trimmed with black velvet, climbed the steps into the high pulpit. When he began his address in French, his voice shook a little, but as he got into his subject, pointing out that God's Grace alone remits sins, it steadied and resounded loudly in the vast arched space. His brown eyes glowed, and his gestures were eloquent as he explained the plan of salvation *by Jesus Christ alone!*

Bodies stiffened, brows arched, and sleepy eyes opened. There were mutterings, exchanged looks, and some frowns. But everybody listened.

As soon as he finished, the audience gathered in excited groups to discuss the astounding speech. In some places the discussions went on into the night. The Sorbonne, it was whispered the next day, interpreted the Inaugural as a manifesto against the Catholic Church.

That evening John met Nicholas at the Pelican for supper.

"Now that it's over, I feel better," Nicholas confided, while they waited for Nerien to bring the venison. "As I spoke yesterday, the conviction came that you had showed me God's will. You are overpowering when you think you're right."

"I'm glad you have no regrets."

"Wait a minute, John, I didn't say that. I am certain we did God's will. Even in Parliament today men discussed Christ's Gospel. But I regret I had to be the one to bring all this about, because I am in trouble now!"

A cold fear struck at John's heart. "What do you mean?"

"The monks have accused me of heresy. I am summoned to appear before Parliament tomorrow."

"What will happen?"

"God alone knows." Nicholas shook his head. "I have hopes that my own faculty, the professors of the medical school, will stand by me, also those of the arts school. The faculties of the philosophy and the divinity schools will undoubtedly denounce me."

"What if you are condemned to the stake?"

"When Queen Marguerite learns I am in trouble, she will intercede. One afternoon when I went to see my father at the royal palace, I had a visit with her. I told her then about the Inaugural."

"Did she approve?"

"Heartily. I think the King will listen to her."

"What if he won't?"

"Then I guess I'll burn," Nicholas said glumly.

The sun was warm the next morning as Nicholas Cop marched behind the long-nosed beadle who had come to escort him to the Palace of Justice. Nicholas was frankly terrified. His hands shook as he straightened his scholar's cap. To make matters worse John Calvin had insisted he would attend Parliament, too. If John, who never minced words, were moved to become embroiled in the controversy, they might both end up at the stake. Nicholas had done his best to deter his friend, but nothing could stop John when he made up his mind. Like Hercules he stood ready to subdue the mightiest monsters, and this by what he called that mightiest of all clubs, the Word of God.

Suddenly the sound of singing broke into his thoughts:

> "Some ten or twenty times a day,
> To bustle to the town with speed,
> To dabble in what dirt he may,—
> Friar Lubin's the man you need!"

The Protestant signal of danger! Danger of the gravest sort. Were the voices trying to tell him not to go before Parliament, that his death was prearranged? He slowed his steps, and looked about cautiously.

Three men staggered toward him around a curve in the street. One, a drunken reveler, was singing "Friar Lubin." Could the hate-mongers have learned the secret warning and under its cover sent an assassin to plunge a dagger into his heart, so that there would never have to be a public trial?

One of the men blocked the bridge ahead. He looked like Triboulet, the King's fool, whom Nicholas often saw at the palace. The other two shouted loudly and danced in front of the irate beadle, grabbing his staff. Nicholas walked slowly toward the bridge, his heart thumping. The man there *was* Triboulet, sober but feigning drunkenness, Nicholas was sure, for the fellow winked at him, and came close to say warningly, "Queen Marguerite begs to inform you that Parliament intends to throw you in the dungeon without a fair hearing, as it did Berquin. You must flee. Under no circumstances return to your chambers. They mean to kill you!"

The King's fool pranced away to dance with his noisy colleagues around the beadle. Nicholas did not wait to make excuse. He threw off his scholar's cap and gown, and ran toward St. Martin's Gate.

"*Mon Dieu!* The prisoner has escaped," the befuddled beadle shrieked when he realized what was happening.

But Nicholas Cop had crossed the bridge and kindly trees along the opposite bank enveloped him.

When Nicholas failed to show up at the morning session of Parliament, John made inquiries in an effort to find out why. All answers were vague. Cop's chambers and his office held no clues. With fear tugging at him, John went to the Pelican at the usual time for supper, but again there was no Nicholas.

While John sat anxiously scanning everyone who entered, Clement Marot came in. He sauntered toward John's table and leaned down to whisper the news that Nicholas had fled the city.

"Everything is in turmoil. We have to have a meeting tonight, but not at the same place. A piece of scarlet ribbon tied to the latch outside will mean a gathering at the Black Horse Tavern at the same hour, midnight."

After a meager supper, John went back to his room and tried to study, but he found concentration impossible. He kept thinking about Nicholas, wondering if he had been captured. When at last it was time to start for the Black Horse, he made his way through the smelly darkness, praying that Nicholas would be spared.

The faces of the group that greeted John in the tavern cookhouse were solemn. Only Clement was cheerful.

"Beda is back," he clowned. "Into my hole I'll go, I do not want to be meat for crow."

No one smiled.

News spread that Parliament had offered a reward of three hundred crowns for Nicholas, dead or alive.

"Beda's return means an increase in persecution," Dr. Poitent said gravely. "He will have his revenge!"

"*Par Dieu!*" Clement rolled his brown eyes. "Being a Protestant calls for too much fortitude. I cannot relish the thought of being fried alive. From now on, I, for one, am outwardly a loyal Papist!"

"That is the trouble with too many of us." Nerien spoke boldly. "If we stand together, can the Papists burn us all? There wouldn't be room enough on the Place du Grève."

"I have seen too much death." Michael Sept, the public executioner, complained. He stood a frowning six feet four, tousled black hair hanging over his brow. "I think I will leave Paris and go to Geneva. I cannot stand any more!"

"There is still work to be done in Paris," Dr. Poitent told them. "If necessary, we can change the place of meeting so frequently that the cruel head of the Gendarmerie, Lieutenant Morin, and his men cannot possibly spy upon so many locations. But I shall never pretend to attend Mass, not even to save my life!"

John ran his fingers distractedly through his hair. Nobody said anything about trying to find a common meeting ground. Essentially these who protested certain abuses in the Church and those within it who disagreed were of the same religion. It was the extremists in both groups who were causing the hatred, the bloodshed. There were scoundrels, too, who masqueraded under the name of Protestant. Finally he said, "There are good Christians within the Church who are working to bring reform. Remember our common denominator, Christ and his salvation!"

"Just tell Lieutenant Morin's men that when they come to arrest you. It could be any day now, any hour. Just tell them that!" Terror etched Clement's Puckish features.

"When they come to arrest me? Do you think they will?" John felt himself break into an icy sweat.

He realized, before Clement could answer, that spies might have discovered that he had written the Inaugural! Why I am more frightened than Clement, he thought in disgust. But I must not be afraid.

" 'If God be for us, *who* can be against us?' " he quoted in a firm, deep voice. " '*Who can be* against us?' "

The following afternoon when John returned from his classes, he found a note on the table in his room. A pleasant perfume rose from the folded parchment. When he broke the seal—a marigold on a field of blue—his curious eyes saw the signature of Marguerite, Queen of Navarre! The message was brief:

The Queen of Navarre would like to talk to you at your earliest convenience. Present your name at the southern gate to the Louvre. The sentry has been instructed to let you pass and to summon a page to guide you to my apartments.

What could a queen want with him?

The next afternoon, after his last class, he bathed and put on his best doublet, a pale blue pourpoint with a white ruffled neckband. His shirt was white; his breeches and shoes, black. The curling white feather which crested his black hat gave the whole costume an impressive finishing touch. He had never met a queen before and he wanted to look his best to meet this one, for without her the Protestants of France would be in a terrible plight. He paused before the looking glass, to survey the effect. His slim black beard and mustache were neatly clipped. His eyes sparkled with excitement. He looked almost gay. He smiled to himself when he thought of his friends' amazement, if they knew he had been summoned to the Louvre.

As he started down the stairs, a frenzied thought congealed his blood. What if the summons had not come from Queen Marguerite? What if this were a trap to lure him to the palace, so that he could not escape as Nicholas had? He ran back, hurriedly grabbed up the scented note, and read it again. Only a queen could afford such perfume. And her seal was there, too. He closed the door quietly behind him, descended the stairs, and strode toward the royal palace.

When he approached the southern gate, which faced the Church of St. Germain l'Auxerrois, he saw that the portcullus was up, guarded by a sentry in bright armor. Again doubts assailed him. Why should a queen send for him? He had left the note in his room; he could not bolster his courage by rereading it. But he could disappear and his friends and family would never be certain he had come to Louvre.

"My name is John Calvin," he told the sentry in a voice that shook. "The Queen of Navarre has sent for me."

"Dr. Calvin"—the man stood at attention—"her Majesty is expecting you."

A page was summoned and John, saying a silent prayer, followed him under a wide arch, past guards in gold and scarlet uniforms. Through iron-hinged doors they entered a massive building with five rows of casements, where the page announced to still another guard that Queen Marguerite had sent for Dr. Calvin.

Another page appeared, and John stared. This boy looked like one of the King's messengers. His scarlet doublet was crested with a gold salamander. The white linen shirt was piped with gold, in the same manner as his white tights and scarlet hat.

The youth bowed formally. "Follow me, please. This way."

As they climbed the grand staircase, John visualized the beggars sitting at the doors of Notre Dame. The price of this boy's elegant suit would give them all a banquet.

There was a loud roaring in the distance and John jumped.

"Do not be frightened," the boy said. "Those are only the King's lions. They are taken into the woods, turned loose, and hunted for sport."

History would be repeating itself, John thought, if the hate-mongers ever persuaded King Francis to throw the Christians to his lions. The page seeing his expression, added reassuringly, "They are caged. Do not fear."

They entered a great draughty room, with fine furniture upholstered in blue brocade, heavy hangings of gold cloth and large wall tapestries. At the far end of the room a fire blazed in an enormous cowled fireplace. The page bowed and backed out.

The Queen advanced to meet her guest, her dark eyes glowing softly. Her plain black silk gown swept the stone floor. Beneath a sheer gauze cap, her brown hair was parted in the middle and gathered in a chignon at her neck. Her only ornament was a jeweled crucifix. The Queen of Navarre's pale, plaintive face was not beautiful, but her smile was warm. She held out her hand, and John's heart beat fast as he bent to kiss it.

"Why, Dr. Calvin!" Her throaty voice was pleasant to the ear. "I believe you are blushing. From what I have heard, it doesn't seem in character for you to kiss a lady's hand."

"I'm afraid I'm not very courtly, your Majesty."

She laughed. "Come, we'll sit by the fire and talk."

John followed her to a blue sofa before the fireplace, and the Queen introduced her lady in waiting, who sat nearby on a stool before an embroidery frame.

"We can talk freely," the Queen said. "First, I must thank you for coming to my defense at the play the students of Navarre gave. That was gallant."

"You know about that?"

She nodded. "The Sorbonne summoned me before them when my book, *The Mirror of a Sinful Soul*, was first published. Since they have no authority to summon a member of the royal family, I ignored them. The play was their way of striking at me."

"So Nicholas Cop told me."

"That is one reason I sent for you. Nicholas asked the men who helped him escape to send word to you that he will go to his native Basle. As soon as possible he will communicate with you. And he said to have no regrets, that he has none."

John sighed. "I hope he will be safe."

"The other reason I sent for you is to discuss your safety. You came to my defense, now it's my turn to befriend you."

"My safety!" John stroked his beard with nervous fingers. "Am I in danger?"

"Perhaps not too seriously at the moment, but it is rumored here in the palace that you wrote Nicholas Cop's Inaugural."

"Then Parliament will summon me?"

"It is only rumored. You will likely be under surveillance. But should I learn of any imminent threat to your safety, I will send Clement or the Court Fool, Triboulet."

"But your brother is the King. You can influence him to intercede with Parliament!"

She shook her head. "Not any more. He is in a foul mood. Cardinal Duprat is ruling him, and the cardinal's sympathies are, of course, with the most conservative among the clergy."

"I had hoped the King would show tolerance!"

"He cannot forget that France is surrounded by the Emperor's territories. The Cardinal has convinced his Majesty, that the freedom of thought nurtured by the Protestants is a threat to the absolutism of the crown."

John shook his head. "It is hard to understand how a king who has built schools, and libraries, and encouraged learning in every form, could fail to see that the Protestants are his loyal subjects."

"I tremble for what could happen to them," the Queen whispered. "Have a care!"

John rose to leave. "How can I ever repay you for your warning, your Majesty?"

"Just say an occasional prayer for me, Dr. Calvin. When my little son died three years ago, I wondered if I wanted to live. It was Dr. James Le Fèvre and that cousin of yours, Olivétan, who pointed out that God had a place for me in life, and made me realize there is more to living than life at court." She stared down at the tips of her black shoes, "I read the Bible over and over. If I were not convinced that it contains truth to live by, I would not be so concerned about what happens to an honest scholar like you."

"Thank you for your thoughtfulness." Again he bent over her hand, and this time he did not blush.

"One more bit of advice, Dr. Calvin. Why not go to Nerac to visit my former tutor, Dr. Le Fèvre? He is there under my protection. Someday go to him. Talk to him. Consult him about any problems that perplex. And take care of yourself, Dr. Calvin. God bless you!"

In the days that followed, a white-faced pudgy man appeared wherever John went, but he continued to remind himself that God was watching over him.

The feeling persisted that he was called to write a manual of Christian faith, but there were times when the enormity of the task overwhelmed him. Words were words; paper was cold, not warm like the fire in his heart. He, an ordinary man, was attempting to expound the words of eternal life! If only the King would read the book, believe, and show some tolerance for the Protestants! If only he, John Calvin, could see Christ's face in all its dazzling purity! Sometimes his longing to have the veil of error pulled aside became an ache within him.

The outline for the manual grew slowly, carefully, until it was complete in scope—six chapters: prayer, faith, law, the real sacraments, the false ones, and Christian liberty. *Institutio Religionis Christianae* would be the title and, as was the custom, the first edition would be in Latin. Later he would translate it into French, so that the common people would have it to study along with their French Bibles.

By early January the outline was clear and concise, and John began to write, carefully annotating each chapter with references from the Bible. Night after night he sat at his table, choosing his words with care. He was so involved with the important work he was doing, he even forgot to tremble when he thought of the King's man who followed him about.

One night toward the end of the month, he was working on a passage dealing with Grace in the chapter on faith. It would have to be very clear. He bowed his head in prayer, asking guidance of the Holy Spirit. As he lifted his head, he heard hasty footsteps on the stairs. On they came past the second floor. Up. Toward his room. There was a loud pounding on the door and he leaped to his feet. In imagination he could see a soldier standing there with lifted halberd, come to take him to the dungeon. Then he heard a voice.

"Quick, John. I come from the Queen of Navarre with an important message!"

John ran to unbolt the door. Clement Marot reeled into the room, closed the door behind him, and leaned against the heavy oak for support.

"Her Majesty says to flee for your life. Lieutenant Morin is on his way to seize you. There is no time to pack!"

Outside there was the sound of marching feet, followed by the roar of shouting men.

"Mary, preserve us. We are too late!" Clement pointed to the window. "The only way. Here. Fasten the end of the coverlet to the table leg. I'll tie the bedclothes together. It's our only chance!"

For a desperate instant John's legs felt like lead. The tower window was square and small, the table too wide to be pulled through the casement, but was it strong enough to hold together? Clement shoved the table over, swung the coverlet, with the twisted sheets tied to it across the sill.

"Go first. I'll follow."

John came to life, thrust the pile of finished manuscript inside his doublet, climbed over the table, and grabbed the hurriedly improvised rope. Gritting his teeth, he went down hand over hand until he reached the end of the sheets. There, swinging in the air like an acrobat on the flagpole at a fair, he looked down and shuddered. The ground was almost a story's length below, but he let go. As he landed, agonizing pain shot through his feet and legs and for a moment he couldn't move.

Clement, breathing hard, landed on the ground beside him. Someone above them shouted angrily, and looking up, John saw a helmeted head.

"Run that way, John!" Clement pointed toward the south. "Bart Bardeau, the vinedresser, will hide you when you reach the Faubourg St. Victor. Michael Sept has been alerted to watch for you. I'll run the other way. Perhaps I can divert them. God's speed!"

John began to hobble. His ankles ached, but he moved as rapidly as he could until he reached the forest along the River Seine. He was faint, his head swam, but he kept moving. For over an hour he crept through the darkness, picking his way among tall trees and heavy bushes. A little moonlight, filtering through the barren branches, made weird patterns on the sodden earth. A nameless terror hovered over the forest, filling him with unease. The going was hard. Limbs lashed out at him, tearing his clothing. For a time there were no sounds save his heavy breathing, his footfalls, and the cracking of branches as he struggled through.

Then suddenly in the stillness there came the barking of dogs and the shouting of men. John's life depended on his moving, but he was so weak he feared he would fall. Stumbling, lurching, he dragged himself into a nearby creek, wading upstream over the slippery stones so that the bloodhounds would lose his scent. Once he fell with a splash, soaking his clothes. Scrambling up, he hid in a dense copse from which he listened to the thunder of hoofs and watched men on horseback waving torches in the blackness as they searched for him. Red and black shapes with shining helmets. The King's hunting men!

He lay quietly in his sanctuary of bushes and tall grass. He was bruised and his skin was cut. Weariness flowed through him in a dark wave, and he closed his eyes. . . .

Hours later he awoke and looked up, filled with momentary panic. Above him towered a gigantic figure. The sun was high. There was no barking of dogs, no shouting of men. He stared fearfully at the man until, in a flash, he recognized him—Michael Sept, the executioner who hated death.

"The poet sent word you had escaped. When you did not reach Bart Bardeau's cottage, we waited until it was light and then began to search for you."

John struggled to a sitting position. He was sore and stiff. "Where are Lieutenant Morin's men?"

"They returned to the city at sunrise."

Michael helped John to his feet. "Come. You must rest. As soon as you are strong, you can move on disguised and under an assumed name. We will send word to your friends in Paris."

After John had eaten the broth his host, Bart Bardeau, prepared for him, he fell asleep in a warm bed.

The next morning at the crow of the cock, wearing a smock-frock, with a hoe slung over his shoulder and a white cloth wallet at his belt, he began to travel. He was no longer Dr. John Calvin, a chaplain in the good graces of the Church. His new name was Charles d'Epeville, and he was an outlaw sought by Parliament, who must continue to disguise himself. His destination was Saintonge where Louis du Tillet, a former classmate and the curé of Claix, resided. Louis du Tillet was in sympathy with the New Religion, and there John would finish his manual.

With hair grown long and beard untrimmed, John led a secluded life at Saintonge. The curé's library numbered several hundred books. With one, the Bible, always open before him, John finished the first draft of his manual. In exchange for room and board he taught Louis Greek. When he ventured to attend church, the images seemed idolatrous. At sight of others buying indulgences and kissing the feet of statues, as he had so recently done, he felt one with Martin Luther and other reformers.

One cool April night, walking with Louis after a Greek lesson, John brought up the subject of invoking the saints.

"You shelter me, a refugee, and yet you continue customs which are not Christian," he accused.

For a small man, Louis had an unusually large voice. "The custom has grown up," he boomed. "The people expect it."

"Do you mean to tell me that you, a curé, advocate giving them what they expect?"

"Let me show you something when we return to the library," Louis said in a distressed voice.

Back at the house, John followed his host into the library where the curé selected a book from the shelves. He turned several pages, then said, "Here it is. The Council of Carthage forbade the invocation of the saints at the altar. The priests were ordered not to use the expression: 'St. Peter and St. Paul, pray for us!' I know I'm wrong to continue a custom expressly forbidden by the Church, though encouraged by ignorant monks. But it has become the accepted procedure. People follow without reflection."

John's heart sank into his boots. With a canon like Louis taking such an attitude, what hope was there of purging the Church? Of being honest intellectually and spiritually?

"And yet you encourage me to write a manual instructing in the true doctrines of our faith?"

Louis shrugged. "Invoking the saints is harmless. People are used to it."

That fallacy so disturbed John's mind and heart that the constant strain of it affected his health. He began to have headaches, and he lost most of the weight he had gained since coming to Saintonge. Introspective by nature, he spent hours roaming the countryside, meditating about salvation, the visible church, and the Church Invisible.

One day a letter came from Nerien in Paris. It contained the news that Clement Marot had been arrested again, charged with Protestant sympathies, but he had escaped the scaffold because the King refused to believe him guilty; the poet, after all, had been attending Mass regularly. He now owned two parcels of land which he called Clement and Marot. Here he spent his time growing vegetables, which he gave to the peasants. He talked of his land constantly, of the birds there, the small animals, and the verdure. And he spoke often about his wife and three children. They were his reason for denying his beliefs. His "Vineyard Song" was sweeping the nation. Dr. Poitent, Bart Bardeau, and Messire La Farge continued to do everything possible to strengthen the Reform, but the future looked grim.

John was at work on his manuscript late one May afternoon, when Louis entered the library, his brows drawn together in a frown, his small, hazel eyes clouded.

"John, sinister rumors have started about you. The priests say you are a tool of the Huguenots, an iconoclast, a destroyer of images, that you are injuring people's souls."

"And my presence here is dangerous to your career?"

Louis's eyes would not meet John's. "I am in a delicate position. I fear the authorities will confiscate my fine library. Summer is coming. One of my servants, Zippo, who can be trusted, will swing a hammock for you in one of the grottoes a few leagues from here. I will provide a chair, table, and candles."

"Thank you, Louis. As soon as the book is finished, I will move on."

"Do not misunderstand, John! I just feel that it is dangerous to overthrow the customs of the ages in an hour or a day."

"You do not really believe in my reform?"

"You are wrong about that, John. You are growing bitter, because you deplore the fact that the Gospelers and Roman Catholics have found no common ground to unite. Have you forgotten what the Church has done to uplift mankind?"

Have I forgotten? John thought with a pang. I could never forget. The good influence of the Church has changed history. It was the civilizing force when the Northmen attacked the Roman Empire. Everywhere it has uplifted society. But there are perversions of power and there are errors!

"Louis," he said firmly, "we can never measure the blessing, the faith, the comfort, the Church has given since Christ's crucifixion. It is my Church, but errors have crept in because of man's sinfulness. The starting point of all my thoughts is *God!*"

"The world is in confusion," Louis agreed.

"Closing our eyes to error will never bring it peace."

Heavy clouds wallowed in the heavens the second Friday night in October, lightning glittered, and thunder sounded. A strong wind blew in gusts, tearing at shrubs, rustling fallen leaves, and swinging the signboard above the door of the Black Horse near St. Denis. By midnight the common room was filled and the bolt slid back only upon the prearranged signal, the two-line jingle:

Let him be taken!
He ate the bacon.

"We must not do something we will all regret," Dr. Poitent said, pointing to a pile of tracts and placards on the long, wooden table—William Farel's protest against superstition, corruption and error. "These are inflammatory. Ever since the Pope pronounced against Henry the Eighth's divorce last March, King Francis has been inclined to rebel against the authority of the Church, too. Now extreme Protestants are alarmed at the efforts to form a united church of Europe!"

"We could have a united church only on the Pope's terms, and he claims to rule by divine right!" a ferry boatman said in a rough voice.

"Our brother, William Farel, wrote these tracts in wrath," Messire La Farge protested. "They will only stir hatred."

"But don't we want to spread this New Gospel? Why not nail these tracts everywhere, on the doors to the King's chamber at the palace, at his château at Blois, on the gates, and on the walls of the Louvre?" Clement shouted excitedly, his large eyes gleaming.

Eli Corault, a large-boned ex-priest with craggy face and failing eyesight, asked pertinently, "If these are the truths we profess, why are we afraid?"

Clement nodded eagerly. "We can post the tracts after nightfall. Nobody will see us!"

"Should we cringe for our own safety?" Matthew Cordier demanded. "Isn't the Gospel bigger than any of us?"

Clement threw back his shoulders. "I vow to have more courage. For months I have attended Mass, but I won't any longer."

Eli Corault spoke again. "My good friends, if the poet be right, if God is calling us to action, let us advance!"

"Before we act with rashness, allow me to read some parts of the tracts," Messire La Farge pleaded.

"By Mass, the preaching of the Gospel is made impossible. There is only bell-ringing, chanting, howling, empty ceremonies, candles, incense, fraud, and all manner of superstitions. . . ."

"The Holy Supper of Christ makes us remember his great love, and how he cleansed us with his blood. Allow the Mass to be forbidden in the churches, and the Lord's supper restored. . . .

"Every Christian knows that our Lord and Saviour Jesus Christ gave his body and soul, his life and blood for our sanctification, by a perfect sacrifice, yet there are evil priests who set themselves in Christ's seat, as if they are our redeemer and pretend to offer in the Mass an acceptable sacrifice to God for the salvation of the living as well as the dead. . . .

"Surely these tracts are not something we wish to affix in public places to be read by people who cannot understand!"

"Yes." "Up with the placards!" "There have been too many executions!" "This is a way to strike back!" "Let's show Beda and his Papists we are ready to fight!"

Messire La Farge crumpled up as if he had been hit on the head. "There have already been too many executions! These will cause more. Exercise prudence. Beware of hatred, I beg of you!"

"To back down now would be cowardice," Eli Corault insisted. "As we leave, each of us can secrete some of the placards and tracts under his cloak!"

"We can plaster Paris with them!" Clement echoed.

8

November, 1534-1535

The wind cast snow against John Calvin's face, powdered his heavy black cloak, fur cap, and woolen stockings. The frosty November air chilled his bones, as the hired black horse thudded across the bridge. Ahead the road widened suddenly. Naked woods and round brown hills appeared on one side, on the other a creek eddied and swirled.

His excitement increased as he galloped toward Nerac. There he would consult Dr. James Le Fèvre, the Father of the Reformation in his beloved France, as Queen Marguerite had suggested a year ago. Tired of his exile, his manuscript finished, John wanted Dr. Le Fèvre's help in deciding what he should do next.

As he rode, his mind revolved around the persecutions in Paris, where it was impossible to be intellectually or spiritually honest. Nerien had written only the past week that the long-smoldering hatred had burst into flame. Rashly the Protestants who met in secret had fanned that flame by posting some of William Farel's tracts and placards all over the city. The King had been wroth to find his bed-chamber door at Blois plastered with them. A bricklayer by the name of Pouillet had been arrested. It was feared he would be tortured in an effort to force him to reveal the names of the Prottestants. His wife thought he would break under the torture. . . . Then how many scaffolds would be erected? What would happen to Messire La Farge, Nerien, Matthew Cordier, and Dr. Poitent?

John rode into the city, tied his horse to the hitching-rail in front of Dr. Le Fèvre's modest cottage, and knocked on the worn door. A little man stooped with age, opened it. He had long, white hair, a white beard, and black eyes peered through a pair of narrow spectacles.

"And you, young sir?" he wheezed. "You must be a student. Come in. I am delighted to see you."

John asked if he could put his horse in the stable, and the old man told him there was an empty stall. When he returned after tending the animal, the odor of cooking filled the little house, and John suddenly realized it was time for the evening meal. He was so chilled that his teeth were chattering like a trapped woodchuck's.

"If y-you are about to sit down at the t-table, I can sit by the f-fire until you are through," he managed.

"No. No. No. Sup with me. You will be doing an old man a kindness. You see I have my books and my memories, but I get very lonely."

"Thank you. Something warm would be appreciated."

"You must not mind dining in my kitchen. I do my own cooking. A woman comes twice a week to clean. Queen Marguerite owns this house, and is kind." He paused. "But your name, young sir? Have we met before?"

John shook his head. "I am John Calvin. I have come for advice."

The old man started. "John Calvin? Are you—no, you couldn't be. You're too young!"

"I am twenty-five, but I feel fifty, Dr. Le Fèvre. I have some awful problems."

Dr. Le Fèvre noted that his visitor had a serious face with shining black eyes, a full mouth with a sensuous lower lip, lofty brow, and long nose. Olivétan's cousin who had fled Paris to escape the wrath of Parliament—a French scholar, had written two little treatises, *Pschopannychia* (Sleep of the Soul) and *De Clementia* (a commentary on Seneca, dedicated to the young Abbot of St. Eloi,

Claude de Hangest). Seldom had the elderly reformer seen more concise writing on religious themes. Such a mind could do what he had been unable to do in purging the Church of errors.

"Are you a cousin of Olivétan?" Dr. Le Fèvre held his breath.

The young man nodded. "We are fellow Picards."

"Oh, my friend, there is so much I want to say to you!"

John saw that the old man was trembling. He was over ninety, but apparently his mind was as keen as in his days in Paris. John helped him put out the food. They sat down at the round table, and after the host had said Grace and thanked God for sending this guest, they began to talk. He answered all John's questions about the persecution he had suffered. At the age of fifty he had abandoned Aristotle and mathematics for theology. A few years later, in 1512, he had translated Paul's Epistles and written a commentary on Corinthians, asserting that there was no merit in human works without the grace of God. In a later commentary on the Epistle to the Hebrews, he had stirred up a fierce controversy.

"How did you ever come to your conclusions?"

"While I was studying in Rome, after I received my degree in the arts, I saw sights that stood my hair on end. I heard enough blasphemy out of the mouths of some of the priests to curl it. The battle was spreading and I knew I had to open my mind and my heart to truth."

"That is just the way I feel. It is the way my cousin, Peter Robert, feels. Called of God and therefore invincible. But I am not sure now what He wants me to do."

"Have you seen your cousin's French Bible?"

John's heart quickened. "Peter Robert's Bible? No, I haven't seen one."

They pushed back their chairs, and John followed Dr. Le Fèvre into the front room where a fire crackled and popped. The elderly man went to his bookshelves and lifted down a large volume bound in black leather. John took it wonderingly and sat down at the round table. It had been published only four months ago, and MD XXXV was engraved in gold on the cover, the custom being to put on a volume released after August 1, the date of the following year. Tooled in gold, above the figures, was "Neufchâtel."

Tenderly John opened the book. A small design of tooled gold ran around the inside edge of the cover. On the back of the seventh sheet he found his own name on the Preface. Tears came to his eyes and the lettering blurred as he remembered Peter Robert's words: "Will you write a preface for the French Bible? . . . You are my favorite cousin. It would mean a great deal to me, John. . . . Following Christ is worth any price, John; even the scaffold. . . . Only as the pure light of Christ shines from these pages will France, her people, and the Church be great! . . . The people need the truth!" Slowly, lovingly, John continued to turn the pages, aware that what he held in his hands was Peter Robert's life work.

"I think I had a small part in bringing that into being," Dr. Le Fèvre said proudly. "Olivétan says I inspired it."

John leaned forward. "I'm sure you did. Please tell me what I must do. I have lived in a cave. I have hidden in trees and watched the King's soldiers around Saintonge beating the thickets for me. Can I take my vows as a priest and try to bring internal reform from within my Church?"

Now tears appeared in the old man's eyes. "Young sir," he said in a voice that broke, "I am despised, libeled, persecuted, disgraced. But the Roman Catholic Church is my Church. How can I desert it now, as I approach the end of my earthly pilgrimage?" He paused, wiping his cheek with the back of his hand.

"And you recommend that I follow your example?"

"Since Rome persists in closing ears and eyes to internal reform, it might be wise for you to withdraw, and work with those within the Church who feel they must work from within. Chief among them is James Sadolet, a good and brilliant man, who writes of salvation by faith as the Protestants do and who frequently quotes from Philipp Melanchthon's writings. Of course you know Melanchthon is Dr. Luther's co-worker, but he is more pliable than Luther. Sadolet's Commentary on the Epistle to the Romans proclaims salvation by faith, and could have been written by a Protestant, but Sadolet is urging the Pope to set up a special commission to reform the Church."

"What if he, too, is taught to fear the seed of discord and is silenced?"

"He is a strong man. Of course he is a man, and not God, and therefore human. He may be promised a cardinal's hat or silenced for the sake of peace."

"I sympathize with him! I know what he is going through!"

"I, too, know what it means to take a stand," Dr. Le Fèvre said sadly.

"I must stand for truth. There is no question about that. But should I try to stay in the Church as I stand?"

"If I had it to do again, I would do what I see you are straining to do—sever all ties with Rome."

When John rose to leave, Dr. Le Fèvre shuffled after him to the door. His hand trembled in John's for an instant. "I give you my work, John Calvin. You will succeed where I have failed!"

And in that instant John knew he could never take his vows as a priest. Surely God was calling him to resign his benefices at Pont l'Évêque and La Gesine Chapel. The great church was the Church Invisible! If only good men like James Sadolet can continue to work within the Church, seeing it in the Reformed light, together we may bring unity among Christians! The thought brought some comfort, though there was still the pain of a lost dream. For John Calvin had never loved the Holy Roman Church more than he did in this moment of rejection.

Rain dripped through the thick foliage; dampness was everywhere. Through the black rows of trunks the woods seemed to belch smoke. The trees and the fog shut John and his sleeping traveling companions in like a high protective wall. His brother, Anthony, had decided to journey to Strasbourg with him to meet Dr. Bucer, and John had persuaded Louis du Tillet to talk to the great reformer of Strasbourg. The canon's servant, Pierre Daquet, snored on the opposite side of the chapel steps. When the storm had overtaken them and visibility had become too bad for travel, they had stretched out under the jutting roof of the deserted chapel to wait for dawn. For a long time John had listened to the dripping rain and the whistling wind, but at last he, too, had fallen asleep.

When he awoke with a start, the sun was slanting down through the tall trees. Anthony and Louis sat up, too, and looked about, soon realizing that Pierre Daquet had disappeared and one of the horses with him.

Louis rummaged through the contents of the travel-box under his saddle, and shook his little round head. "I don't know how to tell you this, but our community purse is gone with Pierre."

Anthony echoed his dismay. "That means we will have to beg our way to Strasbourg."

Gloomily they started on. Although the rain had stopped, they rode all day on still muddy roads, watching for the King's men. At an Augustinian monastery they begged lodging for the night, and the good monks gave them supper, beds, and breakfast. Mounting once more, they rode on until they arrived at Strasbourg.

Louis had a classmate who was in one of the churches, and he and Anthony went there, while John rode alone to Martin Bucer's. The afternoon was warm and the sun was drying the puddles. John quivered with excitement as his horse moved through the twisting streets. Everyone had talked of Dr. Bucer, a gentle theological professor who had helped Wolfgang Capito reform the city. At the age of seven, Bucer had entered the Order of Dominicans, but while he was a young instructor at the University of Heidelburg, Martin Luther had swept him off his feet.

Even as John lifted the lion-head knocker, the door swung back and Dr. Bucer, who looked much like a happy penguin, stood before him. John introduced himself, extending his hand. Dr. Bucer took it, but the next instant, without warning, John felt the ground coming up to meet him. . . .

"I didn't realize how exhausted I was from the long trip," he apologized as soon as he recovered. "I was so anxious to meet you, I came directly here."

"Stay as my guest, and tomorrow, when you feel stronger, we will talk."

Despite John's protests, Dr. Bucer and a servingman led him, wobbling, up a flight of stairs to a bedchamber where he lay down on a curtained bed. The servant lit the fire in the wide fireplace, and then he and Dr. Bucer tiptoed out, closing the door behind them.

The next afternoon, seated in his host's parlor, John asked for news of Peter Robert.

"When I was in Geneva recently," said Dr. Bucer, "he seemed obsessed with carrying the Gospel to Italy. He was counting on the Duchess of Ferrara, Renée of France, to aid his work."

"He is a man with a purpose."

"He knows God is leading him."

"God led me to you, Dr. Bucer. I had no idea I would be able to stay in your home. You are a scholar I am privileged to consult."

"There are great scholars here—Capito, Oecolampadius, Bullinger, Gyraneous, and others. They, too, will be glad to discuss the Reformation with you."

"You failed to mention the most famous of them all—Dr. Erasmus."

John's host frowned. "Perhaps I had better tell you, Dr. Calvin, that he has little use for you. He is old and cantankerous."

"Of all the scholars here, I would rather talk to him."

Dr. Bucer smiled uncertainly. "Then we will visit him tomorrow, but be prepared for anything."

They chatted on for several hours. The Gospel advocated by Dr. Bucer was the community of love in action. That was the goal of the Strasbourg reformers, and all their efforts were directed toward it.

The next day, as John followed Dr. Bucer into the long drawing room of Dr. Erasmus, it seemed like a dream. Everywhere John had traveled discussions had centered around the works of this famous Dutch scholar, and now he, John Calvin, was facing this greatest of the Humanists, the most famous thinker of them all.

Dr. Erasmus sat in front of a wide window with diamond-shaped panes. The desk before him was cluttered. The room smelled of leather and smoke.

Dr. Bucer introduced John, and the scholar lifted his eyes from a leather-bound book to peer at his visitors over the rim of his spectacles. The thin lips set, the sharp nose lifted, as he asked rudely, "Is this the idiot who is said to have written the rector's speech which fired all Paris?"

Calvin was astounded. "Dr. Erasmus, I came here to talk to you about religion. All I can say is that I doubt you have very much and your manners do not equal your intelligence!"

Dr. Bucer gasped. "Now, gentlemen——" he began in a soft voice.

Dr. Erasmus waved a square hand. "Martin, I will say what I have to say to this—this young fool. You came uninvited. I will have my servant show you out!" He rose with difficulty and yanked angrily on the bell cord. "Martin, should you care to call without this impertinent hothead, you will always be welcome."

"Before you throw me out, Dr. Erasmus," John said, "there is something I will say! You write of truth, but you compromise your beliefs by doing nothing about them. I think the sight of a man who represents truth is painful to you!"

"You—you . . ." Trembling, his eyes blazing, Dr. Erasmus shook his finger at John. "I see a great pestilence arising in the Church against the Church," he prophesied in a voice of doom. "I want no part of you, young Calvin, or your opinions!" He turned and stalked out of the room, his head high, his back straight, his brocade house robe rustling.

Dr. Bucer was red to his small, flat ears. "I am sorry, Dr. Calvin. Do not let his rudeness make you bitter. I think you hit his sore spot. He knows he compromises his beliefs. But kindle a little love in your heart and he, in turn, will love you."

John snorted. "I care little whether he likes me. I don't like him. He is the rudest man I've ever met."

Dr. Bucer shook his head sadly. "God commands us to love our fellow men."

"He does not say we have to like them. I could never like Dr. Erasmus!"

"In judging other men, Dr. Calvin, you must learn to use the Christian yardstick."

"The Christian yardstick? What on earth is that?"

"First you remember that people are human. Then you remember that there is human frailty. Using that yardstick will mellow you. That is the community of love in action."

Long shadows were lengthening over Basle the day John, Anthony, and Louis arrived there. It was a city of tranquil streets lined with chestnut trees in bloom, lovely churches, and houses with dormered windows where giant storks nestled in the gables like white sentinels guarding the people. Red geraniums brightened the well-scrubbed doorsteps, windows sparkled, and the river reflected the green of its verdant banks.

The first thing John did, after bathing and unpacking his box, was to go in search of his old friend, Nicholas Cop, who was just leaving the school as John came up the walk.

"It *is* you, John," Nicholas cried joyfully. "I thought the Papists would have finished you long ago!"

"Where is your faith?"

"I should have known God would preserve you for a special task. How about having supper with me and talking as we used to do?"

They walked back to the inn where John was staying and found a quiet corner. John talked with his friend of the encounter with Dr. Erasmus, of his visit to Dr. Le Fèvre, and of his book, *The Institutes of the Christian Religion.*

"I don't know just how to tell you this, John." The gently inquiring eyes brightened. "But time and time again when I think about our escapades in Paris, I thank God for your inspiration, and I vow to live nobly, selflessly."

John swallowed the lump in his throat. Nicholas meant what he said. "Thank you, my dear friend."

"If you need money to help pay for the printing of the book, I would like to give it to you in gratitude for what you have done for me and for the Reformation."

John said he would call on the printer the next day, and if money was necessary, he would let Nicholas know.

Early in the morning, John and Anthony set out for the establishment of Professor Thomas Plater, the printer everyone recommended. It was on a quiet street running off a square near the river. The apprentices, setting type at a large press in an oblong room, bowed pleasantly.

Professor Plater came forward to greet them. He was a handsome man, with strong features, a high forehead, graying combed-back hair, clear gray eyes, and a full gray beard. His figure was trim, though his shoulders stooped. He wore a black doublet cut in the latest style, long black breeches, and a chemise which had a round white collar and cuffs. John was aware of the professor's fashionable garb, but he did not feel ill at ease in his own worn doublet and old-fashioned breeches. Clothes, he thought, were designed primarily to cover you.

Professor Plater's office was furnished with a plain wooden desk, several chairs, and many shelves where manuscripts were stacked.

"I have brought you a book which I hope will pay for itself," John said as soon as they were seated. "It is a manual of the Christian faith, authenticated by passages from the Scriptures."

"The Reformed faith?"

"The New Faith, which is really the old faith, whatever men choose to call it."

The printer thumbed through the manuscript, pausing to read aloud: " 'I come not to bring peace, but a sword.' Then this is a controversial book?"

"Yes."

"Your first?"

"My third. I wrote a commentary on Seneca and a brief book on the subject of the sleep of the soul after death."

"You are an ambitious young man. What made you think you were capable of writing a book presenting the Reformed faith?"

"I believed it was God's will. Too many people today are confused, even in the Church."

"H-m-m! I do not have the time to read it now. You can see how work is piled up here. If I think it will sell, we can make some arrangements. I will get in touch with you."

Anthony spoke, his deep voice charged with eagerness. "You will find it a good book, sir. My brother can do anything."

My brother can do anything. Anthony had echoed that over and over. Anthony had faith in him. Dear, loyal Anthony!

"I will read it," Professor Plater said brusquely.

"I wish to learn the book-binding trade," Anthony said, leaning forward. "Will you take me as an apprentice? Then, if you publish my brother's book, I will work at night, too, binding it to cut down the expense."

"Do you wish to make this your life work?" Professor Plater asked, watching Anthony intently.

"Yes. Without books men would be poor indeed."

"Then I will be delighted to have you with me. I believe you are in earnest. So I will send you to the Guild Hall to arrange your apprenticeship. Come Monday morning ready to start."

At dusk the following Friday, a frowning Nicholas Cop appeared at John's door with a letter. "This just came from my father in Paris. Eli Corault brought it with him, having escaped just before he was to be arrested. The ex-priest is full of tragic news, and so is this letter. You'd better sit down, John."

"Is it that bad?" John asked, as they sat down facing each other.

"Yes. A wholesale extermination has been taking place in Paris. The inflammatory tracts and placards the Protestants have been posting everywhere so excited the authorities that scaffold after scaffold has risen!

"On January twenty-fifth, seventy-five people were accused of heresy and cited, by the blowing of the trumpet at the crossroads, to appear before the court. Clement Marot was one of them. He had to flee to Geneva, leaving his wife, and three children. His property has been confiscated, and he will be burned if he returns to France."

"I have heard he idolized little Michael!"

"The Queen of Navarre gave the poet money to escape and has taken the boy as a page at Navarre. The message Clement sent back to Paris with a friend was pathetic: 'Encourage Michael that he walk in his father's way and be not mute.'" Nicholas closed his eyes as if to shut out a terrible vision.

"Yes, Nicholas? What else?"

"Now the soldiers are being ordered to fasten iron chains to a seesaw affair on which they tie the victim. This is swung up and down, in and out of the flames until the victim faints. Then the executioner cuts the ropes and the condemned drops into the fire."

John found it difficult to speak.

"Nerien?" he managed at last. "Messire La Farge?"

Nicholas looked grave. "Nerien escaped with Clement. He didn't want to leave Messire, but La Farge insisted. Nerien thought he would head for Ferrara where the Duchess harbors Protestants. As for Étienne La Farge——"

"Yes, Nicholas? Was he executed?"

Nicholas nodded sadly. "By this hideous method. Eli was still in Paris when the executions took place. He died quietly, urging the people gathered on the Place du Grève to read the Bible for themselves, and if they couldn't read, to learn."

John felt cold terror gripping him. If I had stayed in Paris, he thought, if the rector's Inaugural had not driven me out, I would have died a heretic's death, too.

"Who else?" he whispered.

"Pouillet, the bricklayer, although it was he who named La Farge, Nerien, and Clement. There were others convicted, most of whom we do not know. More recent converts. About eighteen in all."

"Did Pouillet reveal the places of meeting?"

Nicholas frowned. "Some of them. Several were arrested in the midst of a prayer session, herded off, given a quick trial, and burned at once."

"Those may be the lucky ones. Poor Pouillet! I have always heard the torture is unbearable."

Nicholas shuddered. "Nails pulled from fingers and toes, the body stretched and torn on the rack, torches set to the feet, and water poured down the victim's throat, choking the breath!"

John gazed at Nicholas in horror. He felt weak all over, as if life were slowly being drained from him.

"I am overjoyed that Eli, Clement, and Nerien were spared, and I am grateful that I escaped. What can I do to vindicate the faith of these saints?"

"You might try to persuade the King that those of us who are Protestants are among his most loyal subjects."

The King? John thought. Somebody should try to convince him, now that he refuses to listen to Queen Marguerite. Excitement lifted John to his feet, facing Nicholas. "I could write a preface to my manual and address it to the King! The purpose would be to point out the facts."

"You know, John, that might work. When could you write it?"

"Now. At once!"

Stalking to the desk, he sat down, and began to write. Nicholas sat without interrupting, thumbing through Martin Luther's *Babylonian Captivity of the Church*, which he had taken from the table. The only sound in the large square chamber was the scratching of quill on parchment until John finished what he had to say. Then he jumped up, waving the sheets under the nose of his friend.

"I have it. 'To his most Christian Majesty of France, to his prince and sovereign, John Calvin desires peace and salvation in Christ.' "

Nicholas interrupted. "His 'most Christian Majesty'?"

John shook an instructing finger. "That is the title of the King of France."

"I understand. Go on."

"When I commenced this manual I thought of nothing, Sire, but to put down the truths that would come before your Majesty.

"My sole intention was to present some instruction to the ones who long to be God's children, chiefly among my fellow countrymen. For my eyes have seen many in France hunger and thirst after Christ, yet few who received the true knowledge of him. The simple, facile style of this book signifies to my intention.

"But now I perceive that the fury of Godless men in your realm is growing so fierce that there is no place for the pure doctrine, so that this writing should at the same time exhibit before men a confession of faith. May you learn from it what is the nature of this faith which drives the fury of the heretic-hunters to destroy your kingdom with fire and sword. . . . It is up to you, Sire, not to turn away your heart and mind where such grave matters are at stake; to maintain God's honor on earth, to preserve the honor of truth, and to continue the honor of Christ among us. . . . A true king administers his kingdom as a servant of the Lord. Whoever rules otherwise is a robber. . . .

"Should it please your Majesty to read this confession, without ill will or anger, then I pray we will regain your favor. Should this not occur because you leave the power in the hands of those who fight against us with dungeon, whip, torture, fire, and sword, so that we shall continue like sheep to be led to the slaughter, then we shall keep our souls in patience, waiting for God's mighty hand which, when the time is fulfilled, will appear with a sword to deliver us from tribulation and to punish the proud and malicious.

"The King of Kings protect your throne in righteousness."

"John, is it wise to speak so boldly? You are addressing the King!"

John gave a rueful smile. "If it had not been for what you call my boldness, you would have been living safely in Paris in the bosom of your family and in the favor of the Court. But frank-

123

ness is a requisite of a servant of God. There is no room for duplicity. Before God, the King stands as other men."

John sent the preface to Thomas Plater the following Monday when Anthony went to work. But days passed into weeks and the printer sent no word. John tried to be patient, sure that God had called him to write the manual, and that somebody would print it.

On the morning of the last day of May, that year of 1535, John was in the inn yard feeding the birds. He was very tired and his head ached dully. Another long, hard day lay ahead of him, preparing for a Bible class he had promised Nicholas he would teach. As he threw the last crumbs from his hand, he heard the garden gate creak and footsteps pounding on the path.

Anthony ran up, crying, "Professor Plater wishes to speak with you at once!"

"Is he going to publish my book?"

"He didn't say. When he came in this morning, he had it with him. He threw it down on his desk and called to me, 'Go and tell your brother to come at once!' So here I am."

John hastily put on his best doublet and went off to the printer's with Anthony. Professor Plater's clear gray eyes lit up when they entered. He rose from his desk and strode around it, extending both hands.

"Dr. Calvin! You have indeed written a book!"

"Then you will print it?"

"I will, yes, yes. I am sorry I took so long to read it. If I had known——"

"Do you think it will convince others that salvation is what the Protestants think it is?"

"It will have a profound influence. The logic is indisputable. The scholarship is superior. The writing is concise. Oh, yes, Dr. Calvin, your book will have a large circulation. It might even sell five thousand copies! It should pay for itself."

"I am happy," John said simply, relief sweeping through him. "But five thousand! That seems like a lot of books. Yet—with God all things are possible."

9

Summer of 1535

Toward the end of July, John set out for Ferrara, again accompanied by Louis and Anthony. And in his saddlebags was the first bound copy of his book, which he was taking to the duchess. Th' question he had asked Nicholas when he had first learned of the multiple executions in Paris had persisted in his mind: How can I vindicate the faith of such Christians? He remembered that, in Ferrara, Renée, the daughter of Louis XII, was sympathetic toward their faith. If he could convince her that the manual instructed in that faith, she might be willing to help distribute it among the refugees from France and others. Then, too, Nerien and Clement were now in Ferrara!

It was a clear afternoon when Anthony led the way along the narrow trail over the Bernina Peak. Louis followed him, and John came last. They drew rein suddenly, as a commotion at the side of the road caught their attention.

Two horses grazed in a clearing where two men struggled, a huge obese man and a little priest. The big man was lowering a dagger to the ear of the priest, who writhed and shrieked.

"No! No! For the love of God. Oh, please, no!"

"Stop!" John shouted. "Leave the priest alone!"

The bully paused, dagger in mid-air. John slid to the ground, and grabbed his wrist, shaking the dagger free. With a quick movement the man's huge arms grabbed him and threw him aside. The dagger dug into John's arm. Freed, the priest scrambled to his feet and stood shaking, his teeth chattering.

"Mind your own business, Papists," the big man thundered, his eyes flashing, his nostrils distended.

He lunged at John, but Anthony quickly placed his large body between them. Louis, too, moved closer. Anthony held his riding whip in one hand and a bared blade in the other. The big man, seeing himself outnumbered, paused, scowling.

"Why were you attacking this priest?" John demanded.

"I am a Protestant," the bully said defiantly. Then from his belt he drew a string of dirty white objects. "Priest's ears," he boasted. "I collect them." His expression was diabolical.

"Why don't we horsewhip him?" Anthony was eager.

"No!" John turned to the so-called Protestant. "If ever we hear of your committing further mutilations, we will be back to deal with you. Go now, but remember that our Lord said to love our brethren. Your hatred is of the Devil!"

The man muttered to himself, but he lost no time in scrambling off.

John, looking at the priest, was so choked by anger and grief that he could barely say, "I am glad we got here in time. Please do not judge all Protestants by a man like that."

"We met on the trail. When he spoke disrespectfully of the Church, I told him I had vowed to serve it. Without warning he grabbed me off my horse, and we hit the ground together. . . . How can I ever repay you?"

"By remembering that your highest loyalty is to the Lord Jesus Christ."

The priest's eyes widened, then narrowed. "But I serve Christ! What do you mean?"

"Be sure he is the *center* of your faith."

"Why are you saying this to me?"

John remembered the copy of his manual. He went to his saddlebag, drew it out, and handed it to the clergyman. "Will you read this book?"

"I will do anything you ask."

"Then it is settled. Come. We will ride on together."

As the journey progressed, Father Bernardo revealed that he, too, was on the way to Ferrara, and that he was trusted there. John inquired about the duchess.

"She is watched by a Carmelite monk, Hyeronymous Bolsec. Have a care. Anyone who attempts to discuss religion is suspect."

"Are Protestants sentenced to death by the Inquisition?"

Father Bernardo shook his head. "Pope Paul III would not tolerate that, though some are imprisoned or banished. The Inquisitor Ory and the Jesuits are on the alert for heretics, but there is not the cruelty that is current in Paris."

"How do you know so much about the Inquisition, Father Bernardo?"

The little cleric shrugged. "You are my friends. You saved my ears, perhaps my life, so I will tell the truth. I am employed by the Holy Inquisition to obtain information."

"Then you are really a spy?"

"I would rather have you think of me as a legate."

John was quiet for a long moment. Then he said, "Would you sacrifice us, if need be, to the cause?"

Father Bernardo shook his head quickly. "My first loyalty must be, as you have said, to the Lord Jesus Christ. And I am sure in my heart that He would not want any harm to come to you."

The late afternoon sun slanted down through the treetops and the green forest shrouded the travelers as they dismounted a few leagues outside Ferrara. John and Anthony put on some of Louis' clerical robes over their breeches and doublets. Father Bernardo looked them up and down, then shook his cropped head. "Those will never do. The Jesuits would know in a minute that you are frauds. Your habit is too short, Monsieur Anthony. You should not try to disguise yourself as a cleric. It would never fool anyone." He pointed at John. "The curé is much wider than you. His habit does not fit you." He walked to his own saddlebags and took out a vestment. "This will be a bit short, but put it on. It will announce you as a Jesuit."

John obeyed. Then they mounted their horses and continued until they reached the gates of Ferrara. There men with arquebuses stopped them. "Halt! Give your names. State your business." John gave his favorite fictitious name, Charles d'Epeville. Louis gave his own. Anthony said, "Anthony d'Epeville," just as if it were his right name. When the guards recognized Father Bernardo, they waved a greeting, lifted the portcullis, and stepped back. One by one the four horses clattered across the wooden bridge. The portcullis fell behind them. There was no turning back now. Ahead were the Grand Inquisitors, their legates, and the court of the Duke of Ferrara, Hercules II, the son of a Borgia.

The stench of a decaying animal mingled with the odors of privies and garbage in the streets. Everything was in darkness except the castle, where lanterns swung from the gateposts of the courtyard. Here the odor of spices erased the stench. At the stables, a bedraggled groom took their horses. The prospect of seeing Nerien and Clement and possibly Peter Robert again lifted John's spirits as he stepped after Father Bernardo toward the tower entrance. The priest explained to the men-at-arms, who blocked their way, that his friends were to remain a short time.

After a while steps sounded, heavy steps, and an erect man of dark complexion and medium stature appeared. He wore yellow satin and carried a massed candelabra. "What do you seek in Ferrara?" he asked rudely, staring with sharp, black eyes.

Louis took a step forward. His round, shaved head shone in the candlelight as he bowed low, his hands folded in the sleeves of his cassock. "I am a canon of Angoulême. We have come a long way and are very tired."

"Just what is your business here? You're not Protestants?"

"Your Grace"—Father Bernardo advanced until he stood beside Louis—"these friends came to my aid when a violent Protestant tried to hack my ears from my head!"

"Ah, Father Bernardo." A kindly look crossed the hard brown face. "Since you vouch for them they are welcome." The dark man bowed and stood back. "You know my wife finds Protestants exciting, so we have to be careful."

The great banquet hall was illumined by torches in wall brackets, revealing a dais at one end where two canopied chairs had been placed at the center of a table spread with massive plate. The old-fashioned hearth in the middle of the floor was strewn with rushes. Oiled linen edged with bits of colored glass filled the latticed windows. Upon the high ceiling were frescoes of cherubs and voluptuous women. The odors of roasting meat and baking bread permeated the screened end of the hall where the kitchen was hidden. When John came down to supper later that night, he scanned the groups chatting about the room. He couldn't see Peter Robert, Nerien, or Clement among them. The duke and duchess entered, and everyone rose. John looked with interest at the woman who had almost married both the Emperor Charles V, and later Henry VIII, before she had become the bride of her Borgia duke. Her auburn hair, in tight curls about her slim shoulders, set off her fluffy white dress and black veil. As John, followed by Louis and Anthony, advanced to be presented, her deep-set eyes measured him. If it were not for the slight hump on her back, she would be beautiful, he thought, as she smiled and held out her hand.

Father Bernardo pattered up to relate his terrifying experience.

"That was one who merely called himself a Protestant," the duchess said firmly.

The duke glowered at her and she stared back with lifted chin as he said, "My dear, unless you show more discretion as to those you champion, I shall be forced to conclude it wise to have our children reared away from the heretical influence you exert on them."

Just then the strains of a lute sounded and a voice began to sing:

"Some ten or twenty times a day,
  To bustle to the town with speed,
  To dabble in what dirt he may,—
  Friar Lubin's the man you need."

A good deal of confusion followed as minstrels, jesters, parrots, and pages in bright costumes moved about the long table. A buffoon with a kangaroo on a chain leaped from one maid to another, kissing their cheeks. The singer was Clement Marot, a Clement who would not meet John's gaze! Later, seated below the dais, facing the duke and duchess, with Louis and Anthony on either side of him, John watched the poet.

Clothed in purple doublet, bright yellow breeches, and a yellow tam with a green feather, Clement strutted around the hall in time to the music. Not once did his eyes meet John's even briefly.

All the next day John had a feeling of unease. He went outside to walk in the courtyard, where fountains green with age sprayed dirty water. At one end, under a spreading olive tree, sat a young man and two children, a boy and a girl. The man was Nerien. He was reading aloud from a leather-bound book, and the children were listening intently.

Concealing his excitement, John strolled casually in their direction, pausing before them to tie the thong of his shoe. "I suppose you are a tutor, young man," he said in a low voice.

"Yes. Yes, I am. These are the duke's children. See. I am forbidden to read the Holy Scriptures to them." He lifted the book so John could see that it was Peter Robert's Bible!

"Yes, I see. What can I find to do here?"

"Do not tarry now. Move off!" Nerien said softly.

John strolled out of the courtyard, past the stables redolent of leather, straw, and manure. He understood: Nerien was being watched. Here in Ferrara spies watched everybody. He himself felt like a lamb in an arena circled by wolves.

That night at supper the feeling of unease grew stronger. A hostile-eyed Carmelite sitting across from John stared at him awhile, then whispered to a cardinal who was nearby.

After supper the Carmelite came up to John. "I am Brother Bolsec. I have the feeling we have met before, in Paris," he said in a voice furred with cat softness. He was a huge monsterlike man with bulging eyeballs.

"I always remember a face," John said, careful not to show his anxiety. "And yours is one I could never forget."

Brother Bolsec licked his wide mouth with a small coated tongue. "Perhaps I am mistaken, but I was sure you were somebody I ought to know."

John took a deep breath. "You must have me mixed up with someone else."

As John and Anthony were preparing for bed that night, Father Bernardo came to their room.

"Are you the author of the book you gave me?" he asked, looking at John.

"Yes, Father Bernardo, I am John Calvin."

"But you are infamous! You are considered a threat to the Church. Yet you came to my defense!"

"Sit down. Forget we saved your ears. Just open your mind and hear me out."

The little priest sat down nervously. Anthony stood at the end of the bed frowning.

John drew up a chair, took a deep breath, and began: "You agreed that the first loyalty of a priest should be to Christ. You also said you were sure He would not want any harm to come to me. Have you changed your mind?"

Father Bernardo shifted on the oak chair. There was a look of bewilderment on his brown, honest face.

"You are the enemy of the Church. You speak ill of the Virgin, of the saints, and even, I am told, of the Mass. Then how can you expect me, a priest of the Church, to protect you?"

"I have never spoken ill of the good and blessed Virgin, but I want her son given the glory He deserves, as she would wish."

Father Bernardo looked puzzled. "I have read the preface and the first chapter of your manual. There will be a reaction throughout the world to such a book!"

"Can you understand it?"

"Anyone could understand. But the Church does not teach that way!"

"There is nothing in it which cannot be found in the Bible."

"Oh, dear!" Father Bernardo wailed. "I don't know what to do."

"Then I will tell you. Go back to your room and finish reading the book. If you are not convinced it is the truth, I will confess my identity and give you credit for unmasking me."

For an instant the priest's face relaxed. "You are a brave man. I

131

will do as you say. But you understand, do you not, that I must do what I think is right?"

"Yes. And whatever you decide, we will still be friends."

"God in Heaven," the little priest moaned as he scuttled out. "Even if I turn him over to the Inquisition, we will still be friends. What kind of religion is that?"

Dawn was creeping through the grilled windows when John opened his eyes. Anthony snored on. Stretching, John greeted the newborn day with the prayer that Father Bernardo would know the truth when it was shown him.

In a few minutes he heard the door open. Two figures crept in—Clement and Nerien.

"At last!" John whispered. "Is Peter Robert here?"

"We took a chance in coming, Master John." Nerien's voice was low. "We cannot stay long. As for Peter Robert, he left to go south."

"Oh! I longed to talk to him." John's disappointment was sharp.

"The duchess bid me to invite you to stay in Ferrara. She wants to talk to you, but she is closely watched."

"Her husband never forgets that when Dr. Le Fèvre was her tutor, he influenced her. Even her letters to him and others are destroyed," Clement said.

"I came to Ferrara to talk to her and see you both. Is there any chance of a true Reformation in Italy?"

"There is the good Bishop Sadolet. There is Cardinal Caraffe. Both speak of salvation by faith, as the Protestants do. If the Pope would enlist their help, the Reformation would come."

The opening of the door interrupted them. Father Bernardo peered in, and Nerien and Clement stiffened. The priest advanced quietly with a strange trancelike expression on his face.

"There can be only one decision, my friend," he said to John. "I am convinced you are a man of God."

"Salvation is God's free gift, Bernardo. The papacy cannot forbid God to give it, nor can the Pope oppose Christ's own performance of the promise of salvation or the remission of sins!"

"Yes. Yes. The Vulgate says that."

"Then you will help me tell others?"

Father Bernardo hesitated. "Yes," he said at length. He turned to Nerien and Clement, as if seeing them for the first time. "Do you tell others?"

Nerien's face was eager. "A Christian must!"

Clement shifted his feet and looked at the floor.

"Clement," John said, "Father Bernardo has just become one of us."

"I hope he will be a better Christian than I am," Clement said contritely. "When the arm of Rome is not reaching out for me, I tell others. When it is, I go to Mass. Sometimes I am brave. Again I am a Christian only when it's safe. And at such times I hate myself!"

Two mornings later John was awakened by someone shaking him roughly. The face of the figure bending over him was indistinguishable in the shadows, for dawn was just beginning to break.

"John, the duchess is waiting in the chapel. Hurry!" It was Clement's rolling voice.

John got out of bed, drew on Father Bernardo's habit, put on his shoes, and picking up the copy of his manual, which Father Bernardo had returned, followed the poet into the chilly corridor.

Treading softly, ears straining for the sound of footsteps other than Clement's, John moved along the passage to a high-arched door which stood open.

"The duchess is here in her chapel. If I knock three times, she will tell you what to do."

The door clicked shut behind him, and John looked about with excitement and awe. The faint gray dawn was the only light penetrating the gloom as the Duchess of Ferrara limped to greet him, her hands outstretched. They were alone except for her lady in waiting.

"Master Calvin, a proper welcome. I am sorry it had to be delayed."

"I have brought you a gift. It contains the truths found in the Holy Scriptures. This is the first bound copy."

She took the book. "Thank you, my friend. I am glad you have come. Would that it were under happier circumstances, but the duke has me watched constantly."

"From what I have seen we are in a nest of bigots."

She smiled gently. "Even my husband watches me. The Carmelite Bolsec follows like a bull after a red petticoat. I am weary."

"Your life is not in danger?"

"The duke happens to love me, in spite of what he calls my 'absurd religion' and my disfiguration. Besides, he believes his attitude toward the Protestants is right."

"Then you cannot try your Christian beliefs on the Court?"

"I try them. They do not avail. 'Roma locuta est; causa finita est' (Rome has spoken; the case is settled)."

"I know."

"There is much I would like to discuss, but we dare not linger here too long. In Venice last year everyone was talking about you, saying that you have the courage dear Dr. Le Fèvre lacked."

"He had great courage. In his day it took even greater courage to teach our beliefs than it does now. He was singled out, persecuted. He stood almost alone. Compare him to Dr. Erasmus!"

"Understand, Dr. Calvin, that I admire Dr. Le Fèvre."

"We all do. In fact, I wonder if I have his courage. When I am in the midst of the intrigue here at your court, I am very frightened."

"I sent for you to show you what to do should a crisis arise. . . . Come to this chapel. I had a secret exit constructed recently when my husband was in Rome. Some French refugees built it for me to aid escaping Christians. Come. Let me show you."

He followed her into the nave, where she placed both hands against a panel in the wall behind the altar and pushed. It swung back revealing a passageway.

"Count the panels. Remember this is the seventh from the doorway. It could be your passport to freedom."

John nodded. "Thank you. I hope I never have to use it."

"So do I. Now I must return to my chambers before the duke rises and misses me. Let us meet here again just before dawn next Friday, one week from today."

The week passed with Brother Bolsec hovering near like a vulture, but there were no incidents. Just before dawn on Friday, John dressed and went quietly into the little chapel to wait for the duchess. It was almost light when she came, followed by her lady in waiting. The duchess rushed toward him, her skirts rustling as they swept the floor.

"Oh, Master Calvin, your book will do much to erase error and bring faith! One cannot read it without being compelled to kneel and thank God for his greatest gift!"

"I pray that others will find it helpful. A French edition will soon follow. Many cannot read Latin with ease."

"How old are you, Master Calvin?"

"Twenty-seven."

She sighed. "God is calling you to be a leader among men."

"Whatever he calls me to, I will obey."

"If only——"

The door burst open and Father Bernardo ran toward them. "Leave Ferrara at once, John Calvin. Do not wait to inform your brother and friend. Your identity has been discovered!"

John was palsied with fear. "Bolsec?"

"Who else? A priest from Basle reported you were coming here. The duke has just given orders that you are not to be allowed to leave. If you make haste——"

"But my brother? Louis?"

"Neither is the one they seek. Go quickly!"

The duchess took command. "Fetch a scholar's gown, Father." The priest scurried out. "We will tell your friend, the canon, and your brother to follow you to Modena, Parma, Piedmont. The Inquisition has little strength there."

In less than fifteen minutes, John, his heart thumping, went through the secret passageway, sauntered past the sleepy soldiers at the city gate, and walked on until he was out of sight. Then he began to run, and kept on until he reached some tall pines where he hid and watched the duke's men charging by.

It was almost twilight when he came out of hiding and started walking toward the Modena road, passing fields blanketed with grapevines and hills studded with olive trees. With darkness came the wails and snorts of unseen animals. He had to spend one night in a tree, but he finally reached the Valley of St. Paul of Grand near Salizzo. Here he gathered men, women, and children on the hillside and taught the doctrines of grace and salvation while he waited for Louis and Anthony to appear.

"I've had enough," Louis said sheepishly the night he and Anthony arrived in the valley. "I am going back to Angoulême and work within the Church. I've decided all this reform you prate about is not worth the strain."

John felt as if a donkey had kicked him in the head. Louis is bending to pressure just like Bishop Briconnet, he thought. "If that is your decision, good speed," he said stiffly. "Every man is answerable to his own conscience."

"You despise my lack of fortitude."

"That depends on what you do when you reach Angoulême. You can stand like a goat chewing tin, making meaningless sounds, or use the voice God gave you to teach about His Salvation!"

After Louis left the following day, Anthony clapped John on the shoulder. "He's not dead, you know."

"I'm glad of that, but I had grown very fond of him."

"Well, forget him. Cheer up. A traveler on the trail told us that an Edict of Couchy and a royal pardon of Lyon grants a six months' reprieve to all heretics that they may consider their sins! We could go back to Paris as you have been longing to do!"

"Then let us return. Maybe we can help those who have been enduring the awful trials there."

But when John and Anthony stopped at the cottage of Bart Bardeau, the vinedresser, before entering the city, he told them, "It was a mistake to come back! The pardon terminates in a few days!"

"And Beda would see that we were detained!" John said angrily.

"Not Beda. He is a prisoner at Mont St. Michael. The King decided he was a threat to the royal power. But others have taken the rector's place. The persecution has only begun."

"But where can we go?" John's voice was a sob.

"We could seek asylum in Strasbourg," Anthony suggested. "Dr. Bucer would welcome you again. He needs teachers, and you have been saying you want to teach and write. There we will be safe."

10

July, 1536

As the brothers galloped along the dusty road in the predawn grayness, the morning breeze refreshed their saddle-weary bodies. For several days they had traveled, but now the hardest part of their journey was behind them. Ahead lay Strasbourg, the city of brotherly love, where men were judged with the Christian yardstick and the community exemplified the Gospel in action.

"I wish I never had to sit the saddle again!" John said feelingly.

Anthony lifted his hand. "Rein your horse, John! There's a man on the road waving something."

John recognized the standard in the soldier's hand—a gold salamander on a field of scarlet, the King's standard—and a flicker of dismay went through him.

There was the noise of hoofs and a clatter of spurs as a company of men-at-arms passed at breakneck speed. They wore tilting armor, visored and helmeted, with metal encasing them from head to toe. Because of their lances and heavy swords they sat the saddle awkwardly.

"You will have to turn back!" the foot soldier with the standard shouted. "The King fights the soldiers of the Emperor. Dead and wounded are lying everywhere. No one can pass."

"Can't we take the Campaigne Road?" Anthony cupped his hands to call.

"No, it is blocked."

John's heart sank. The only other way they could reach Strasbourg would be to circle through the borders of Savoy by way of Lyon and Geneva! This would lengthen the journey by days, but there was nothing to do except wheel the horses.

That afternoon it rained. Thunder rumbled and lightning flashed crimson, but they rode on. By nightfall the roads were a sea of mire. Two inns where they asked for accommodations were filled with the King's men. One of the innkeepers sold them a small wedge of cheese, and they had to be content with that for their supper. The night was spent in an old church where rats scampered.

The storm seemed to follow them, and by the time they neared Geneva, John was so tired he felt as if he would fall from the saddle. Their first sight of that city evoked a whistle from Anthony.

"No wonder Peter Robert wrote it was the most beautiful place on earth!"

John forgot his aching bones, his weariness. "What a song I could write to the Creator of such beauty if I had the talent of Francis of Assisi!" he murmured.

They rode on quietly until they reached an old cracked wall and the Cornavin Gate, which bore a coat of arms of a wine-cellar key, a gaming bird, an eagle. The key probably represented Peter. Peter and Paul were the city's patron saints. Patron saints, John thought. *Post tenebras lucem* (After darkness, light)! With William Farel triumphing and truth spreading, that should be a marginal inscription on the plaque.

A young man with a round, short body stepped from the sentry box and clanked up, very martial and important.

"State your names, your business, and the length of your stay in Geneva."

John lifted his eyes to the mountains. Geneva, he thought. Here a man can give his right name!

"John Calvin. *Master* Calvin and Anthony Calvin. Our destination is Strasbourg, but the Campaigne Road is blocked with fighting. We will be here tonight."

"You will find an inn down by the river in the Rue Contana," the repulsive little strutting pigeon of a sentry said, lowering his arquebus.

As they approached the inn, a man eating an apple on the bank beside the swift blue Rhône, rose and came toward them. In his scholar's dark gown, he moved with the proud bearing of a nobleman. Monsieur Viret's blue eyes smiled with the rest of his face as he introduced himself, saying that if he could do anything to make their stay happier, they had but to let him know.

"Thank you, Monsieur. I am John Calvin and this is my brother, Anthony."

Peter Viret's long jaw dropped. "Not *the* John Calvin? The author of the *Institutes?*"

John nodded, feeling his ears grow warm.

"Why, you are one of the great! Your book is helping the people of Geneva. Although they celebrated their freedom two months ago, making Christianity a part of their lives is another matter. I must tell William Farel you are here."

As soon as they were shown to their room, John took off his dusty clothes and climbed into bed, certain that he had never been so tired in his life. He drew the covers up around his neck and was soon asleep.

It seemed only a moment, however, before somebody was shaking him awake. A man with fiery red hair, a square florid face, and brilliant blue eyes stood over him. He had the look of a bristling red dog.

"Wake up," he said rudely, and John wished he would go away. "I am here on the Lord's business!"

Elation filled William Farel as he stared down at one of the most famous men of the age. He decided that John Calvin looked stubborn but honest . . . there was something in the pitch of his chin. His face, with long nose, generous lips, and tiny lines between keen black eyes, had sensitivity and strength. People everywhere were discussing his book. If there was one man in the world who could save Geneva, this was the man. And here he was, looking like a hungry gaming bird as he regarded his visitor with annoyance and curiosity.

Scowling, he sat up. "Who are you?" he demanded. "Why do you stare at me that way?"

"Because I wonder if I'm dreaming. You are the answer to my prayer."

"*I* am?"

William pulled up a chair. "My name is William Farel. . . . Perhaps you are aware that three factions divide the people of Geneva —the Protestants, the Catholics, and the Nationalists or Libertines. The Libertines were the soldiers who fought for freedom, and they resent so many French refugees."

"I suppose that is natural." John yawned.

"Have you no questions?"

"The fighting going on here is no concern of mine. I leave in the morning."

"Some people affirmed the Protestant beliefs only to escape the tyranny of their temporal rulers. Few know the meaning of their faith."

"And you are struggling to convert them to the teachings of our Lord?"

William nodded. "With little success. Your duty, John Calvin, is to stay here and save the people, organize the new church and the government."

A look of horror twisted across John Calvin's intelligent face like a writhing serpent. "But I am too young. I have just turned twenty-seven. I am a scholar. I hate strife. I must have solitude!"

"Only a leader can save Geneva. There is a proper foundation. The right of gathering in General Assembly to elect administrative officers was secured in 1387. A Little Council of twenty-five senators or councilmen is at work. The Council of Sixty discusses matters too difficult to debate in a large assembly or Council of Two Hundred."

The scholar waved his hand. "I am not your man, Farel. I do not get along easily with people. I am too outspoken."

"You recognize your faults. That is encouraging. So few do."

What if this is God's will, John thought with an awful fluttering in his heart. "God, surely thou art not speaking through this red-haired revolutionary."

William tried another thrust. "In your *Institutes* you point out that *obedience* is the key to the Christian life. If it is God's will, you must stay."

John Calvin shook his head. "No. I am going to Strasbourg where there is no strife!"

"Is it God's will you seek, or John Calvin's?"

"In the name of the Lord have pity on me! Cease torturing me. Allow me to serve God in my own way!"

"Then it is John Calvin's will you choose?"

John sat up straight, striking out with unreined anger. "You are an impudent man, sir. Daring to tell *me* God's will for *my* life. Do you think you are God?" He stopped abruptly, ashamed of his impetuous outburst.

William rose and stood over him, hammering on the bed table with his mighty fist.

"In the name of Almighty God, John Calvin, I say to you that your writing and studies are a pretext. If you refuse to obey Him by staying here, He will curse you, for you seek John Calvin's will instead of God's."

In that instant John felt as if God's awful hand had seized him. My will, he thought in horror, and not God's. To obey blindly has been my prayer. His mind reeled through the maze of events. He had returned to Paris believing it was God's command, yet the termination of the pardon had kept him from entering the city. Already God had given his book wings. This revolutionary standing over him had written the placards that had fanned the hatred and increased persecution. John had heard how he had laid his hands on images, smashing them in violence. He certainly needed help in building a church. Could this be God's call?

Like a prophet of Israel, William Farel stood there, waiting for his answer. There could be only one.

John sighed deeply. "I don't want to stay, Farel. I would rather be burned on the Place du Grève before Notre Dame or stretched on the rack until I was torn limb from limb. No, I don't want to stay. But you're right—I must!"

11

Fall of 1536

In September, through William's influence, John was appointed Professor of Sacred Letters to the Church in Geneva, but no salary was given him. Anthony secured a position at a local bookshop, but John would not allow his brother to carry the burden of his support. Occasionally he earned a little money by doing secretarial work for some of the councilmen. But he knew he was going to have to learn a trade, and began considering what it should be. His daily classes on the Epistles of Paul, which were held in St. Peter's, grew steadily, but there were times when doubts assailed him. Could it have been William Farel's thundering voice he had heard and not God's?

At his living quarters in the Rue de la Treille he often climbed up to the roof from which he could see the spire on St. Peter's Church, blue Lake Leman, and in the distance, the snow-crested Juras and Alps. Sometimes in his loneliness he walked to the Town Hall, a few steps from his house, and tried to make friends with the councilmen. But he was received coldly: a foreigner, another refugee from France.

One night when he turned into St. Peter's Square, he found it crowded with men and women dancing. Torches set in pails of earth circled the scene with a reddish glow. Couples sprawled over the church steps, or nestled close on the seats built around the chestnut trees. John paused to watch the peculiar leaping step, the lively motion, the bright whirling petticoats and slashed breeches.

Suddenly he felt that someone was watching him, and turned to see a young woman coming toward him. Black hair streamed straight around her slim shoulders and she walked as if on air. When she paused in front of him, her pungent perfume sickened him. Under her insolent regard he felt himself crimson.

"Want to dance?" she asked.

John stood for a moment looking down at her, wanting to pull her scarlet gown up over her naked shoulders. Then compassion welled within him.

"Do you like that dance?"

"Oui, Monsieur. It is said to have originated with a troubadour named Rigard, Monsieur. That is the rigadoon."

"It is horrible, and besides I do not dance."

"We like it, Monsieur. I could teach you."

He thought: This girl has no idea there is more to life than vulgar dancing, the pleasuring of the senses. How can I help her?

"What is your name?" he asked.

"Francesca Favre. My father fought the Savoys. He is a member of the General Council."

John had heard of the Favres. William had spoken of the unruly draper and his incorrigible children.

"Are you going to dance with me or not, Monsieur?" she pouted.

"No, I am not going to dance. And I cannot help but think that you could be an attractive girl if you would make some changes in your life."

She winced as if he had struck her. "Oh, come now, Monsieur. Don't you want people to be happy?" She sidled closer. "What is there about me that bothers you?"

He moved back, repelled. "Any young girl who decks herself out in such a dress could never bother a gentleman!"

Her black eyes began to glitter, and her face paled under its heavy splotches of rouge. "Now get this, Monsieur—you don't have to insult a girl just because you don't approve of her. Who are you?"

"I am Master Calvin. I am sorry I was rude, but I teach that people have souls as well as bodies!"

"Well, now. I'm waiting. Plead with me to go to the gloomy cathedral every day to listen to that red-haired gloomy!"

"Everyone should attend church. That is one place souls are fed."

"Surely, Master Calvin, you do not wish to be so droll." Her voice was wheedling now. "Do not be like Pastor Farel! You are young and have wonderful eyes."

John was about to remonstrate further when a doltish creature moved between them. Where had he seen this comic little Caesar? Oh, yes! This was the obnoxious sentry who had been at the gate when he arrived at Geneva. His name was Ami Perrin.

"A-ha!" He wagged a stubby white finger. "The timid Professor of Sacred Letters whiles away the hours with the gay Francesca. Tsch! Tsch!"

He rolled his little round eyes and John wanted to slap him. Francesca snickered, and John frowned at her.

"Your spiritual welfare is a serious matter, Mademoiselle. It affects your immortal soul. I only want to help save it."

For an instant she sobered. "I suppose you are right."

"I am right. Never forget that the pleasures of sin have a terrible price!"

"What do you want me to do?"

"Attend church with regularity. Feed your soul just as you feed your body. Learn to pray."

"How boring!" Ami said.

Francesca was standing still now, her expression almost wistful. Ami broke the silence by coughing. She shoved him aside.

"You know, Monsieur, it's the first time anyone ever reminded me that I have a soul. But please, oh, please, do not look at me like that. As if you read my soul and saw it black!"

John shook his head. "Mademoiselle, you are wrong. I was just seeing you as you could be in Christ."

"Tell the psalm singer to go away," Ami's grating voice interrupted. "Come, Francesca, dance with me. The professor is just a dead saint!"

"No, I do not want to dance with you, Ami. I want to dance with the professor."

The lutes were sending out a provocative rhythm. She held out her arms, once more the bare-shouldered girl who knew her physical charms. For an instant she looked pretty. Her lips, parted in a smile, were bright red and her eyes sparkled. John realized with a shock that he wanted to take her in his arms and whirl away to the beat of the dance. The call of the flesh, he thought. Firmly he shook his head.

"Mademoiselle, there is much more to life than dancing and seeking pleasure. That must be my message for Geneva. My message to you."

She stared at him. "All right, Monsieur. Wait until you meet my brother, Gaspard. Try to tell him that." She extended her hand. "Good night, Monsieur Calvin. You go your way and the Favres will go theirs. Our way may lead to that Hell you will surely predict for us, but we'll have fun on the way."

It was the last day of September, in the year 1537. John, riding into Vaud, Lausanne, behind William Farel, noticed the ancient towers, the high arches, dwellings rebuilt after the recent fire, and old sun-bleached structures. The streets and squares swarmed with citizens and clergymen—priests in fiddle-shaped habits, ministers in ankle-length gowns and velvet skullcaps, hooded monks; peasants in coarse cloth; mountain people in starched coats, gowns with laced bodices and puffed sleeves, velvet breeches; burghers in multicolored breeches and doublets.

The crowd was so large that the horses had to move with the people, but at last the two men tied their mounts to the staples in the yard at the Inn of the Lion. By the time they were shown to their beds, John's head pounded and his throat ached.

"I am a sick man, William. I may not be able to help you debate against the priests in the morning."

"What's the matter with you?" William demanded, scowling in disgust as he unpacked. "I am twenty years older than you, and I'm not even tired!" He flung open the casement. "All you need is some fresh air."

"Maybe, if I get a good night's sleep, I'll be all right in the morning."

"God predestines your presence at the cathedral to fight His battle. He needs us both. That is why I insisted that you come."

When William had left to visit some theologians, John bathed in cold water from the basin on the rough board table and then stretched out on his bed, brooding. William was unreasonable in his obsession with the debate, which was to begin at sunrise between the priests and ministers, to help the people make up their minds about joining the so-called New Church or continuing in the Church of Rome.

When dawn slanted through the window the next morning, John's chest felt heavy and he ached all over. The thought of debating before a vast crowd made him shudder. William was up early, stamping around the room. He cut some black bread, meat, and cheese; he poured some goat's milk.

"All right. Get up. Breakfast is ready."

John forced himself to crawl out of bed, but he was shaking as he took his seat opposite William.

"Have you decided what the Lord wills you to do, John?" With ferocity William impaled a slice of meat with his knife. "Return to bed and nurse your aches, or dress and enter the arena of the cathedral to defend His Truth? Three hundred priests will attack it."

John was still deliberating, when William left with a final word of admonishment. "Don't be late, John. I will save you a seat. You do not want to miss your most challenging opportunity to witness!"

Later, as John wobbled along the street to the cathedral, he remembered that William had grown up in the mountains of Dauphiny. When he had come under the influence of Dr. Le Févre in Paris, he had become so ardent against error that he sometimes acted with violence. But he had a good heart, and he seemed to have no doubts. He was sure God had called him to champion His Truth.

The tower clock was striking seven as John entered the crowded cathedral. People were standing around the walls and even in the vestibule. William saw him, and motioned him toward the empty chair next to his own.

A few minutes later William moved to the front, faced the as-

146

semblage, and began to blast the ears of the crowd with the redis-covered doctrine of salvation by faith. Works, he repeated over and over, would never save anyone. The canons sat quietly, star-ing in concentration. When William sat down, a big priest rose to challenge him, insisting that works gave merits toward a salvation the Church pronounced could be earned. John stayed quietly on the bench while the arguments went on and on.

"Why didn't you help us?" William growled as they supped that night.

"You presented the arguments with great skill. I felt no com-pulsion."

"Your will again, and not God's?" William asked scathingly.

The next morning a priest with apple cheeks and honest blue eyes read an indictment charging the Protestants with ignorance and neglect of the teachings of the Roman Church, and claiming that it was wicked to challenge the authority of the Pope, since "he came a light into the world."

Then compulsion lifted John to his feet. "When the mind is addled," he roared, "the purple glare is so bright that truth is hid-den. Assuredly a bad tree can produce only bad fruit. The priest was, in all probability, sincere when he made the statement the Pope came a light into the world. . . . That comment palpably falsifies Holy Writ. The Pope a light into the world? Blasphemous mouth!" He pointed sternly at the astonished priest. "You apply to that fetid monster, Paul Third, the sacred terms applicable to none but the Son of God?"

Turning back to the assemblage while the priest stood with open mouth, John expounded other Reformed beliefs, which excluded the doctrine of transubstantiation and pointed out that the bread and wine do not become the actual flesh and blood of Christ. He went further than that, stating that to believe in this doctrine was a form of cannibalism!

John's explanations, following William Farel's arguments of the day before, won many new members to the Protestant cause. Priests, ministers, and citizens circled John to tell him they had been con-vinced.

John Tandi, the Cordelier who had spoken, lingered after everyone else had gone. "Your power came from God!" he said. "The Protestant Church is the church of the early disciples revived. I want to have a part in it."

John sat alone in the simple rooms he shared with Anthony in Geneva. Time had moved on, and the snows had melted into puddles. Young shoots were breaking through the earth. Spring had come to Geneva. John had just returned from a walk, during which he had outlined his sermon for the following Sunday. Ever since his success at Vaud, he had preached regularly, urging the people to live in obedience to God. As he lifted his quill to put his sermon on parchment, there was a knock on the door. He put down the quill, and went to open it. Michael Sept stood there.

John was grateful for everything this gigantic man did to influence the French refugees toward Christian living. Because he could flatten an iron bar on an anvil or a big man with his fist, the rougher refugees respected him.

"We have trouble, Master Calvin," he blurted.

"Come in. Tell me about it."

Michael took a chair, stretching his mighty legs out before him. "Last night I caught a family man entering the Bordel. When I remonstrated, he informed me that the Council elects the woman who runs it, that it is legal, approved by the city leaders."

"Surely the Council does not approve of such a place!"

"I investigated, and I found that prostitution *is* legalized and that the Council *does* elect La Reine du Bordel."

John was dismayed. He had had no idea such vice was legalized. Something would have to be done about it. A decent community could not tolerate it.

The next afternoon he called on Councilman Favre and his son, Gaspard, neither of whom had the grace to show any repentance.

"Men will be men," Councilman Favre said with a shrug and an oily smile. "If I were you, I would stick to preaching the Gospel!"

"I would remind you, sir, that anything which affects the souls of the people is the affair of the ministers. Our religion includes the concerns of everyday life—business, politics, education, culture, community, and family. It insists upon active participation in day-by-day affairs."

148

"The ministers had better not meddle in politics!"

John stood still for an instant, the veins in his temples swelling. "Monsieur Favre, I am appalled at the thought of any so-called Christianity that would neglect the field of politics, believing it beneath a Christian. *Christ's Kingdom is over all the earth!*"

That night John talked to William. "We ought to uphold the separation of Church and State," William said, "but many do not understand the doctrine. They think it means Christians have nothing to do with politics."

"We will keep telling them. The few followers of Christ are the Church; the State includes everybody. Every citizen is a part of the State, though not every citizen is a part of the Church. A Christian, however, must be a responsible citizen."

"What are you going to do about the Bordel?"

"I'll do something!"

"Have a care. Money means more to some men than souls."

As John sat at his desk the next night, there was the sound of hurried steps approaching his open door, and a man he had never seen before appeared, breathing hard.

"Master Calvin?"

John nodded.

"For the love of God, come quickly. A woman is dying and wishes your prayers."

"I'll go with you," John said.

The man's legs, longer than his, seemed to skim over the rough streets in the darkness, and John had difficulty in keeping up with him. An unseen cat howled as they crossed the Court of St. Peter, and John felt an uneasy stirring. Where was this unknown messenger taking him? At night this way and unexpectedly? William's warning sounded in his ears: "Have a care. . . ." Now I'm imagining things, he thought, as the guide turned into a dark, twisting street and paused before a large house behind a high wall. The man held the iron gate open and stood back to let John enter, which he did, warily. The grounds were in blackness and only a dim light shone in the window beyond.

When he reached the open door, he was assailed by the odor of

149

strong, cheap perfume mixed with the smell of stale air. The entrance yawned like the hole to a grotto.

"Give me your hand," his guide said. "Come."

All is not well, John thought in panic. That inner sense tells me.

"I must get Master Farel," he said quickly, and he turned and stumbled back down the path.

He could hear the man shouting after him, but he did not stop until he reached St. Peter's. He found William in the tower study and told him breathlessly of the strange summons and his suspicions.

"If a woman really is dying, I have to go back," he ended. "But I have to be sure."

"Take me to this place."

A few minutes later they stood side by side outside the iron gate, and John pointed in disbelief at the house. Light streamed from all the windows now, and the sound of voices and raucous laughter came from within.

William stared in amazement. "John, are you sure this is the house?"

"Yes."

"And you almost went in?"

"I was about to when I got an odd feeling."

"I should think you would. In God's holy name, John, don't be so naïve! Do you know what this is?"

John shook his head.

"Geneva's Bordel. If you had been discovered there at this hour of the night, your preaching days would have been over. Let us leave before someone sees us hanging about, and never tell anyone you have been here!"

Angry blood warmed John's cheeks. "We will go now, but I will *not* keep this a secret. On Sunday morning I shall enter the pulpit of God's Church and tell His people exactly what happened tonight. I'll ask them to join me in insisting that the Council close this place."

"What if they will not believe you? Many do not have a conception of what Christianity is. Some try to atone for their private vices by religious bigotry."

"They cannot condemn God. What I do, I do in His name."

"At last there is hope for a great Geneva!" a tall man with silver hair and military bearing said as he came up to speak to John at the conclusion of the service on the following Sunday. "I am Francis Bonivard. Your courage will have its effects. For many years some of us have struggled for righteousness."

John's heart lifted. Francis Bonivard. The brave prisoner of Chillon who, with two other Christian patriots, Benzanson Hughes and Philibert Berthelier, had waged the fight for liberty and godliness. His good blue eyes, in a young face grown old with suffering, looked steadily at John.

"I first heard of you when my cousin, Olivétan, wrote from this place, telling me of the struggle you were waging. And you are still ready to fight for a good city!"

Francis Bonivard nodded. "My body grows weary, but my spirit? Never! Men must keep fighting for those things in which they trust."

"Then we can count on you?"

"Of course. I have a little influence with some members of the Council. Right always wins sooner or later. And you can count on me."

At last John and William had completed a Confession, or set of rules, and an oath to follow them. The beadle was sent out to bring the people to the Town Hall in groups of ten to sign the agreement to conform. Ami Perrin, the last to be brought in, complained loudly that the articles included the weapon of excommunication used by the Catholic Church. Amusements, he protested, were not sins and he wanted no part of a joyless religion. Why couldn't people dance and play cards if they wanted to?

"Dancing and card-playing in themselves are not sins," John said slowly. "But pleasures have come to so dominate that they are too frequently engaged in. Where vice has become a habit of long standing, everything which could lead to the danger of overindulgence should be eliminated."

"Men of the clergy!" Ami scoffed, as he reluctantly signed the oath. "What do you do for fun?"

That summer the gambling houses were closed, despite the threats of Pierre Ameaux, a gaming-card manufacturer. Dancing was no longer permitted in the streets. The Bordel and other places of prostitution were emptied. The slit breeches had to go. Drunkenness was no longer tolerated. In defiance, a chinless reprobate, Jake Camaret, marched down the aisle in St. Peter's one Sunday morning, followed by one of the women from the Bordel, whose dress and walk plainly showed the lack of any shame. Plunking themselves down on the front bench, they turned to smirk at those around them.

John's first impulse was to denounce their blasphemy. But the thought occurred that God would want this opportunity used to tell them about Him. Calmly he opened the Bible and read of the woman at the well. He finished the worship service as if there had been no brazen attempt to dishonor God and man.

The next morning, as the clock struck nine, he appeared at the Council meeting in the Town Hall and insisted that the couple would have to be punished if the Church was to be respected.

"I have told you before, and I tell you again," Monsieur Favre said rudely. "Stick to the preaching of the Gospel!"

John stiffened in anger. "That is the answer the ungodly will always make when the Church points its fingers at their sins. I say to you that the Church will ever decry evil!"

John's reply was like a declaration of war. Monsieur Favre sat down in his high-backed stall, lips compressed, eyes glinting. Ablard Corne, a short man with a rotunda of stomach, rose. Every eye was on him as he began to speak.

"What Master Calvin says is true. How can we have a good city unless we respect morality?"

Abel Poupin, a tall man with sunken cheeks and deep-set eyes, got to his feet. "We all know that Jake Camaret and the woman are brazenly living together. It would be well to show the populace how we deal with adulterers."

Philibert Berthelier, the son of the famous patriot, disagreed. "Do not listen to that Frenchman. He is throttling the liberty my father gave his life to win!"

John was quietly insistent. "There can be no compromise when souls are in jeopardy."

A week later the sentence of the Council was carried out: Jake Camaret and the woman were marched naked through the streets past a mocking populace. Before them stalked the beadle, proclaiming as he went, "Thus the Council deals with those who break its laws—adulterers, thieves, murderers, and lewd persons. Let evildoers contemplate their ways, and let every man beware!"

John's thoughts raced painfully into the past as he read the letter he had just received from his sister Mary. Charles had died two weeks before, in early November, without being reconciled to the Church. The canons, in a body, had tried to force him on his deathbed to let them give him the last rites of the Church, but he had died still proclaiming salvation by faith. Burial had taken place at night in the ground at the public crossroads under the gibbet, so that his enemies could not find his body and have it dug up and burned. The Abbot of St. Eloi, Claude de Mommor, had been a good friend, but not even he thought Charles deserved burial in hallowed ground.

John closed his eyes and saw once again the little niche in his mother's bedroom, where she had knelt to tell the good Virgin of her needs. The blue-draped Virgin was still there, but no one knelt before her now. Not even Varnessa; she, too, prayed only to God. For an instant John longed for the sound of the bells of Noyon-la-Sainte, the touch of his mother's hand, the lilt of Charles's voice in the square raftered rooms, his father's bass tones rumbling to the canons, and the sight of the beloved bishop. But he had to follow the light. Unless God expected a man to believe the Holy Scriptures, why had He given them to him?

The white-clad trees stood like specters in the February night. Snow buried the streets and covered the slanting rooftops, as John trudged toward St. Peter's. A carriage crunched by, its dim lights filtering through the gloom. The sharp wind slapped at him and his feet felt like ice as the snow penetrated the holes of his shoes, his only ones, now patched with folded parchment. The city had recently given him a small salary, but it was not enough to supply even necessities.

As he neared the square, a round figure muffled in a long,

black cape whisked by. John recognized Ablard Corne and called out a greeting. How grateful he was to such men! There were several on the Council who tried to live like Christians. Despite their efforts, the problems seemed to grow graver all the time. Quickening his steps, John entered the vast church and climbed the tower steps to the bells. Underneath the big one, in the silent moonlight, lay a dead pigeon, and on the smaller bell, the *Clemence*, two gray and white birds slept huddled together in the cold winter air.

John leaned upon the stone balustrade. He brushed back his black hair, shoving it under his pastor's cap to keep it from blowing in his eyes. Below the moon-splashed world rolled away to insurmountable white peaks; above him the deep blue sky glittered with stars. He stood very still, his arms at his sides, staring up at the heavens, then down at the blinking lights below.

"How long, my Lord? How long? I have never asked for an easy task, but I am weary of the strife."

Sleep was difficult these days. Indigestion plagued him. Severe headaches were frequent. Loneliness tore through him like a physical pain whenever he thought of Peter Robert, Nerien, Nicholas Cop, Martin Bucer, and even the compromising Louis du Tillet. An occasional traveler from Italy brought news of Peter Robert, who was now distributing his Bible among the Waldensian peasants. Letters came regularly from Nerien, Nicholas, and Martin. He had Anthony and William to confide in and consult. But William continued to find a bitter joy in smashing images and tearing down symbols sacred to the Old Church. John found it difficult, but he held him in check. And Anthony was busy most of the time courting this girl and that. His easy good looks made him a favorite with the ladies.

Geneva, instead of becoming the City of God, as John had dreamed, had in the two years since he had been there, continued to be a godless place where all manner of vice flourished. Refugees poured in, signing the Confession and rules in order to remain, and then disregarding them. Dice rolled, prostitutes plied their trade, thieves stole, murderers stabbed, and the ungodly blasphemed. Catholics who were truly Christians longed for the simple penance of days gone by. Libertines recalled the heroism of the past and demanded: "Are we going to allow the Protestant Pope, Master Calvin, to curtail our liberty? . . . Why, oh why, doesn't he stick to preaching the Gospel, instead of meddling in civic affairs, politics, economics, and social issues that are no concern of the Church?" And John's reply was always the same: "Anything that affects souls is the concern of the Church! We will have righteousness!"

Tears burned behind his eyes as he prayed and meditated tonight. Unless the confusion cleared, he would not be coming here much longer. Monsieur Favre's threat would become a reality, for he continued to proclaim loudly that the city must rid itself of "that Frenchman."

The slow tapping of a cane on the stone steps coming up to the tower interrupted his reverie. Faint at first, the tapping grew until it sounded loud against the wind. Eli Corault! John thought. What is he doing here at this hour? He started down the steps to meet the near-blind preacher, who had been one of the early Gospelers in Paris.

"John? Is that you? I came to warn you of a plot!"

John stood above him, his face ashen. What now? Slowly, like a man grown old, he took Eli's hand and led him below to the tower study, guiding him to a chair beside the little hearth where a fire still burned.

"Plot?" John asked tiredly.

"Monsieur Favre just paid me a visit. I went to your rooms, and Anthony told me you were here. Two Anabaptists, Caroli and Benoit, are to challenge you and William to a debate before the Council. It is to be a trap. You know the law: if you lose the debate after accepting a challenge, you will be banished!"

"What will be the subject?"

"You are to be accused of Arianism to confuse the religious who remain loyal."

Anger and fear fused in John. Ever since the fourth century a controversy had raged over the person of Christ. Those who refused to believe that He was the eternal Son of God were termed Arianists. Peter Caroli had come to Geneva, saying that he had been a bishop of the Church of Rome and had been persecuted in Paris for his Reformed faith. He asked to be appointed a preacher. But Mi-

155

chael Sept had unmasked him, revealing he had never been a bishop, but was an Anabaptist, afraid to state his faith, because he knew John Calvin had written a book against their belief that the soul slept after death. So John had refused to agree to his appointment as a preacher, and now Caroli sought revenge.

John sighed. "If William agrees, we should insist on a public debate," he said at length.

"There is more to the conspiracy. Bern demands that the Lord's Supper be administered here as it used to be, with unleavened bread. Furthermore, Bern decrees that we must do as we are ordered by the Council, preach only the word of God and stop meddling in politics!"

"It was always the spirit with Christ; matters such as leavened or unleavened bread are inconsequential. Geneva must remain a sovereign state. We will not yield to the demands of Bern!"

The firelight played over Eli's flowing white locks and rugged features. "Monsieur Favre indicated that if I would co-operate, after you and William are banished, following the debate, I will be given a place of influence."

"What was your reply to that?"

"That I would rather be banished with two such Christians than be made the Chief Syndic!"

The following morning, as John entered the Place Molard on his way to visit a sick refugee, he had a premonition of danger. Then suddenly a group of men and dogs circled him. He wanted to run, but he knew that if he did, he would be lost. He stood very still, his heart thumping wildly. On the outskirts of the rabble the Camaret brothers and Gaspard Favre shook their fists.

"Are you going to comply with the demands of Bern?" the chinless Jake called.

"Arianist!" a rowdy with a big blob of a nose roared. "Heretic!"

John lifted his hand for silence. "Know this: the ministers will not yield to the demands of Bern." His voice shook a little.

Somebody heaved a stone. For an instant John was stunned. When he felt the side of his head, his fingers came away covered with blood. Before he could duck, another stone struck him. And another.

"Let him be now!" Pierre Ameaux, the gaming-card manufacturer said, his little pig eyes glaring. "We have taught him a lesson."

The crowd moved back and John started dizzily down the hill. Fists pummeled him as he staggered forward. Then he slipped and went down on his hands and knees in the melting snow. At once a bevy of dogs was snapping and snarling around him. One, more horrible than the rest, lunged, growling deep in his throat, his hair bristling. With great difficulty John clambered to his feet and started to run, sweat pouring down his face.

"Get him!" a harsh voice yelled.

John could hear the angry beast padding after him. His legs were weak, but he whirled and stood waiting like an early Christian facing one of the lions. The animal leaped again, eyes ominous, hungry jaws parted, showing long, spiked teeth. John took an involuntary step backward, lifting his arms. The dog reared and, with its front feet, threw its weight against him, knocking him down. John kicked out, but the jaws found his windpipe and closed on it, ripping through the flesh. With all the strength he could muster he struggled to push the beast off, but the weakness spread until he had no strength at all.

"O God, help me!" he prayed.

Suddenly the animal twitched, thrashed about, and went limp. Through half-closed lids John could see a man standing over him. An impish face came into focus, the face of Clement Marot. He was holding a mighty cudgel, and John realized that his assailants had fled.

"Where did you come from?" he said weakly.

Clement's grin flashed. "I look a lot braver than I am. One might say the angels sent me. And just in time. I struck the beast on the head. The mob thought you were dead. Ha! Ha! What a rhyme!"

John groaned. "I am losing a lot of blood . . . please find a physician." The blackness settled down again. . . .

When he opened his eyes, he was in a strange bed in a strange room. Clement, in a chair beside him, leaned forward to say, "A Dr. Tertor was here; he washed and bound your wounds. A miracle, he said, that you hadn't bled to death."

"Where am I?"

"In my room at the inn."

"My dear friend, I am grateful!"

Clement left then to find Anthony, promising they would have a long talk when John felt stronger.

Early the following morning, Anthony came with a cart to take his brother home, and that afternoon Clement called to see the patient.

John's first question was about Nerien. He had, it seemed, insisted upon staying in Ferrara with the duke's children until they were taken from their mother to be reared away from Protestant influences. The feeling had been growing among loyal Catholics that her sympathies with the Reformers were having a bad influence on the young. "It's your cousin, Peter Robert, you need to worry about," Clement said.

John's heart raced. "Peter Robert?"

"He works like a man who knows he is condemned and wants to accomplish all he can before the end comes. I saw him in Modena. He had just come from Rome where he went to talk to Cardinal Sadolet in an effort to persuade him to continue to plead for internal as well as external reform."

"Did you say *Cardinal* Sadolet?"

"Oh, yes, he has been made a cardinal. But that has not stopped him from working to purge the Church."

John moaned. "If anything happened to Peter Robert——"

"Prepare yourself. He is helping the Waldensians distribute a large printing of his Bible. They are sending the books over the mountains into Italy."

"Oh, Clement, he expected so much of me! He thought I was being called to lead, but I am making a mess of everything. I fear I will have to flee Geneva!"

"But you are standing firm. I keep praying I will do that. Then I get frightened. At first I thought this New Faith exciting. But as I read the Bible and translate the psalms, I know it has become a part of me, and I yearn to live it."

It took John a long time to go to sleep that night. "When will Peter Robert's work be done?" he kept asking himself. And each time the thought swept anguish through his mind. As he tossed, there was a loud explosion. The blast had sounded close! He swung his legs over the side of the bed, staggering on bare feet toward the open casement. As he leaned out, footsteps thudded down the street toward the lake. Someone must have fired an arquebus. Why? To frighten him so that he would leave the city? Or as a warning that he had better give up his dream of a reformed Geneva?

The next night, as he sat in a chair reading, a dog collar came hurtling through the window. With a trembling hand he picked it up. A name was lettered on the metal: John Calvin!

A few days later as he walked in the withered garden behind the house, he heard some scraping sounds on the other side of the high wall. Two pairs of round eyes in childish faces peered over it.

"Hello," John called. "What are you doing up there?"

"We want to see Master Calvin's devils," one little boy said in a small, frightened voice. "Are you one of them?"

John went to debate with the Anabaptists, feeling that he would rather be in his grave. For two days it continued, while the Libertines chanted, "To the Rhône with the preachers! Drown them!" And sometimes the crowd took up the chant: "Drown them! Drown them!" When William or John spoke, it was to the sound of booing and the stamping of feet. Their only course was to keep on speaking, although the din drowned their words. On Saturday the disputation was postponed until Monday.

"I wish we could think of some way to force the Council to act fairly," William said despairingly as they walked slowly away from the Convent of the Cordeliers where the debate was taking place.

"Perhaps there is," John told him. "There will soon be an election. If we point out to the councilmen that many influential citizens are alarmed at the failure of the Protestants to hold to their beliefs, and that the plot to rid Geneva of her ministers may result in a return to the domination of Rome, the councilmen may change their minds!"

"Above anything else they fear the old yoke. We will ask for a special meeting of the Council at once and tell them this!"

"Expediency! We must be forthright, too. We must speak of repentance!"

"Yes. Christian principles are above Machiavelli's," William agreed.

"I'll go with you to the Council and insist on something else, that the members cease denying the ministers the right of excommunication." John's jaw set. "Easter is coming and I will not allow it to be desecrated by those with no repentance in their hearts!"

Shortly afterwards the Council reluctantly issued a decree stating that the Anabaptists had created a disturbance of the peace and had failed to prove their accusations against God's ministers. The pious document ordered Caroli and Benoit to leave. In bewilderment and chagrin they packed their belongings and rode in haste through the Cornavin Gate, still wondering at the change in the attitude of their fellow conspirators on the Little Council.

John was sitting down for the evening meat and bread the following Wednesday when Eli came tapping in, accompanied by the boy who led him around the city. Anthony helped Eli to a chair, and the boy squatted on the floor beside the table, looking up hopefully. John invited them both to share the meal.

"Speak, Eli. I can see you are disturbed. Food will be more palatable if you first tell us what's on your mind."

Eli shook his leonine mane. "Through Monsieur Favre's influence the Council has put me under a ban which forbids me to preach."

"But why?" asked John.

"He fears if I enter the pulpit I will reveal the plot against you and William."

"What are you going to do?"

"Enter the pulpit as usual."

John thought of the angry voices and the cold blue Rhone. "The State has no right to interfere with the Church! If we allow mob rule, how can we expect to lead people to Christ? Yet all this is terrifying!"

"William may have trouble at his church, too. There are rumors. And a week from Sunday is Easter!"

During the meal they discussed possible strategy, concluding that, whatever happened, they would insist on the separation of Church and State.

"Are you, William, and Anthony, to have the midday meal Sunday, here in your rooms as usual?" Eli asked as he rose to leave.

"Yes. Will you join us and compare notes?"

He nodded. "We must figure some way of bringing peace to the churches before Easter!"

Sunshine warmed John the following Sunday morning as he started for St. Peter's. Although feeling ran high, it was difficult to believe the Libertines would harm a blind man like Eli. Surely, he thought, they will be ashamed to do him violence.

As he came to the slant-roofed house where the Camaret brothers lived, he heard a hateful laugh above him. He looked up, and something soft, wet, and putrid splashed down on his upturned face, onto his gown, his worn shoes, and the cobbles. The stench was horrible and he began to gag. Above him Jake Camaret leaned over the casement holding an upturned chamber pot. His brother leered ghoulishly behind him.

In cold fury, John marched back to his rooms to wash. He had only the one gown, and all he could do was to try to clean it with water. While Anthony helped him, they held a gloomy conference. The smell made them sick, but they kept wiping the cloth until the excretions had been removed. Even when they finished, John continued to shake with anger.

"Try to control yourself, John," Anthony said sympathetically. "I don't blame you for feeling dragonlike, but you are a minister; you are supposed to forgive."

Control myself! John thought in fury, as he strode back toward the church, his black sleeves wet and flapping. There is a limit to a man's control! With his back ramrod straight, he swept into the church and down the aisle to his chair behind the communion table. When the time came, he mounted the steps, and looked about to see if the Camarets were there. Yes. There they sat at the rear next to the gaming-card manufacturer and his gaudily dressed wife. The chinless Jake and his bearded brother had the audacity to grin when they saw John glancing in their direction.

He looked them squarely in the face and his voice struck like a blow. "Pour your chamber pots on my head! Fire your muskets! Set your curs on me. Name them John Calvin. I shall fear no man. And the Church will not yield her spiritual authority!"

For an instant he had to lean on the pulpit for support. "If God be for us, who can be against us?" he asked himself. . . . The peo-

161

ple were waiting to hear a sermon. He took a deep breath and began to preach about Jesus entering Jerusalem and the need to prepare the heart for Easter.

"It will be only a matter of time, William, before God's enemies force us to leave Geneva," John announced sadly as they sat down to the midday meal. Then he told him about the threat to Eli and the blind man's defiance of the Council's ban.

"We may be beaten; God is not!"

"But where shall we go?" John asked.

"There will be work for us someplace," William said, but he did not look very happy.

"Eli was coming. He should have been here half an hour ago! Shall I go and look for him?" Anthony suggested.

"He would have sent his boy to tell us if he had changed his plans. He must have been detained."

At that very moment someone pounded on the door and Anthony ran to open it. Eli's boy stood there in shredded clothes, his face bruised and streaked with tears.

"Master Calvin! Master Calvin!" he cried, darting in. "Somebody beat Monsieur Corault and left him lying in the cloister. When the police came, one of them struck him. I tried to kick him, but he beat me, too. They have dragged the pastor to jail."

"We will see about that!" John thundered. "The time has come to find out where the real authority is!"

Anthony and William nodded in agreement.

Francesca Perrin, Councilman Favre's daughter, who recently had become the bride of the rising Ami Perrin, was in her father's draper's shop on Monday morning when the curious procession went by. Master Calvin led it, his black gown flying behind him. Sometimes he looked like a hungry gaming bird, but this morning he looked like a king, his head high, his step purposeful, his eyes as fiery as the beard of Master Farel, who with clenched fists, marched behind. Then followed the huge blacksmith, Michael Sept, some lusty outlaws and French refugees, and a long line of church-minded citizens—the scum and the elite of the city.

Francesca's heart lurched as it always did when she saw the Frenchman. Angry, he was so dynamic he left her breathless. This row, whatever it was, had the promise of becoming a real battle. "If that daft Frenchman shows his blasted face at the Council Chamber today, we'll banish him from the city," her father had vowed that morning. "We are making an example of the blind preacher, and the Frenchman is fool enough to try to interfere."

Madame Perrin went outside and moved along beside Master Calvin, but he did not notice her. His black eyes looked straight ahead, sparking in his angry face. He had never treated her as a woman, but as a piece of wood he wanted to save from the flames. Today she would have the satisfaction of seeing him get what was coming to him.

John led the procession up the stairs at the Town Hall, past the carved lion guarding the entrance to the Council Chamber, and threw wide the wooden doors. Eyes bugged, and whispers ran around the chamber: "I knew it!" "Master Calvin!" "The preachers!" "That foreigner!"

Lifting his arms so that his black sleeves spread like the wings of the Imperial Bird on the city gates, John pointed the finger on which he wore his seal ring at the trembling men on the high-backed chairs.

"You have done an iniquitous thing!" He pounded the long wooden table until the rafters shook. Words rushed from his mouth like water down a mountain in the spring. "Beating a helpless blind man! Striking a defenseless child! Interfering with the work of God over which the State has no control! A minister must preach when God directs and as He directs, and never to please the ears that hear him. You must release the minister at once!"

The syndics looked at one another in complete helplessness, their faces as white as the enormous ruffs around their necks.

"Mother of God!" Francesca heard her father say. "This Frenchman dares order the Council?"

Her husband, Ami, rose and made a stiff bow. "Master Calvin, we find your demands offensive. We are the authorities here!" he said ineffectually, and Francesca wondered with distaste why she had ever married him.

"All we ask is that you and the other ministers conform to the demands of Bern," another councilman said with deference. "If you agree, we will release Monsieur Corault."

Master Calvin went red with rage. "We are the ones to decide questions of religion in Geneva and not your Council or the Council of Bern."

Abel Poupin was distressed. "If only you would comply with these demands, we could worship in peace on Holy Easter."

"Peace at your price? The State shall *not* dictate to the Church! It is the duty of the ministers to attend to the affairs of the soul! Never will we yield our authority!"

That night John heard resounding hoofbeats on the street outside, followed a moment later by knocking on his door. When he threw it open, the Town Herald stood there in his blue and gold uniform and three-cornered blue hat. He carried a gold-topped staff.

"Geneva needs the good will of Bern, Master Calvin. The Council has sent me to inform you that this is the last chance it will give you to agree to conform to the demands of Bern."

"I will have to consult Master Farel."

"If you will not give me your assurance at once, in the name of the syndics I forbid you to conduct a service on Sunday."

"Tell the syndics I will be the judge of whether or not to conduct a service!"

"They are not going to like it." Shaking his head ominously the man in blue rode off down the hill.

When William came in later, John told him of the herald's ultimatum. William's eyes began to shine. "We will show the Council that the true authority is God. We shall hold services as usual on Sunday, and not according to the demands of Bern!"

Vast crowds surged toward the churches that Easter morning. Those accustomed to attending services reluctantly, on this day went eagerly. There was the hurried click of soles on the cobbled streets, the buzz of voices, and the uproar of an excited populace.

From his window John Calvin saw the crowds surging by, but when he noticed wooden staves and cudgels protruding from cloaks and doublets, he was tempted to stay at home.

With closed eyes he prayed: "Dear God! Give me courage. Forgive my mistakes. When I vowed to take up thy Cross, I knew persecution would follow. But this is Easter morning, the day thy Son rose from the dead. Not even the Council is going to prevent me from proclaiming thy truth. The protests of the Libertines will not stop me. I will go and tell them He is risen and to rejoice! . . ."

When he opened his eyes, he saw Michael Sept approaching the house, surrounded by a dozen refugees, all strong-bodied, stalwart men.

"Come, Master Calvin!" Michael's smile was boyish when John met him at the door. "Your guard of honor awaits you for what promises to be an unusual Easter!"

"But we want no violence on such a day. You know that, Michael!"

"I know that and you know it, but those men with weapons don't know it. So we will just march along beside you."

John put on his pastor's hat and, with shoulders thrown back, he started for St. Peter's, surrounded by Michael and his men. Libertines, brandishing guns and other weapons, shouted threats across the Court of St. Peter's. The air was charged with accumulated bitterness as John moved past venomous eyes in hate-filled faces, lips that hissed and blasphemed, and loaded arquebuses. Down the long aisle he went, to take his accustomed place behind the communion table. And when the time came to mount the high pulpit, he forgot himself in the might of overpowering truth, as he preached about the Cross and the crucified but living Christ.

When the Town Herald appeared at John's door the next afternoon, John met him quietly. He was a young man, a friend of Gaspard Favre's, but his manner was not unkind as he unrolled the official parchment and read the Council's decree. William and John were given three days to get out of Geneva. Eli would be banished with them. They were not to come back.

"At least we serve God, not man!" John said as he, William, and Eli rode together three nights later toward the city gates.

But William was wild with fury. That the Council should dare! That they should banish their ministers, declaring them all hotheads! John breathed a sigh of relief as the Cornavin Gate loomed up in the twilight. He had been afraid William might do someone physical violence. Their destination was Bern, where they would put their case before the synod. If the synod refused to order Geneva to take them back, they would seek asylum elsewhere, probably in Basle—but, oh, how John longed to remain!

With a last look at the lights, he spurred his horse down the darkening road. Some words he had read in Philipp Melanchthon's *Apology* flashed in his mind: *"Scias me positurun animam citius quam fidem!"* (You know that I would rather lay down my life than my faith!) Melanchthon, the reformer, and his dear friend, Martin Luther, would understand the pain of this moment. But they would understand, too, that there was no joy to equal that of risking one's all to uphold God's Glory.

12

1538-1541

In the gloomy little room John rented at Basle, he pushed open the mullioned window to let in the soft summer air. He had been in this city seven weeks, since the Synod of Bern had decided that he and William should not return to Geneva. If they were allowed to return, the ministers said, their rule would be as despotic as that of the Roman hierarchy. William was considering accepting a church at Neufchâtel, and John had grown so used to his company, he felt that the separation would be unbearable. True, he would be near Nicholas, but he knew he would sorely miss William.

His mind constantly went back to Geneva. Over and over he asked himself what mistakes he had made. He could see himself standing in the high pulpit of St. Peter's, pleading for righteousness, demanding it. He could hear once again the angry voices speaking of him as "that foreigner" or "that Frenchman." He could see the hate-filled faces. Then he remembered people like Abel Poupin and Ablard Corne, who tried to live like Christians. He vowed to concentrate on his writing; the more books he could write and get scattered over the world, the faster the truth would spread. But he had the feeling, too, that God was about to call him to some additional work. And he prayed to be shown His will.

The sun was bright and John went out to the garden to relax for a few minutes before sitting down again at his desk. There was something about a garden that refreshed a man and made him feel close to eternal values. Birds flitted about as John walked between the bright-foliaged plants, clustered blooms in pink, white, and yellow. Ivy covered the old wall; a lilac sprayed purple against it. With the gentle wind came a familiar scent like that of cloves, bringing with it painful memories of the Libertines who had adopted gilliflowers as their symbol. And there they were growing along the path.

"John!" William Farel came through the low gate, holding a letter. His face was grave. "This just came from Peter Viret, who is visiting in Neufchâtel. He says that Eli Corault died there suddenly, as if from poison!"

"Eli?" John's heart missed a beat. "When?"

"A fortnight ago. You remember, when he left us at the crossroads after we rode away from Geneva, he told us he was going to visit relatives at Thonon. On the way he stayed in Neufchâtel at an inn. Later his body was found behind a clump of bushes on the highway."

John ground his teeth. "If I thought——"

"We'll never know. Don't torture yourself. There's nothing we can do for him now."

John took a deep breath and exhaled slowly. "Maybe Eli was rash at times. He said he told the Libertines that last Sunday that they were like rats among straw. But he was a brave man, willing 'to lay down his life before his faith.'"

"Amen to that." William was quiet, remembering. At length he said, "I've accepted the call to Neufchâtel, and I'll be leaving Basle in four days."

"So soon? Will you miss me, William? Our tempestuous life together?"

William nodded solemnly. "I guess the Lord knows what he's doing in separating us. You know Bucer's frankness. He thinks that for the sake of peace and Christianity we should preach in different places!"

"I understand his logic."

"Yes. We're too much alike, too severe and too easily carried away."

"Then I never want to grow as fond of anyone again. I have rebuked you, William, when you wanted to destroy images or tear down symbols such as the cardinal's crest on the outside of St. Peter's, but our parting will be difficult."

"We'll write often, and we can visit each other. If you send for me, I promise I'll come."

"The time may arrive when I'll hold you to that promise."

William sighed. "I wonder where you'll go."

"I don't know. I'll surely write though. I believe I'll be called to do other work, and I keep wondering what it will be."

"Why don't you ask God?"

"I do. A dozen times a day. And I often think that perhaps He is telling me never to preach again!"

John looked steadily at Dr. Bucer as they sat in the Strasbourg minister's drawing room the first day of September, 1538. A few days after William had left Basle, a letter had arrived from Dr. Bucer, inviting John to Strasbourg to organize a church for the French refugees. The thought of such an undertaking had sent chills up and down his spine. But here he was. The Voice had spoken.

"What you are trying to say kindly, Martin, is that I failed in Geneva because I was too harsh with sinners. Is that right?"

Martin Bucer nodded. "John, you must employ that Christian yardstick I told you about. Never forget that the Christian Community is the Gospel in Action."

"Yes, I must remember human frailty."

"People should want to go to church to hear the Good News of salvation. They should go with joy!"

"But the Lord's Supper should be only for those who repent of their sins and promise to lead a more Christian life. One reason we are forced to be so severe in Geneva was that sinners came wanting to partake, but showing no repentance and no desire to lead a holy life, now or ever. Such have no place at His table. For people like these excommunication should be employed."

Martin nodded. "I agree. You cannot serve the Lord's Supper to

169

those who are not his disciples, 'of the household of faith.' I'm sure you had serious problems."

"The more frightened I was, the more severe I was. I keep asking myself why we failed."

"If God had intended you to make Geneva godly, you would have succeeded. Maybe organizing a church here is His way of giving you another chance."

John looked down at his tight-clasped hands. "I realize I lose my temper sometimes, but I cannot tolerate sin in any form, and I despise my sin most of all."

"Love is the greatest power in transforming men."

"I shall remember that," John said meekly.

The Church of the Penitents was filled the next Sunday morning when John preached, trying meanwhile to keep his legs hidden, since he had no stockings and no money to buy any. He was here to organize this congregation of poor refugees. While each Swiss state paid the ministers salaries which would supply their necessities, the City of Strasbourg had not made any provision for him, and he would have been embarrassed to let Martin know that he was in such desperate need.

That night after he got in bed he thought again that he must learn a trade, so that he could meet his financial needs while he continued teaching and preaching. Tailoring was a good trade. You cut cloth and sewed careful seams, and the garments you produced kept people warm. John believed that competitive trade built character in men and a better state, so that he would be proud to be a part of such business enterprise.

Early Monday morning he made out an application for citizenship, since only a burgher or citizen could be a tradesman. Then he went to the Guild Hall of the tailors.

"The cost of joining the Tailors' Guild as an apprentice is twenty florins," the young clerk told him kindly.

Twenty florins! That is a great deal of money, John thought in dismay. But perhaps I can get part-time work as a secretary and pay it gradually.

"Is it permissible to pay a little at a time?" he asked.

A tall, homely man standing at the window turned and came

toward him. "My name is John Storder. I need an apprentice. I will lend you the twenty florins."

When John Storder smiled, crinkling up the corners of his deep blue eyes, he was no longer homely.

"I accept, Monsieur Storder. But please keep my secret. I am one of the city's preachers, but no salary is provided for the minister of the New Church for French refugees. I am happy to serve in organizing a new church here, and the lack of money must not stop me. But I have to earn my support by learning a trade."

"I understand. It will be our secret."

Less than a week later, on Friday night, Monsieur Storder invited John and Martin to his home for supper.

When they knocked on the door, John Storder's wife opened it. She was wearing a gown of soft gray material and a wide, red apron. Her eyes were brown; her hair, the color of golden wheat, formed a braided halo around her head. Small of body, with pink, healthy skin, she gave John a sense of tranquillity.

She curtsied. "Dr. Bucer. Master Calvin. Good evening to you both."

John Storder came into the hall and the next instant there was the sound of running feet and two children appeared—a girl about five, with eyes as stormy blue as her father's, and a boy of eight. The little girl grabbed her mother's skirts, peering at the visitors from this safe haven. She curtsied when she was told to, and the boy bent in a stiff bow.

The delicious odors of roasting beef and baking bread permeated the rooms, and Madame Storder excused herself to finish preparing the meal.

In the drawing room, where a cheery fire blazed, John seated himself on a red brocade sofa. Martin sat next to him, and their host, puffing a long-stemmed pipe, took a high-backed oaken chair opposite. This was a friendly house, with the laughter of children echoing through it, and John felt secure, at peace, almost as if he belonged there.

"Supper is ready," Madame Storder announced after a few minutes, and led the way to a long table covered with a fine embroidered cloth. The food tasted as good as it smelled: brown beef, thick gravy, hot homemade bread, potted fruit, cheese, and milk served from a tall blue pitcher.

After the bountiful meal, Madame Storder tidied up, put the children to bed, and came to sit with the men beside the crackling fire. When Martin excused himself and left for a conference with a young preacher, John decided to see how strong his host and hostess were in the faith. He found that the Storders, Anabaptists from Liége, did not share the belief of the members of that faith in an after-death Purgatory similar to that of the Roman Catholic Church. Nor did this family believe, as most Anabaptists did, that one was not a Christian if he failed literally to imitate Christ in all respects; also they refused to believe that infant baptism was error. Madame Storder asked some very intelligent questions, and the outcome of the evening's conversation was that the Storders agreed they wanted to participate actively in the Strasbourg Church.

"There is one thing I want to make clear, Master Calvin," Madame Storder said frankly. "The main beliefs of most Anabaptists are Scriptural; many have died for their faith. I have an idea you have met some pretty poor Anabaptists!"

"I have," John said with feeling, as he remembered Caroli and Benoit.

The months passed while John Calvin painstakingly learned his trade. By spring he could cut and sew a doublet and fashion a cloak. He rose before dawn every morning, ate a quick breakfast in his room, and walked to John Storder's establishment to work until half past ten, when he went to the Church of St. Nicholas to teach a class in the New Testament. His church grew, and his duties increased. As at Geneva, many of the new converts knew little of the meaning of their faith. The instruction had to be thorough. There were daily calls, too, to be made. Into the building of the church body went much prayer, thought, and the zest John Calvin brought to anything he did.

Every Friday he had supper with the Storders. During these evenings, he found himself growing very fond of the children, especially small Judith, who would climb up on his lap, begging him to tell her a story. She liked particularly tales about the bushy-tailed squirrels that scampered up and down the tree trunks in the garden. Her mother had a fine sense of humor, too, and she would laugh and laugh when the squirrels "in person" came to sit on their haunches, their long bibs very white against their gray fur, their "hands" lifted like the beggars at the church door. John always left there rested and happy. In a measure John Storder, Idelette, and the children erased the familiar ache of loneliness.

On the fifth of May, 1539, John was sitting before the open window, looking down the hilly street, when a man rode up on a black horse, dismounted, and tied the animal to the hitching-post. Although he was splashed with mud and had lost some weight, John recognized him at once.

"Nerien! Nerien!" he shouted, racing to the door.

Joyfully they embraced, and John led his friend upstairs to his room, where he helped him out of his mud-caked doublet, gave him a towel and water with which to freshen up.

"Your ribs stick out, Nerien. Was your stay in Ferrara so terrible?"

Nerien, drying his face on the clean linen towel, turned and shook his head. "They finally took the children away from the duchess to be educated as proper young Roman Catholics, so my work in Ferrara came to an end. The duke never relished having French Protestants overrunning the palace, but he came as near to liking me as he did any of the foreigners who stayed there. I have great sympathy for the duchess. The only thing she can do to get the children back is to deny her faith. She has thought of that."

"I will write her a letter to bolster her courage."

Nerien pulled on the clean shirt John supplied, fastened it, and stood frowning.

"John, can you stand a shock?"

"Yes." John smiled. "Are you to be married?"

"No, John. I bring bad news. Peter Robert is dead."

John sat down quickly, feeling as if the pain through his body—sharper than any physical pain—would smother him. "Not murdered?"

"Cardinal Sadolet, who was in Ferrara a month ago, said he died in the saddle. There had been no sign of previous illness. He was very much loved in the Alps. The Waldensians commemorated his life by a week of prayer and Bible study. The cardinal told me himself that Peter Robert was one of the greatest men he had ever met."

"He found God's will and did it."

"The duchess is sure he was poisoned."

Did it matter how he had died? He was dead, but his work had not died with him. Through the Bible he had given the people, he would live. From its pages light would continue to dispel darkness.

> The body they may kill
> God's Truth abideth still
> His Kingdom is forever!

For days that hymn kept beating through John's brain. Music has such mystic power to move hearts, he thought. The Church should have a psalter. Clement Marot began a collection in 1532, a psalter or French book of praise. We can build on that.

So it was that, during 1539, the best French and German hymns for use in the singing school were collected, translated and published: *Alcuns Pseaulmes et Cantiques mys en chant*.

John worked even harder at everything now, as if to make up for the work Peter Robert could not do. He began a commentary on the Book of Romans. Night after night he spent revising the Latin edition of the *Institutes of the Christian Religion*. When it was finished, he arranged for the revised printing with Windelin Richel in the Rue St. Barbe. He continued to put in the required hours at John Storder's tailoring shop. He translated the Song of Simeon. Then he worked out a liturgy from the best of William Farel's service, Martin Bucer's German liturgy, and his own ideas, including portions of a service for a weekly Lord's Supper. The result was a worship service consisting of an invocation, confession, free prayer, a psalm or hymn, a long prayer, sermon, and a benediction. No images or tapers were permitted.

John was at Martin Bucer's, in March of the following year, when a student burst in to announce that Noel Beda was dead. "The world is a better place," John said.

Martin shook his head sadly. "You are forgetting the Christian yardstick!"

"I thought that was for measuring human beings!" John said tartly.

It was about that time that John rented a house, and began to take in boarders to help with expenses. He tried to use the Christian yardstick in his dealing with them, but he found it difficult to teach, write books, and keep house. The boarders threw their belongings about until the disorder was unbearable. When he asked them to co-operate, they ignored him. Only one paid the rent on time.

In the midst of his trouble, he had a visit from Anthony, who said, "What you need is a wife. I have met a nobleman who visits in Geneva and wants to marry his sister off. They are from the Province of Alsace. Her dowry should be large enough to hire servants."

John snorted. "Dowry! I do not intend to sell myself."

"That is up to you. A dowry is the custom. Anyway, I suggest you see her."

Everything went wrong on the spring afternoon John expected the lady and her brother. Two of the boarders got into an argument and he had to intervene. Men wandered about in the common room scantily clothed. Somebody cooked cabbage, and the house was filled with its strong smell. A bird flew in at an open window and sprayed the furniture before someone caught it and put it out. How this house needs a woman! John thought in desperation.

The knocker sounded and his heart knocked with it. When he threw the door open, the count and his sister stood there. She wore a blue dress of shining silk with a white velvet underskirt. Her hat was blue velvet with a gray plume. Her eyes were green and narrow. She was regal, and at least as old as John was.

She swept past him with a nod, her brother stalking straight-backed behind her. John pointed to a marred oak chair. The countess seated herself and sat staring at him, her nose tilted. The two men sat opposite her. John waited eagerly to hear her voice, but to his consternation, when she addressed him, her words were in German, high-pitched and hard.

"Doesn't your sister speak French?" John asked the count, who was regarding him coolly.

"Not one word," said the count, whose French was excellent.

"Then we could never converse. I cannot speak German—only French and Latin."

The count turned abruptly to his sister, speaking to her in fast German. Her face flushed, she gesticulated, tossing her head. John gathered that her brother was threatening her, telling her she might never have another chance.

The count shrugged his slim shoulders. "Greta is spoiled. She says she will not study French, but she finds you most attractive."

John knew he lied. Only that morning he had appraised himself as he stood before the copper mirror trimming his beard. Though he was only thirty years old, his struggles in Geneva had taken a toll. There were hollows in his cheeks and he was too thin. Of course, the fact that he was known throughout Europe might attract some women, and Greta wanted a husband—any husband. He hesitated, picturing long, lonely evenings with boarders wandering about, creating confusion and disorder. He longed for loving companionship. For a wife!

"Perhaps we should get to know each other before we decide on marriage," he said slowly. "When it comes to something that important, one should not be rash."

The count translated. His sister stood up, stamping one foot, rapid German tumbling from her lips.

The count reluctantly rose, also. Again he shrugged. "My sister will not be kept waiting. She must know your decision now."

"I do not think I wish to marry your sister," John said directly. "We would not be happy. I am not the type of insane lover who could cover her faults with kisses. But thank you both for coming."

The count scowled, clicked the heels of his shining black boots and bowed. Greta loosed another rush of words and swept indignantly toward the door. As it slammed behind them, John breathed a sigh of relief, even as he thought wistfully: I wish she had been the right woman.

With dragging feet, he climbed the stairs to his cheerless room and began making the bed; he loathed unmade beds. He remembered that there had been no time to wash the dishes after the noonday meal, and made his way to the raftered kitchen and the table piled with dirty utensils and plates. The food left on them was hard

176

and caked. Happily married men are fortunate indeed, he thought. How I envy them!

"Anne Le Fert has a friend of marriageable age," Anthony told John in January. "Are you interested?"

John's heart leaped. Then he remembered that he didn't like Anne. She wore low-cut gowns and cheap baubles. His brother had spent some time courting her. Anthony was entitled to make his own decisions, so John had kept his feelings to himself.

"I wonder if I should take a wife."

"You know you're yearning for one."

"I have given the matter some thought."

"Anne tells me her friend, whose name is Halna, is very lovely. She has large, beautiful blue eyes and is sought after by many men. She sounds like a good prospect."

"When you see her, if she is all Anne says she is, ask her for me. If she agrees, we can set the wedding date for early March. Be honest. Tell her of my need. Tell her what my house is like."

"I'll tell her all that. But I'll tell her, too, what a lucky woman she'd be to marry one of God's great."

John shook his head in horror. "Don't mislead her. God set the way; I followed. Anthony, I have never had any desire for fame; what has come has been thrust on me like an unwanted cloak!"

"I think Halna wants to marry somebody like you."

After Anthony had left for Vaud where Anne and Halna lived, John went about in a state of oblivion, dreaming of Halna. He said her name over and over. It was a beautiful name. All that week, every time he heard a horse galloping up, he hoped it was Anthony with good news.

When he heard approaching hoofbeats on Saturday, he raced to open the door. But it was only a messenger with a package which contained a copy of the *Institutes*.

Thumbing through it, John found blasphemous taunts all over the margins: "Thou liest!" "Thou dreamest!" "Thou art an idiot!" "Thou art Simon Magus, a sorcerer." Page after page was filled with ribaldry and insult against God. John ground his teeth. How could any man be filled with such venom?

The notes were unsigned, but only one man of John's acquaintance wrote with those curling flourishes. Michael Servetus, who had challenged John to a debate in Paris and then failed to appear.

Lost in his thoughts, John did not notice the arrival of little Jacques Storder, with tears streaming down his face.

"Papa is dying!" the child sobbed. "Mama wants you to come."

Disturbed and almost weeping, John rushed through the streets after Jacques.

At the Storder home, he found Madame Storder at her husband's bedside. Her eyes were tearless, her face as white as the sheet the doctor was pulling over the newly dead. John had never felt so inadequate. John Storder's soul was safe, for he was Christ's. But what did a minister say to a woman who had loved a husband so much and lost him?

Before he could find words, she lifted her chin. "Don't look so pained, Master Calvin. You might pray with me. That will help."

He knelt at the bedside with her. At first the words stuck in his throat, but he managed to ask God to bless her and give her strength. And when he was quiet, she began to pray in her soft, gentle voice, and the words ripped his heart: "And, O loving and ever-merciful Father, thy servant thanks thee for giving her such a good man as John Storder for even a little while!"

Life alternates between sorrow and happiness, John thought a few days later as he prepared for his wedding. Halna had accepted him and was coming to Strasbourg for the vows. He wouldn't be lonely any more.

The Monday before the marriage was to take place, one of John's students came to see him.

"How do you know you want to marry Mademoiselle Halna?" he asked, red-faced.

"Why have you come here?" John asked.

The stripling shook his head. "I will say what I have to say and leave," he said, throwing his shoulders back. "If you had not been so kind to me, or if you were anybody else, I could not tell you this. You won't like what I have to say, but I have to say it."

"And what do you have to say, young man?"

"You are being made a fool of. Halna Mallinae is not the kind of woman for a good man to marry. I know. I come from Vaud."

"You made up this lie!"

"Oh, no, Dr. Calvin. Everybody knows but you. People are laughing behind your back. Ask Dr. Bucer."

"Forgive me. I will investigate. If what you say is true, it took courage."

After the youth left, John threw on his cloak and went directly to Martin's to tell him of the student's visit.

Martin sat staring down at his plump white hands, crossed on his ample stomach. At last he lifted his eyes. "How could I approach you with the gossip? I would be doubting the power of Christ to make a life new. I hear your betrothed has started attending church. She seems to to be a new creature in Christ. She wants a new life."

John threw up his hands. "You carry this Gospel of Love a little too far. Is that all your friendship means? Even if I could stomach a woman with a past like that, others could never forget. I am sorry for her. I hope she is truly changed. But it would never work!"

John ran all the way home, and hastily despatched Anthony to call off the wedding. But in the days that followed he was more aware than ever of his loneliness.

"Maybe I should play Cupid for you as Martin Luther did for Philipp Melanchthon," Martin Bucer said brightly one April afternoon, as they were returning from the singing school. "Luther says man is only half a man without a helpmeet."

John rubbed his cheek and gave an embarrassed smile. "From the etchings I have seen of Dr. Luther, I would say he has the figure for the part."

"As I do! Now, in that case let me see . . ."

John held up a hand. "No, Martin. Spare me. Anthony tried it. I do not wish to go through that again."

"John, I am Cupid personified! I know just the wife for you: one who would tolerate your work, who would never interfere, who would understand you, and care for you!"

In spite of himself, John's heart began to pound. "Martin, *who?*"

"None other than the Widow Storder. It is a year since John died. Spring is a great time for courting. Why not court her?"

Madame Storder! John thought wistfully. In all Strasbourg there is no finer woman.

"She is everything any man could ask, but I do not want to do anything in haste, Martin."

"No, I guess you wouldn't!" The minister grinned. "Take my advice. If you decide to court her, rush her off her feet."

"I'll think about it," John said pensively.

And he did think about Madame Storder the rest of that week. He remembered her gentle ministrations, the serenity of her presence, the light in her warm brown eyes. When he had called on her after her husband's funeral, he had come away reminding himself that he must work even harder to help the people in his pastoral care to discover such faith as hers.

On Sunday morning he noticed her sitting in the congregation, and even in her mourning clothes she was lovely. His heart fluttered a little as he looked at her, and he had to rebuke himself for his irreverence. But it was difficult to keep his mind on his sermon.

That afternoon he brushed the dust off the ministerial gown, which he had designed to distinguish Protestant clergymen from Roman Catholic priests, wiped his shoes, and put on a small velvet tam. Before he started out he inspected himself in the mirror. Although he was not yet thirty-two, his hair was beginning to gray around the temples, his shoulders sagged, and he was too thin. Well, he thought, John Storder was no fair knight either and Idelette married him. With purposeful step he walked to her home.

A lark on a tree was singing as he lifted the knocker. Somewhere a cowbell tinkled. The door opened, and Idelette stood there, solemn-eyed and still wearing mourning cloth. As she recognized him, her face came alive.

"Master Calvin! Come in!"

John followed her, his knees knocking together. Excitement left him speechless. She glided ahead of him to the comfortable sofa beside the chimney piece. He sat down beside her, and looked into her eyes, which were shining now. When she spoke, her voice was even sweeter than he remembered it.

"Are you still busy converting Anabaptists?" Her eyes twinkled.

He began to talk as he never had to a woman, telling her of

the confusion of his house and his loneliness. It was comforting to have a sympathetic woman listening to him.

From that evening on he visited her often, and he was the one who always seemed to do the talking while she listened with glowing eyes. He found himself dreaming of his good friend's widow.

One day when he went to her home to take her walking, he noticed that she had discarded her dull black and widow's wimple.

"Idelette, do you enjoy our hours together as much as I do?" he asked shyly.

"Yes. Yes, I do, John." Her face colored crimson like a cup of wine. She was watching him, waiting, waiting. His breath began to come faster. He wanted to speak, but he couldn't; the words stuck in his throat. They walked back to her house in silence.

Her small daughter, Judith, met them, looking like a Raphael cherub, with a wreath of flowers in her hair. "This is my birthday, Dr. Calvin. I am seven. Will you stay for supper?"

The meal was merry, and later, after Judith had been tucked in bed, John sat contentedly beside Idelette on the sofa. There was so much work he should be doing, but this was peace, and he didn't want to break the spell. Her face glowed as the firelight played upon it, and how warm her eyes were as they met his!

"Idelette, when I am here like this with you, I forget my problems. I feel content. Do you—would you—Idelette, could you——?"

"Oh, yes, John dear. Of course I could!"

He lifted her small white hand to his lips; then, bending toward her, he touched her mouth, soft and willing, in a brief kiss. This is the first time I have ever kissed a woman, he thought. In a flash of intuitive awareness he stared at the lady who had just promised to become his. Why, he was just like the insane lovers he talked about! He wasn't just seeking someone to bring order to his house, and be a companion—he was a man in love!

John and Idelette were married in August, 1540, and William Farel came from Neufchâtel to perform the ceremony. Anthony beamed as he stood beside John and handed him the ring. Martin Bucer bustled about looking complacent. Peter Viret had brought Philipp Melanchthon with whom John had been corresponding.

"A happy bride and lucky groom," Melanchthon said, after the ceremony. "It seems only yesterday that I was as happy!"

John knew he was thinking about Kathy Krapp, the mayor's daughter, to whom Martin Luther had introduced him many years ago—the wife he had lost and missed.

But this is no time for sadness, this is my wedding day, John thought. And my wife is at my side. My radiant wife! Her hair was twisted in a circling braid. The simple fullness of her blue silk dress with its white collar set off her loveliness, a loveliness that came from her soul.

After the banquet which the ministers of Strasbourg gave them, Philipp Melanchthon read some love ballads from a worn old book. Judith and Jacques scampered about enjoying the music that poured from Clement Marot's lute, yet all in all they behaved surprisingly well and appeared as happy to have John a member of the family as their mother did.

Within two weeks the house had been transformed, and John had slipped, like a swimmer in sunlit Lake Leman, into the care Idelette gave him. The comfortable red sofa, as well as her other furniture, and some fine linens had been added to his meager belongings. There was no longer any need to work at his trade, for she collected the rent from their boarders and made the small salary the city now gave him cover the necessities. He finished one commentary after another. His zest for writing knew no bounds, and the manuscripts piled up at the printer's.

Then the City of Strasbourg appointed him its delegate to a Convocation of Catholics and Protestants to be held at the Hotel des Saxons in Worms that fall.

"Martin Luther and your friend Philipp Melanchthon will be there," Martin Bucer said happily. "They were the leaders who started this Reformation. You have carried it on!"

Martin Luther! John's heart skipped a beat. How often he had longed to ask this great man some questions! What a privilege it would be to talk to him face to face! Eagerly John packed his saddlebags, mounted a hired horse, and set out.

However, disappointment awaited him, for Dr. Luther had not come to the Convocation; he was too busy with other matters and his health had been poor. But Nicholas Cop was there as a delegate from Basle, and John enjoyed his companionship.

For several weeks arguments went on between Protestants and Catholics. Most of them were futile. Unity seemed impossible, and John was filled with regret. There was a common denominator— Christ's saving love for man. Why couldn't Christians unite on that?

While a professor from Wittenberg was expounding some empty arguments, John watched a roach plodding over the plank floor at his feet. Beside him, Nicholas sighed.

"What a waste of time," he whispered. "We are getting nowhere. It looks as if the Convocation will drag on for months."

Just then an Augustinian monk walked down the aisle and whispered to the young priest who was presiding. He rose immediately, interrupting the boring Protestant from Wittenberg to announce: "Dr. Calvin is wanted in the anteroom."

John edged his way nervously along the row to the aisle. Something must be wrong with Idelette or the children. The weeks of separation had seemed an eternity.

In the anteroom stood three men—Abel Poupin, Ami Perrin, and Pierre Ameaux. John felt weak with relief when he saw them, though he could hardly believe his eyes. A delegation from Geneva! Steel spurs clicked as Ami stepped forward to embrace him, his fatuous face wreathed with a big smile.

"The City of Geneva, now repentant, has sent us as a deputation to pray you to return," Ami said.

Incredible, John thought. He had never in his wildest fancies dreamed that the people who had cast him out, hating him, would ask him to come back.

"What happened?" he asked quietly.

Abel answered. "To be honest, Geneva needs you desperately. Let us gather about a table in the tavern, and we will explain."

When they were seated on some backless benches, on either side of a scarred table, Abel continued:

"In March, the Roman Catholics, led by the ousted bishop, began appealing to the people. Cardinal Sadolet has great eloquence, even in writing. He has been addressing the citizens, and they are wavering. There is not a man in the city learned enough to reply to the good cardinal!" Abel shook his head. "The fear of Bern is smothering us, too. Bern would have a hearty respect for you."

"Unless you come back, the Catholics will win. Geneva will soon be under their domination again," Pierre pleaded. "You must return."

"Must?" John's eyes became hard black stones. "Geneva banished me."

"Then you do not care what happens to Geneva?" Abel pressed.

"Do I care what happens to Geneva?" John asked himself. "Geneva of the blue Rhone, the blue lake, and the confused, stumbling people. Oh, I do." Nevertheless he shook his head.

"Strasbourg needs me now. I will compose a letter to Cardinal Sadolet, which can be read to the people in assemblage."

The delegates from Geneva gave him many reasons why he should comply with their invitation. But he was firm, sure that God had called him to work in Strasbourg.

After supper with Nicholas Cop that night, John wrote an open letter to the cardinal:

We indeed have many faults [it confessed]. Too often we sin. Still, though truth would, modesty will not permit me to boast how far we excel you in every respect, unless perchance you ignore Rome, that famous abode of sanctity, which having burst asunder the cords of pure discipline and trodden all honor under foot, has so overflowed with all kinds of iniquity that scarcely anything so abominable has ever been before. . . . May the Lord grant, Sadolet, that you and all your party may at length perceive that the only true bond of Christian unity is Christ the Lord!

It was a June evening. John sat in the small garden at home in Strasbourg, where fireflies sparked the twilight and a mockingbird sang. Martin Bucer's voice, less gentle than usual, echoed in John's ears, saying as it had that afternoon when Martin had come to see him: "Jonah refused to listen to God, and the judgment of the Almighty descended. John, God is speaking to you through the letters and the visits you have received from the Genevans. Jonah refused to preach to the Ninevites. You must not be like Jonah. If you do, His judgment will descend on you!"

John closed his eyes and leaned against a big tree trunk. In agony he poured out his soul: "O God, show me thy will. Just show me thy will . . . !"

Steps sounded on the path. When he opened his eyes, his wife stood there in a full white gown, and behind her in the twilight was a chunky figure—William Farel.

With a bound John was off the bench. "William. William. Just when I need you!"

Idelette excused herself to put the children to bed, and William, seating himself beside John, wasted no time in saying what he had come all the way from Neufchâtel to say.

"So many letters have come to me, John, asking why you refuse to obey God and return to Geneva. The city has promised you such power that you can direct the church as you wish. You have been ignoring letters from others urging you to go back. You are ignoring God, too."

"I have not been sure it is His will."

"That's a poor excuse! You are afraid to return, afraid you will fail again. Nothing but a miracle could have opened the way for you. God is calling you, John, to make Geneva the city you once vowed to make it. John, God bids you go!"

13

1541-1545

On Sunday, September 18, 1541, St. Peter's Cathedral was filled to the doors. People stood at the back and along the sides of the sanctuary, watching the door leading from the tower study. There was a stir when Master Calvin came through it and walked with purposeful tread to a seat behind the communion table. The new robe they had promised him had not yet been fashioned, but his old one was brushed and clean. In the three years he had been absent, his hair had acquired some gray streaks. His face was more lined, but his eyes were just as bright and penetrating.

Ami Perrin, sitting in the front row beside Francesca, alternately rubbed his fat fingers together and pulled on the gold fringe which adorned his epaulets. What would Master Calvin say when he mounted the newly constructed stairs leading up to the pulpit? Whom would he denounce? The Libertines who had been instrumental in banishing him? The Council had had to make him Master of Geneva indeed to get him back. He had returned with power greater than the duke and the bishop had ever had!

When Master Calvin stood at last before the spiraled columns under the round canopy, there was awed silence. But when he began to speak, to Ami's amazement there was no harshness in his voice as he said he had missed the snow-crested mountains, the beautiful blue lake, the restful valley. He had missed the people even more, for he had learned to love them. His purpose in returning was to help them attain happiness and lead Christian lives. Discipline would be employed when any refused to live according to the laws, civil and spiritual.

"I want you to know that my sojourn of three and a half years in Strasbourg has given me time to think. I have been too severe. I am sorry. I know now that music has a value in worship and I have enlisted the aid of song writers such as Clement Marot, and Theodore de Beza, the author of *Candida.* A singing school will be held on weekdays and the merchants can close their shops and attend. The musicians, Louis Bourgeous and Claude Goudemel, have been employed to set the psalms to metrical versions, assisting the poet Marot. All songs will emphasize the salvation of mankind and the death of Christ for our sins and our redemption."

Master Calvin paused, frowning, then went on to say there was to be no more gambling, drunkenness, lewd dancing, indecent clothing—such as low-cut gowns and slashed breeches, no prostitution, and no conspiracy against the government—civil or spiritual. As he had said time and time again there was pleasure in sin, but the price was terrible! They would find more pleasure in the Christian life than in all their sin, and the reward was great. Not once did Master Calvin bellow and pound the wood as he used to do. A new warmth radiated from him.

"I was not prepared for that," Ami told Francesca, as they left the church.

"Don't underestimate Master Calvin, Ami. You can depend on it, he will rule with an iron fist. The Council has delegated too much authority to him. Why on earth did you have to bring him back?"

John made two journeys back to Strasbourg where Idelette and the children awaited good weather before moving to the house the city of Geneva provided in the Rue des Chanoines. In the spring of 1542, she arrived with the furniture, bedding, and linens in a wagon the city had sent for them, and within a week the large rooms, wide

hallway, study, three bedrooms, and square kitchen were transformed. Once again happiness surrounded John, contentment filled
him, and working was easier.

There was so much to do. Since he had studied law, the Council
had asked his aid in drawing up a Code of Civil Law. He began to
plan for an academy where all would be educated, and men could
be trained for the ministry. He suggested making the clergy independent of the State financially by having the people contribute
to the Church, but the Council would not hear of that. His sermons emphasized God's sovereignty and obedience to Him. The or-
dinances provided for preaching four times every Sunday and once
every other day, so that he had many sermons to prepare for delivery
at the various churches.

The one he was working on tonight dealt with the duties of the
elders in governing the church and the duty of the deacons to
supervise the almsgiving. As usual he was making the sermon brief,
clear, and to the point. He often told the other ministers that long-
winded sermons were a hindrance to the Gospel. He was working,
too, on a plan of home visitation, which included instruction, with
a minister, elder, and deacon calling together. When the door to his
study burst open, John looked up, expecting to see Judith charging
in. Instead Clement Marot stood there, his eyes wide.

"The plague has struck the city. Dr. Tertor says it spreads quickly
in the summer heat!"

John leaped to his feet in dismay. Affairs in the city had been
going well, and now this. "That is terrible, but God will not wipe
out a city he has sent me to convert."

The days that followed were nightmarish. The stricken overflowed the hospital outside the city walls. Twisted, blackened bodies
were seen in the streets. The Protestants prayed. The Papists said
their Pater Nosters and in secret used holy water. Nothing seemed
to check the plague's spread.

How will we manage when the treasury is depleted? John wondered as he plodded from door to door on a warm July afternoon.
Caring for the sick, disposing of bodies, was very costly, and there
were also personal expenses. In about two months a baby would be
coming to the Calvin household. Idelette had a few florins saved,
and John thought: If necessary, I can go back to tailoring.

The moon was full as he started home through the humid dark. His feet burned and one leg ached painfully. When he limped into the Rue des Chanoines, his house was brightly lighted. Something must be wrong!

Inside the floors echoed with the sound of hurrying feet. Several women, huddled in the drawing room, whispered behind cupped hands when they saw him. Upstairs, one with a gray face was carrying a basin toward the bedroom. She paused, looking hard at him. "Are you him?" she demanded.

"I am Master Calvin."

"Yer wife got sick afore her time. Sit like a good husband and don't get in the way. When the baby comes, I'll tell you. There's nothing you can do."

Helplessly he watched the midwife scurry into the bedroom and close the door. A great weakness spread through him, but he managed to cross to another bedroom, bathe, and put on a clean shirt and breeches. He steadied himself with his hand on the slim banister rail as he descended the stairs. The baby is coming too soon, he thought moodily. What if it dies? Avoiding the curious women in the drawing room, he went into the kitchen and sat on a stool, resting his head on the table, letting his thoughts wander.

Once again he saw the joy on Idelette's face when she had announced to him that they were to have a baby. It had been on his second trip to Strasbourg from Geneva. A blasphemous manuscript, denying the divinity of Christ, had come from the Spaniard, Michael Servetus. John had been in a bad mood as he sat writing to Michael, telling him he hoped this was the only copy of the scurrilous manuscript, since he was not going to return it. His anger flamed as he wrote. There was a rustle beside him and a soft voice spoke.

"John. Dear John, there is something I wish to tell you that is important enough to warrant an interruption."

He lifted his eyes. How beautiful she was! A blue gown set off the ruddy glow of her smooth skin. Her eyes were sparkling.

"Yes, Idelette?" His voice was gentle. He even forgot the hateful Spaniard who persisted in plaguing him.

"We are going to have a baby before next fall."

Slowly her words seeped through his consciousness. Then he

leaped to his feet, facing her. "Did you say we are going to have a baby?"

Her face kindled. "Yes, dear, and you will make a wonderful father."

He could only stand there with his mouth wide open.

Her laughter tinkled like bells. "You have months to think about it, dear. Now get back to your letter."

"I can finish that tomorrow. Tonight I would like to sit with you by the fire and dream about our child. Come."

She held out her hand. How warm it was in his, as he led the way downstairs to the drawing room sofa where he had courted her. The hearth fire cracked and popped as they talked about the child God was to give them. . . .

And now it was being born at least two months too soon!

As the time lagged, it eased him to kneel by the wooden stool and pray, remembering that God was good.

The hours seemed unending, but at last a thin wail sounded from the room above, a symbol of life newly come. Trembling with impatience, John mounted the steps two at a time, and paced back and forth before the closed door. He thought the midwife would never open it, but she did at last and came through it with a bundle in her arms.

"A boy," she said, her grin showing yellowed, broken teeth. "A small one, but a boy."

And as John looked down at the little red face, he was filled with ecstasy. First God had given him a wife, and now a son!

The woman's next words spoiled the moment. "Madame seems to have a fever; go for Dr. Tertor."

It took over an hour to find the doctor, who insisted on taking a bath and making a complete change of clothing before he would go near a new mother. In the meantime John went back to the house and sat beside his wife, holding her hand as she slept.

When at last Dr. Tertor arrived, John sat with rapidly beating heart watching the balding, bright-eyed physician as he bent over the bed. Idelette's face against the white ruffled pillow sham was greenish. Her eyes were closed and her breath came fast. The light from the flickering candle on her bedside table made weird shadows on the walls and ceiling. John thought time had never hung so heavy.

When at last she opened her eyes, the doctor nodded at him. He moved forward. "We have a son!" His voice rang with exultation.

"Is he strong, John?"

"I think so. He can yell."

She smiled, and he sank to his knees beside the bed and kissed her.

In the days that followed John regretted ever having to leave Idelette's side. But there was a great deal to do. When he managed to have a few minutes with her, he felt strong enough to shake thrones.

One morning, when the baby was ten days old, John was teaching a Greek class in the chapel auditorium of St. Peter's, when Jacques burst in to say that Dr. Tertor wanted him to come at once. John ran all the way, and Dr. Tertor met him at the door.

"Not Madame Calvin?" John gasped.

Dr. Tertor shook his head. "The boy. He cannot survive."

A few minutes later, John leaned over the infant, who lay, pale and wailing, beside his mother.

"Don't leave us, little son," he whispered. "Stay with us."

Idelette turned her tear-streaked face away, and John dropped to his knees in a huddle of grief as the baby's breathing ceased. In a few minutes he recovered his self-control, and reached for his wife's hand, saying, "My dear one, we know that God is in every drop of rain and everything that happens. The omnipresent power—God!"

"Perhaps we will have another child, John. Perhaps——"

Just then Judith came charging into the room, followed by Jacques. Both were covered with mud. "We have been making the most beautiful tarts, Papa! Oh, Mama, it was such fun."

"Stay with your mother, children, until I return," John said gently. "I have something I must do."

Huge white clouds were sweeping across the sky as John started out to order the coffin and have the grave dug at the Cemetery Plain Palais. His heart echoed the wind's mournful sigh.

As he stepped into the Court of St. Peter, he heard thundering hoofs and a black horse came racing across the square. John leaped back out of its path. The woman rider drew the animal to a halt, causing it to rear and prance. Francesca Perrin looked down at him. The years had sharpened her features; she did not look like a happy woman.

"Master Calvin!" she spewed out in mock homage. "Dr. Tertor just told me that the Lord has taken your son!" There was joy on her face, triumph.

"Yes, Madame. The Lord gave me a son, and He has taken him."

"He is punishing you for making so many people in Geneva miserable. You and your reforms! You are reaping your just reward!"

"I wish I could number you among my spiritual children."

"I thought we settled that long ago. I want no part of your long-faced religion. Your reforms have left many without work. The situation is so desperate that in order to have for themselves what little work there is, there are those who smear pus from the sores of the ill on cloth and wipe it on places others will touch. It's all your fault!"

Horror swept through John. "So in order to give these depraved ones work, we should open the gambling dens and the brothels!" he stormed.

She turned in the saddle to hurl her final blow. "Unless you do something, we will all die!"

With a sinking sensation in his stomach, John watched her ride off, her black cloak sailing behind her like a thundercloud on the tail of a storm. And in that instant a cool lucidity came upon him. His enemies had brought him back, but they were not changed. They had no intention of living as Christians. He had a terrible thought: Would Madame Perrin have ridden me down if I had not jumped out of the way? Can she hate me that much?

By the end of October the corpses lay in mounds outside the city. Great holes were dug and filled with them. Others were burned beyond the city gates. The stench of rotted bodies continued to pollute the air. Each day seemed to bring mounting horror.

"This talk of plague-sowers is not gossip," a bony young minister confided to John. "It is almost certain that there are people working to spread the disease."

192

John ordered the ministers, as they called upon the sick, to be on the alert for such depraved creatures. Monsieur Blanchet, one of the visiting clergy, contracted the plague and died. The Council forbade John to do any more visiting, declaring that the city could not risk his health, since he was desperately needed.

"There is a new rule in this house," John told the children one night. "The front door is to be kept locked."

"Why, Papa?" Jacques asked.

"There are some men and women with sick minds, who try to spread the plague. They are called the 'boute-peste.' Maybe they would not bother us, but it is wise to be careful."

The children, satisfied, kissed their mother and then kissed him, and went off to bed. Idelette sat in an armchair near the open window, looking at the moonlit mountains. She was feeling better now; it was good to see her regaining her strength.

"I can tell when you are worried, John. Is it because of these plague-sowers?"

He nodded, frowning. "Their minds are ill."

"Why can't the police detect them?"

"They are very sly." He shook his head. "Until we find them, this horror will go on and on!"

"You look so tired. Get a good night's sleep, John. For tonight try to forget them."

But it was early morning before John felt sleepy. Tiptoeing into the bedroom, to the cot he had occupied since Idelette had been ill, he suddenly remembered that, in spite of his warning to the children, he had forgotten to bolt the door downstairs.

He turned back and had just reached the foot of the stairs when he heard a sound outside. He rushed to the door and threw it open on two figures shrouded in loose, dark clothes. His eyes went quickly, fiercely over them. He knew them both: a sharp-faced woman and a large man with wild eyes and flowing black locks. In the moonlight he saw that the woman held a dirty rag in her hand. Something wet, dark, and filthy glistened on it. Alarmed at his sudden appearance, the pair fled down the hilly street toward the river.

John could hear the rapid thudding of his own heart. What intuition had made him come down at that particular moment? Had they already covered the door handle with pus? He didn't think so.

He believed he had surprised them in the act. But before he shut the door, he went to the kitchen, found a rag and soap, and scrubbed the doorknob and the painted wood around it. Then he got a spade, buried the rag, and returned to the kitchen to wash.

As he went back to his cot, Idelette called to him. "John, is anything wrong?"

"No, I went to bolt the door. I am sorry I disturbed you." He took her hand.

"I wasn't asleep, John. I've been lying here thinking about those poor people who have the plague. We have so much to be thankful for!"

"You have even more to be thankful for than you know!"

"Gaspard Favre is bragging to the hangers-on at the wineshop that every law you believe in will be broken tonight when the Lects celebrate their daughter's betrothal at their estate at Belle Rive," Michael Sept informed John one night the following spring.

"We need to show where the real authority is!"

"You mean you will go to the party?"

"I haven't been invited, but——"

"I will go with you. I haven't been invited either."

Michael laughed, but John's face was grim.

Night cloaked Geneva, and the terrace overlooking the blue lake, at the Lects' estate, was crowded with guests, come to rejoice at the betrothal. Lanterns, hung from the trees, swayed in the wind as viols strummed a fast melody, and the city treasurer, Ablard Corne, dressed in a robe of state, led the rigadoon with the gay bride-to-be. Francesca and Ami Perrin followed, kicking their heels in abandon. Wine was flowing freely, faces were flushed. Giggles and guffaws were loud as men and women cavorted, and sang in thick voices. It had been a long time since there had been such an orgy, for they were also celebrating the end of the plague.

"*Mon Dieu!*" a shrill voice shouted suddenly. "Master Calvin!"

There was an instant hush. The rhythmic clicking of heels ceased. Even the music stopped. Every eye was on the man in the flowing black gown and cap with velvet ear flaps, who was crossing the terrace, followed by the huge blacksmith, Michael Sept. Since

194

Master Calvin's return almost two years before, nobody had dared defy his laws. Now he stood very still, his black eyes flashing fire as he gazed at the people cowering before him.

Ami's heart beat so fast that he feared he would have a heart attack. He had seen Master Calvin angry, but never so angry as this. Animal rage smoldered in his eyes, his fists were clenched, and he was trembling. The silence was split with a boisterous laugh—Francesca's. Ami tugged on his wife's arm. "Don't do anything foolish, Fran," he pleaded. "He has the upper hand."

Fran jerked herself free, and her husband shuddered as he watched her saunter toward Master Calvin, swinging her hips as only she could do. He remembered how he had been opposing Master Calvin's program to clean up the jail, improve the food given the prisoners, and pay enough to secure a humane jailer. If Fran persisted, Master Calvin would have his chance to show them the inside of the jail as guests!

"Go home to the woman who lived with another man without benefit of wedlock before you married her," she said thickly. "You silly old hypocrite!"

Ami held his breath, as Fran's dart found its mark. He had long suspected that his wife's animosity toward Master Calvin stemmed, not so much from his insistence on morality, as from the fact that he had failed to react to her charms. Madame Calvin had first married according to the Anabaptist custom in which a couple took their own vows. She was a gentle lady and a pure one. Nobody could say that for Fran. Master Calvin was staring at her with incredulity written all over his face.

"You all know better than that," he said in a thundering voice. "It was agreed when I returned to Geneva that there would be no more vulgar dancing and drunkenness! Haven't we had enough trouble here with the plague, the inroads of Bern, and the attempts of Rome to dominate? Don't you want to live like Christians and be happy in obeying God's moral and civil laws? Do I have to police you like naughty children? Here, at the celebration of a betrothal, I find you capering and cavorting and under the influence of drink!" He shook his head sadly.

For an instant Fran dropped her eyes, but only for an instant. Then she shrieked, "You dirty pope, you! Will we never have our freedom back? Swineherd. I, for one, will defy you and all your laws. And there is nothing you can do about it."

Fran turned to her husband, her flashing eyes telling him to be a man and not a worm. He squirmed—he was a worm—but he made himself step forward.

"Asking you to come back did not give you the right to meddle. My wife was just having a little harmless fun. Why don't you preach the Gospel and stop interfering with matters that are no concern of the Church?"

As soon as the words were out of his mouth, he regretted them. If the Church was to have any authority at all, Master Calvin would have to take some drastic action. The Frenchman threw him a look that plainly said: You know you are doing wrong. I will not degrade my office and myself by arguing with you, but we shall see!

Between Fran's ranting and the unease within him, Ami spent a restless night. At noon the following day he, the Captain General of Police, on order of the Council, was arrested by his own men on a charge of public drunkenness. He was marched off to jail to join a violent Fran, who had also been arrested, and who now sat with a hunk of black bread and a tankard of unclean water, her eyes blazing, her hair straggling around her contorted face. And in a littered corner three rats with beady eyes waited to dart for the crumbs.

"If we accuse Master Calvin's French friend, the poet Marot, of breaking some law, Master Calvin will be placed in a most uncomfortable position," Francesca's brother, Gaspard, schemed in the tavern with Pierre Ameaux two days later.

Pierre's fleshy face lit with an evil joy. "How I would love to catch Marot gambling. He makes small wagers. Doesn't the law say there is to be no wagering?"

Gaspard's eyes narrowed. "It just might work. If Master Calvin shows partiality to a close friend, we can force him to be lenient with Fran and Ami. We can command and Master Calvin will be the grasshopper!"

Pierre's face lengthened. "What if it doesn't work? I can't recall a single incident in which Master Calvin has been unjust."

"Master Calvin is only human. He is extremely fond of the poet."

Gaspard was watching in the tavern the next night when Clement Marot began to play backgammon with François Boniard and Michael Sept, the blacksmith. The wager he made was heard by the hangers-on—a quart of wine.

Early the next morning Gaspard accused the poet before the Little Council, and two policemen were sent to arrest him.

"Go to Dr. Calvin's secretary, Nicholas de la Fontaine," Gaspard ordered Pierre Ameaux, "and tell him of the poet's crime."

"Clement Marot is in jail for gambling, accused by Gaspard Favre," the mild-mannered secretary duly reported to Master Calvin. "Shall we try to secure his release? The wager was only a quart of wine."

John was quiet for a moment, considering. Clement had worked hard to please the Council, writing hymns, rhyming psalms, and teaching music. He was paid very little. This was the first time Gaspard had shown any interest in enforcing the gambling laws. Why had he suddenly become the model citizen? But if law was to be respected, it must be fairly enforced with all citizens alike.

"The poet has broken the law, he will have to pay the penalty. He will have to spend a fortnight in jail. I will not interfere."

"Then there is no action you wish to take?"

"You know better than to ask that, Nicholas. A law is made to be obeyed."

The months passed. Another winter came. Pierre Ameaux scowled as he waddled along the street toward St. Peter's on a cold Saturday. The clock on the Town Hall struck two. At this hour Master Calvin would be going over his sermon for the next day. Pierre wished he did not have to go to him for a favor; but he was going in desperation. What if Master Calvin knew he had been conspiring against him? It was said in the city that he knew everything, even a man's innermost thoughts.

He found the minister in his fortresslike tower. Although the small grate was filled with glowing coals, the room was chilly, and

Master Calvin sat at his table wrapped in a heavy black cloak, the Bible open before him.

"Come in, Monsieur Ameaux," he greeted politely, his penetrating eyes going quietly over his guest. Pierre shivered. He felt his throat tighten and his mouth was dry.

"Master Calvin," he whined, "I've come to you as a friend. You know I am your friend."

"Are you, Monsieur Ameaux? I didn't know."

"Oh, yes. Yes, I am. Will you use your influence with the Presbytery to get me a divorce? For a year and a half they have refused."

"Why do you persist?"

"The trouble started when you began stressing the communion of saints. You say it means Christians should share all things in common. So Ameda, my wife, says it is all right for her to share her body with the other saints."

"What a weird interpretation!"

"That's Ameda. She argues, too, that if she is predestined to be saved, no matter what she does, she will be saved. You see, it's all your fault!"

"My fault?" Dr. Calvin roared. "No sensible woman would think like that!"

"Ameda is not very bright."

"That is putting it mildly."

"Well, what do you think?"

"That she is carrying the doctrine of predestination a little too far!"

The Presbytery, or Consistory, which numbered twelve laymen and the five ministers, refused to grant the gaming-card manufacturer's divorce. For several months John pleaded for it until at last the others agreed. Pierre was jubilant.

"I will be grateful to you the rest of my life, Master Calvin," he vowed. "No man could live with a wife like that."

Hour after hour during all those months, John Calvin, in the quiet of his study, considered how to allay the confusion in the minds of some of the Christians about predestination. He had never given the doctrine the importance many insisted on giving

198

it. The ignorant were confusing it with fatalism. There were still those who thought that merely refraining from adultery, murder, theft, and dishonesty would save them. They failed to comprehend that true righteousness could be attained only when a man elected to do everything for God's Glory and according to His will. Redemption by God's Grace made man's mortality righteous, and a Christian thus redeemed served his fellow men for the Glory of God. That was what the Apostle Paul meant and what the Scriptures said. John finally decided to write a book explaining the doctrine.

As he studied the views of Martin Luther and of Augustine, the celebrated Bishop of Hippo, he found that they, too, believed that God alone had the power to save a man, but neither had realized that if God saved some, it was logical to conclude He must also elect that some be damned. Wasn't it blasphemy to question His wisdom? The Scriptures plainly say that God determines all events, even the most insignificant, so that it was certain He determined the most important event, man's salvation.

The days passed; the book was written; John could turn his mind toward other problems that perplexed—and there were so many of them.

Nerien came to the auditorium one September afternoon with some bad news. "A student just back from Turin brings word that Clement Marot was buried last month," he said sadly. "He died very suddenly."

John was stunned. Clement had been in perfect health when he left Geneva in April to go to Chambray and then to Turin where his son was. He would be missed for himself and for his work in translating the psalms, thirteen of which had been printed in the Psalter of 1539. Two years before, an edition of his first thirty psalms had been published, sponsored by the King and Emperor, despite the poet's earlier banishment from Paris, and the Sorbonne had sought to arrest him because of the psalms' Protestant doctrines. One problem his death presented was the need for another musician to continue translating the psalms.

The next morning as John was writing Theodore de Beza at Lausanne to tell him that God was calling him to Geneva to take up Clement's work, a messenger brought a letter from the Duchess of Ferrara, Renée. John paused to read it: "Your poet was poisoned at Turin," she wrote. "There is no doubt of it. All Catholic France has been singing his Protestant songs. He died for what he believed in, the word of God found in the Holy Scriptures. . . ."

John thought of Peter, who had denied his Lord. There were times when Clement had been a hypocrite, too, such as the time he went to Mass after he had eaten bacon on Friday. But Clement at last had made up his mind not "to stand mute," as he had said in the message to Michael, urging the boy to "walk in his father's way." His contribution to the Reformation could never be measured. Everywhere lips sang his hymns, praising and glorifying God. That is the wondrous thing about God's love, John thought exultantly. He works His will through ordinary men like Clement and me. With His power the weakest man can accomplish anything!

Disguised as a monk, Dr. Johann Eck, a professor in the University of Ingolstadt and Martin Luther's most indefatigable opponent, arrived in Geneva during a snowstorm and traced Master Calvin to the singing school. When everyone else had left the church, Dr. Eck called to Master Calvin, who was heading toward a door to the left of the altar in the sanctuary.

The reformer turned, and his brilliant black eyes bored into the visitor one moment and crinkled in a smile the next. The smile transformed the thin, dark face. Dr. Eck melted a little. Dr. Luther had never made him feel this rush of warmth. It made his mission even more difficult.

"You wished to see me?" Master Calvin asked graciously.

"Yes. My name is Eckins. I was in Geneva and I had to come to inquire why you have deserted the Church that nurtured you. Why must you fight the Mother Church at every step?"

"Come. We will sit down where we will not be interrupted."

Dr. Eck followed the Frenchman into a small Gothic chapel, flamboyantly decorated in warm rust and lake blue, the colors repeating themselves in the lovely glass windows.

"How proud you must be of such a shrine!" Dr. Eck exclaimed.

"The architect who designed St. Chapelle in Paris built this. We call it the Chapel of the Maccabees, and the cardinal who ordered it built is buried here."

Dr. Eck noticed that Cardinal de Brogny's crest had been left on the wall. It was on the outside of the church, too. "I am happy that you honor such a good servant of the Roman Catholic Church by keeping his shrine," he murmured. He thought this might be a good way to get back to the subject of Mother Church, but from the way Dr. Calvin frowned, he knew he had said the wrong thing.

"In Geneva we try to recognize that to destroy is never to build. That is why the cardinal's crest remains."

"And you remember Cardinal de Brogny's good work when you worship here. I understand."

"On the contrary, we remember in reverence John Huss, a great immortal, condemned to the stake by De Brogny. In our hearts this chapel is a shrine to the truth John Huss died for. Every time my feet touch these stones I pray that this church will ever teach the Truth of God, declared by men like John Huss, Augustine, Luther, Melanchthon, Bucer, and the Apostle Paul!"

Dr. Eck took a deep breath as he sat down on one of the wooden benches that faced a Protestant altar. John Calvin took a bench in the row ahead, turning to face him.

"Now, back to your question. For years I asked myself: Why not stay in my Church and right the things that need righting?"

"Yet you left your Church. Why?"

"It was the hardest decision I ever made. It was, as I said, *my* Church. For a long time my aim was to help her back to the simple and true religion of the New Testament, to do my utmost to rid her of the error, the greed, the superstition, idolatry, ignorance, and pomp that had crept in. Then suddenly, in my darkness, the light broke! There was the Church I knew and a great church, the Church Invisible. All at once I understood: a Christian's first loyalty is to Christ and not to men. While Cardinal Sadolet and Ignatius Loyola work for the purification and rebirth of the Church of Rome, I pray that we may be united in Christ. If only we could be one!"

"What does the Reformed Church have that the Roman Church lacks?"

"The Reformed Church has the simple Gospel which makes

Christ himself the center of its faith. It needs no relics or saints or Hail Marys to lift men to the Holy Presence. Why make of faith a fetish or a scheme whereby works are given a false place of power and importance?"

"These things are not necessary to salvation?"

"You look like an intelligent man. Any man with God-given intelligence, reading the Holy Scriptures, should realize that Christians are the spiritual descendants of the Israelites to whom God gave His promise. I try to keep that before our people. Salvation is simply coming to Christ, accepting His Grace. Good works must follow. If you are a Christian, Catholic or Protestant, you know He elected you to be saved."

Dr. Eck looked back at the brilliant man whose name was on the lips of the world. For an instant he wanted to nod assent. It all seemed so simple when Dr. Calvin explained it. But he remembered he was on a mission from Pope Paul III, the Holy Father. "If I had half a dozen men like this Calvin," the Pope had said wistfully, "the Church would take the world for Christ. Promise him anything. Even if you have to promise him a cardinal's cap, secure his consent to return. Every man has his price."

Dr. Eck tried another attack. "Is money a problem with the reformers here?"

"I want for nothing. We have had financial problems due to the recent plague. But we worry as little as possible about money."

Ah! Then money is a problem, Dr. Eck thought. Some rationalize, but few can resist it.

"I had better tell you my real name, and why I am here. It's not Eckins, but Eck. I am the professor of theology at Ingolstadt who confounded Dr. Luther."

"Confounded him, Dr. Eck? Are you sure he did not confound you? I was under the impression he had won a debate with you."

Dr. Eck stifled the sharp answer that almost rose to his lips. He managed a suave smile. "Perhaps. Perhaps he did, Dr. Calvin. But we will not quarrel about that."

"I have a confession to make to you, too, Dr. Eck. I knew who you were the minute I saw you. You were at the Convocation at Worms in 1541. Now, don't you think it's time you told me why you have come?"

"I see you are not easily fooled. His Holiness sent me. The Church needs you enough to offer you a high place in Rome and a good stipend if only you will return!"

"I have everything I wish here. Tell the Pope I shall stay in Geneva and continue to preach the Word of God. But tell him, too, that if Rome shows any desire to unite on the true bond, Christ, that he will find me ready to do everything I can to bring unity!"

He rose to signify that the conference was at an end.

As they walked out of the chapel and through the vast church toward the door leading to St. Peter's Square, Dr. Calvin proudly pointed out objects of historic interest. Neither referred to the Pope's offer again, but Dr. Eck thrust into the reformer's hand a heavy purse containing one hundred gold pistoles, a small fortune.

"For books and the needs your Council cannot supply. There need be no accounting to anyone."

John Calvin arched an eyebrow, but he did not toss the gift back. Dr. Eck's heart swelled. Surely the Pope would reward him, he thought happily. Every man really has his price, and soon Dr. Calvin would return to the Church of his fathers where he belonged!

Side by side, in silence, they walked out to the snow-laden square. Four men in robes of state were crossing toward the church, and Dr. Calvin called to them.

"You are right on time as usual, gentlemen. I was coming to meet you. We have a visitor, sent by His Holiness to ask about our Reformed Faith, and he is so impressed that he has presented the city with a purse of gold. Here, Syndic Corne, take his gift to refill the city treasury. There is much need these days. And thank Dr. Eck for his generosity and that of any friend who might have contributed."

A man who is *incorruptible,* Dr. Eck thought in bewilderment. A man whom gold will not taint. Something plucked at his heartstrings. Master Calvin had a remarkable power to rise above the temptations that beset man. Could he be right in his theology? The Pope's emissary hurried back to Rome to report that John Calvin acted like a Christian.

14

1545-1546

When the weather permitted, Idelette sat in the garden sewing or embroidering. Here, one June afternoon, she watched her husband approach with slow-moving feet, as if he were too tired to lift them. And she knew he was. It had been almost four years since they had moved to Geneva and problems continued to mount. Now he was concerned with fire control, the construction of hygienic latrines, new duties for the town watchman, and the repair of the gates and walls. Besides this, some citizens still thwarted all discipline and control.

John's face was drawn as he sat down on a tree stump near her. "Gilliflowers!" he said, sniffing the air. "The Libertines are wearing them in their hats again as a symbol of their revolt."

"Something new has happened! What is it?"

"Monsieur Ameaux had a dinner party yesterday for the city's leaders and attempted to convince them I want to become a bishop. He said I would soon be as evil as a Borgia. Yet he once vowed he would never forget my efforts on behalf of his divorce. He deserved it, and I did not expect gratitude, but that he should hate me so much is hard to understand."

"When you worked against gambling, you struck at his purse. If these men who grow fat on vice, loving money more than souls, can get rid of you again, there will be no more opposition to their money-making."

A blaze of fury filled his eyes. "This attack blasphemed all I teach; it is an attack on the Christian Reformation. I protested to the Council this afternoon, and Monsieur Ameaux was ordered to retract publicly; he was also fined, and sentenced to two months in prison. The sentence is too light. I told the Council just now that I will not enter the pulpit again until he is required to make proper amends."

"But, John, the Council backed you up!"

"If others see him get off so lightly, they will try to uproot everything we have worked for here in Geneva!"

How weary he is, she thought. He had recently finished a commentary on Genesis, and a reply to the Sorbonne's "Articles of Faith" in a book he called the *Antidote Against the Articles of the Sorbonne*. Now there were other writings—a reply to a book by Pighius on Freedom of the Will, which he was dedicating to Martin Luther's intellectual co-worker, Philipp Melanchthon, and a number of commentaries he was planning—in addition to everything else. When her husband was frightened, he got violent. And she knew he was frightened now, for he saw his dream of a City of God fading.

She voiced her fears: "I am sorry there will be another row. As the poet said, 'Fury supplies the armor.' "

"The people must be made to respect the Presbytery and the government."

"John, I worry about you. You do not take even half a day a week off."

"My cousin, Peter Robert, always said, 'God will preserve a man until his work is done.' "

"God expects a man to remember he is a man, and that, as such, he needs proper food and rest."

He smiled. "I must remember that."

But he didn't. The summer passed with no letup in his tasks. There was the church and the work of Geneva at large. There was his writing and his teaching. In desperation he begged Nerien La Farge, who was teaching in Strasbourg, to come to Geneva, and Nerien had agreed to come in September. There were all the people, too, who arrived in a constant stream from every nation to consult Master Calvin. He had no time at all for his family. The world owned him. But living in the same house with him, just seeing him once in a while, having him come home to her at night to tell her of his struggles meant a great deal to Idelette. Even when he was deeply troubled he never raised his voice to her or the children.

As the family walked to the St. Gervais Church the first Sunday in October, Idelette wondered if she could conspire with Dr. Tertor to order John not to work so hard. It probably wouldn't have any effect; the doctor said John was his most difficult patient.

They were nearing the church when she saw him stiffen. His head turned to follow a group riding by with a food basket to picnic in the mountains. His eyes sparked and his gait quickened until the rest of them could hardly keep up with him.

While he conducted the service from behind the communion table, as he always did, Idelette watched and listened. During the hymn he moved restlessly as if his mind was not on it. When he read from the Scriptures, he mispronounced two or three words, something he seldom did. Instead of the text for the sermon he had told her he would preach, he read, in a terrible voice, the warning of Isaiah.

From the pulpit he preached in a thundering tone, which echoed through the church like ocean waves roaring in a storm, hurling reproaches against the godless who made light of Christ's teachings. For a while, before his fury, nobody moved.

Then suddenly Monsieur Ameaux was on his feet. "Master Calvin, you treat us like dumb animals. If men do not wish to attend church, leave them alone. All you do is rant about sin. And to you everything pleasurable is sinful!"

John stood very still, striving for control. After a moment, he lifted his arms; the congregation rose and he pronounced the benediction in a small, tired voice. All the thunder had gone out of him.

Late that afternoon, when Idelette awakened from a nap, she

found him kneeling by a chair in his study. As he lifted his head, she went to him and put her arms around him.

He rose and held her close. "My dear one, when I saw that family ignoring the church worship, fury engulfed me. I made a display of my wrath and have just been praying for God's forgiveness."

"Monsieur Ameaux saw his chance and took it," she said. "That was regrettable."

There was the sound of the door below creaking open and feet pounding up the stairs. Two of the councilmen, Ablard Corne and Abel Poupin, rushed in, their faces whiter than parchment.

"Master Calvin, men with arquebuses are running about the streets shouting threats. Sedition is breaking out everywhere. 'Tis said falsely that you called the Genevans animals at St. Gervais this morning. There is nothing we can do! We'd all better flee before it's too late."

John's eyes flashed fire. "The first thing you have to decide is whether or not your Council is to abdicate in favor of the rabble. Once you have decided you are the syndics in control of the city, order a gallows erected in the center of the square before St. Peter's. Act like men and the revolt will cease!"

The next morning before the citizens were up, a gallows was erected on the square in front of the historic church. After breakfast the syndics, in full regalia, marched by to inspect it, followed by a long procession of curious citizens. The revolt was over.

The following Friday, the Council, its members wearing their slate-colored robes set off by triple white ruffs, sat in solemn tribunal in the courtyard before the Town Hall. The bailiffs appeared, shoving Pierre Ameaux before them, and the citizens stared incredulously. He was wearing nothing but a shift; his head had been shaved, and in one hand he held a torch. His face was as red as a turkey's comb and his eyes were cast down. Reluctantly he knelt, lifting the torch high to symbolize the light of truth. But anyone could see his heart was not in it.

"I have been sentenced to perform the *amende honorable*, because I lied about Master Calvin, who is working for a good church and a fine government in our city. I lied about Master Calvin. Against truth, justice, and God I declared that Master Calvin taught evil doctrine."

At the end of a rope, led by the city herald on horseback, Pierre began a march through the three major squares—the Place St. Gervais, the Bourg-de-Four, and the Place Molard.

At each, before the mocking populace, he declared, "I lied about Master Calvin. I lied . . ."

Pierre was saying his piece, as John entered the Place Molard. How pitiful this is, he thought in compassion, but I had to insist that the Council give him a drastic sentence. Only severity will save Geneva now.

Rumors of plots and conspiracies blanketed the city. The situation was desperate, and John thought of journeying to Wittenberg to consult Dr. Luther. Then toward the end of February, 1546, a traveler brought news that Martin Luther had died on the eighteenth at Eislebien at the age of sixty-two. It was too late to solicit his aid. For days John grieved and worried. What if the Libertines should gain control? What would happen to the city? The unease continued and he advised the syndics to be ready for quick action if further revolt broke out.

As Nerien taught his Latin class one spring morning, there was a loud clatter on the square outside the auditorium. Later, Nerien told John that some of the Libertines had deliberately bowled on the Court of St. Peter's during his teaching hour. The next morning, as John taught Greek, the disturbance occurred again. The students shifted uneasily on the hard benches, looking at one another. At times there was so much noise that Master Calvin could hardly hear his own voice.

When he came out after class, Gaspard Favre, the Camaret brothers, and Francesca were still bowling. As he approached, they smirked at each other and began gathering up the bowls. John decided to do nothing unless the offense was repeated.

On Sunday morning everything was quiet as John began his sermon at St. Peter's A pigeon began flying about above him, and he was grateful for the pulpit canopy. There was no way to keep the birds out, so he always wore his pastor's cap during the service. Suddenly in the middle of the sermon the clatter came again from the square. Those unruly ruffians are playing bowls before the church, insulting God, he thought angrily. Abel Poupin and Ablard Corne rose and faced him with brows raised questioningly. His mind struggled for decision: Shall we ignore this or take some action that will stop such nuisance once and for all? For a moment everything was quiet. Then he heard again the flutter of wings above him, and words from the Scriptures came into his mind: "And I shall give my angels charge over you." As the clatter began once more on the square, a warm, joyous feeling swept through him. He nodded at the councilmen and they went quietly toward the door. Within a few minutes the noise outside ceased, and in the silence, broken only by the flutter of wings, John spoke quietly to his spiritual children. Once more power flowed through him, and he felt invincible. " 'If God be for us, who can be against us?' " he said in a voice charged with triumph. "Who can be against us?"

Through the continuing strife, it was a comfort to John to have at his side Theodore de Beza, who had come from Lausanne to help with the hymns and psalms for use in the worship services. John had persuaded him to preach as well as teach, and he found it helpful, as he wrote his two commentaries on First and Second Corinthians, to have this brilliant younger man to consult. Theodore had devoted his time to pleasure until the light of the New Testament had given his life new meaning. The change wrought in this former foppish man of the world had been miraculous. Filled with a hunger for the Gospel, he charged about with a tyro's enthusiasm, looking for ways to improve the church and the city. He was popular with the councilmen, for he had great charm, and John delegated more and more work to him.

"Something should be done about Gaspard Favre," Theodore insisted one evening. "He is bragging that, although the Presbytery forbids the unrepentant to take the Lord's Supper, he will do so whenever he chooses!"

John had a summons drawn up for Gaspard to appear before the Presbytery at once. The answer came back: "I will not appear."

"Won't Gaspard ever learn?" said Theodore, who was with John when it arrived. "I see no alternative but to call a meeting of the Presbytery to determine what's to be done."

John agreed, and the Presbytery decided to report Gaspard's defiance to the Council. Once again the Libertine was banished, and this time he was informed he would be subject to a death penalty if ever he returned.

John was not optimistic enough to believe that Gaspard's second banishment would bring peace to Geneva. When the Festival of Papegay arrived, commemorating the Libertines' heroism in freeing the city, there was a parade. To John's horror, when he went to view the military display, he saw that Ami's musketeers had new uniforms—tight, brief, with slit breeches. Ami, also wearing the slashed breeches, strutted ahead of his men.

For over a week John deliberated. Then he called another meeting of the Presbytery, telling the ministers and elders that if they ignored Ami's apparent effort to defy their authority, the church in Geneva would be irreparably hurt. It was voted that wearing breeches with immodest slits was against the rules of the Church; they were not to be worn in Geneva again. The Council concurred in the decision of the Presbytery. John was asked to call on Citizen Perrin and warn him that there was to be no further defiance.

When John arrived at the Perrin house, Francesca answered his knock. Her eyes smoldered when she saw him, and with a quick movement she slammed the door in his face. He could hear voices inside, laughter. He pounded the knocker on the wooden door again.

"Open in the name of the Presbytery!" he thundered. "I have something to say to Citizen Perrin."

The door was opened a little, and Ami's frightened face appeared in the crack.

"Captain Perrin, I regret that I have to come to rebuke you. Why did you deliberately choose to wear slashed breeches when they are forbidden?"

Francesca stuck her head over his shoulder. How dissipated she looked these days with dark circles under bloodshot eyes. "That was my idea!" she bragged.

"You might show some toleration," Ami whined.

"I am a servant to whom the law of the Master in Heaven means so much that the cause of no man in this world will induce me to compromise or fail to maintain it!"

"What are you going to do?"

"I shall insist that you keep the promise you made before I would agree to return—to respect the authority of the Presbytery even if you are the commander of the Genevese forces. There have to be rules and laws by which a people live!"

"I understand," Ami said sulkily. "But if the people want to live in one way, and you want to live another, curtailing all personal pleasures, why don't you go back to Strasbourg?"

John knew he must be firm or all would be lost. "You need time to think," he said sternly. "Go to Lausanne and visit Gaspard for a few days. If you go of your own free will, we will not have to banish you. Here the laws will be observed!"

Ami thought for a moment. "Very well," he said almost humbly. "I will leave tomorrow."

It was common report in Geneva that Francesca was infuriated that her husband had been asked to leave the city.

Two weeks later, on Monday morning, a city herald came to John's home to tell him that Abel Poupin had been run down on the Place Molard and carried into a nearby house, where a doctor was in attendance. He was badly hurt, but conscious and asking to see Master Calvin.

John went to him at once, and Abel rolled his eyes when he saw him. "She thought she had killed me, John. She ran her horse right at me yelling, 'Swineherd!' If I had not leaped into a doorway, she would have killed me. *It was attempted murder, John!*"

"Who are you talking about, Abel?" John asked, though he knew the answer before the injured man told him.

"The only thing you can do, Abel, is to file a complaint against Francesca. If we can subdue her, we should have peace."

On the morning of December 16 a flurry of snow swept down from the mountains as a shivering General Assembly, or Council of Two Hundred, met to discuss an emergency. The members converged on St. Peter's Cathedral from all directions to discuss what should be done with a petition from the Perrin-Favre faction, asking permission to return to Geneva. The Consistory, or Presbytery, had voted consistently against it, because the members of the faction showed no signs of repentance. Now, however, the friends of the seditious Libertines were creating a crisis in the city over the Presbytery's refusal.

John walked thoughtfully toward the church, determined to think through the matter carefully, for this was a time of grave crisis.

When he reached the Court of St. Peter's, a noisy rabble armed with swords and muskets was surging all over the square, citizen fighting citizen. For an instant John stood frozen, but only for an instant. Something had to be done to stop bloodshed. He walked swiftly between the drawn blades and lifted his arms. "If blood must flow," he shouted, "take me as a sacrifice. Perhaps that will satisfy your hatred!"

Silence fell as the men hesitated. They lowered their weapons, mouths open in astonishment. Throwing back his shoulders so they would not know how frightened he was, John fixed them with his eyes.

Ablard Corne, peering from the doorway of the church, mopped his brow. The Master of Geneva, who would save the city in spite of itself, crossed calmly toward him. He entered the church, walked up to the stalls where the syndics sat, and sank into an empty one, exhausted by his own emotion. He bowed his head in prayer, and when he lifted it, his eyes held a new strength.

"Why won't they accept Christ's great gift? Why?" he asked in a ragged whisper.

"You marched right between those enraged men, between their drawn blades. You took a terrible risk, John." Ablard was incredulous.

John looked at him with tortured eyes. "I was never so frightened. But I know that a Christian who is doing God's will is invincible! 'If God be for us, who can be against us?' "

15

1546-1552

John continued to insist that his spiritual authority gave him the power not only to teach and preach, but also to censor. Worry intruded on his work, and it took constant vigilance not to yield to melancholy. Such a weakness, he felt, would reflect upon his faith. Although he was still in his thirties, his strength was sapped and persistent headaches made him irritable. Sometimes he felt like a tired old man as he struggled to enforce the law and to refuse the troublemakers who pleaded to return. In vain did the loyal men on the Council declare that he had restored dignity to Church and government, pointing out his progress in social and moral reform. He yearned for infinitely more. The Church of Geneva must become truly independent of the State, and that independence was in constant dispute. He fought fiercely for the power to make the Church what it should be, and he pleaded week after week for funds to build an academy with adequate space for classrooms. The councilmen insisted there was no money. To attain his aims John was striving, working, watching, scheming, hoping, and praying.

Each day brought new cares and problems. The former regent of the schools, Peter Castellio, had become angered, in 1544, when John had refused to approve his appointment as a minister. John did not believe he was grounded in the Christian faith, for Castellio had tried to have parts of the Bible expunged from the canon, including the Song of Solomon, which he declared obscene. Refusing to debate with him, John had left the matter up to the Presbytery and the Council. Both bodies voted to banish the troublesome teacher.

Now Castellio was traveling around the Swiss cantons assailing the Genevan ministers—and John in particular—as fools. John needed Bonivard and Anthony to consult with, but both were being monopolized by their wives. Bonivard's wife, who was his second, had little interest in the church. Anthony's Anne attended the church services cheerfully, but their children required her attention, and her husband worked ten hours a day at his bookshop. The Libertines had become a godless sect, and when John wrote a *Tract Against the Sect of the Libertines,* Queen Marguerite of Navarre rebuked him sharply for his violence. But tantamount among his worries was the need for reforming the Church. There was a rumor that Emperor Charles V had asked the Pope to call a church council to discuss reform. The Waldensian Christians, who lived in the valleys of the Cortian Alps in northern Italy, Southeastern France, and Provence, were being persecuted because they upheld the authority of the Bible, and John could not forget that these people had befriended and aided Peter Robert. One rumor said Francis I was thinking of ordering their extermination.

If it were not for Idelette, life would be so much harder, John often thought. How comforting it was when troubles beat at him from every side to have her to talk to. Sometimes she rebuked him gently, but he knew he needed it, and always he came away from her presence refreshed. Yet physically she had not been strong since the baby's birth, and two more uncompleted pregnancies had weakened her further.

Many of the sermons John preached these days were about the prophets of Israel. It helped to remember that they, also, had been surrounded by foes. He pointed out repeatedly that the Genevans must be as faithful to God as the children of Israel had been, for Christians, too, were the sons and daughters of Abraham by the

Spirit. Abraham had banished the disobedient from the camp; so likewise would Geneva, *the new Israel*. A Christian state had to be a disciplined state. Though he was accused of being too harsh, he clung to this belief, for he was sure that laxity would never bring order.

One July night he was going over his lectures on Second Corinthians, working on a commentary to follow the one he had written on First Corinthians. The notes had been carefully made in Latin, but he reworked, revised, and translated them into vivid French. It was warm and when he got up to close the windows to keep out the bugs which flew in, attracted by the candlelight, he saw a man at the door. It was a messenger, who handed him six letters, one of which was from Thomas Cranmer in England, asking help in drawing up the liturgy for the New Church. Four were from reformers in Germany. Another was from Michael Servetus, saying he wanted to come to Geneva, if it was agreeable.

It's not agreeable, John thought angrily. This man may have a fine mind, but he opposes God's will. His *Errors of the Trinity*, published at Strasbourg when he was twenty, was still read and it confused men. At the time, the heresies had so stirred the authorities everywhere that Servetus had had to flee to Paris and live under an assumed name: Michael Villariovanus. Even then he had continued to expound his unscriptural doctrine. The idea of the Trinity had come from Greek philosophy, Servetus declared. Christ, miraculously begotten, shared none of man's imperfections. The heretic ruled out the belief of one divine essence in three separate beings. The book insisted that man was not saved by personal faith in Christ but by intellectual belief in Jesus as the Son of God. With all the strife in Geneva, the last person who should come here was this man. John decided to dictate a letter in the morning, advising Servetus that if he dared set foot in this city, he would not leave alive.

But John forgot about the dangerous Michael in his concern regarding the work of the Council of Trent, which Paul III had called two years before, in 1545, and which still continued. It was distressing that no Protestants had been invited. Instead of investigating the abuses in the Church, as Cardinal Sadolet and others urged, the group had been called upon to approve some decrees of the Pope, defining the beliefs of the Church, and to sanction certain political alliances. A great opportunity to bring reform to the Old Church was being ignored, John thought when he read the findings. And there seemed no hope of any unity!

The apocryphal books were declared to be of equal value with the canonical. The Vulgate was adopted as the final authority in all disputes, and tradition was pronounced of equal importance with God's Word in the Holy Scriptures. What ignorance! John kept thinking. He decided to do something to combat these errors, and set about writing another book: *Antidote to the Acts of the Council of Trent.*

He was scratching away one April afternoon in 1547, his mind running faster than his quill, as it usually did. No assembly was infallible or binding, he pointed out, quoting support from Augustine's statement at the Council of Nicea. For an hour he wrote on, anger flooding him. Then he read some of his new book to Idelette, as he often did:

"The Pope has become so pious that if he only hears the Protestants are to be left in peace for a while, he is seized with an ague. But it is wonderful to see on the other side with what perfect security he confers with harlots, and how he shrinks not from a profitable treaty. . . . The Pope wishes to prove that there is but one sin worthy of God's anger, and which may be considered as the source of all evil and that one sin is not to do what the Pope says and not to adore *his* holiness instead of the holiness of God. Certain wilt thou, thou foul mouth, thus continue to make a mockery of the Son of God?"

John paused to catch his breath, looking up for Idelette's approval. "What do you think of it?" he demanded brightly.

"John, in marriage, as I have often said, we have a duty to be frank. A wife should not agree with her husband when she thinks he's wrong." She shook her head. "I don't think it's charitable to say all those things about the Pope. And you told me yourself that marked reforms have been accomplished for the priests and the various orders. You're angry because you're disappointed that the Council has not tried to surmount the obstacles separating Catholics and Protestants."

"I am disappointed," he said after a moment. "You're right about that. For the first time I see that we could unite only on the terms of the hierarchy, which would be mental and spiritual suicide. But this is no time to shade the truth. God alone is sovereign and I must say so."

One spring afternoon Ablard Corne and Abel Poupin were shown into John's tower study.

"We have come to tell you of some unpleasant gossip," Ablard began solemnly. "It is being said in the city that while you strive for righteousness for the Genevans, you have failed with your own family."

"What do you mean?" John bristled.

Ablard twisted and untwisted his plump hands. "John, the people who hate you are saying that Anthony's wife is unfaithful. They also say, 'He preaches so much about sin, why doesn't he make a public example of a Calvin? Is sin so shaded that it can be overlooked when a Calvin commits it?' "

John quivered as if a hunter's arrow had struck him. "Anne unfaithful to Anthony? It cannot be!"

Unable to conceal his dismay, he rose and paced back and forth. Perspiration dampened his forehead.

"Is there any evidence?" he asked in a hoarse voice, as he paused in front of them.

"No," Ablard said promptly, "but the gossip is all over the city. When rumors of that sort start and mount, irreparable damage is done."

"Is she then to be condemned without a trial?"

Abel's gaunt face showed his concern. "John, we hoped you wouldn't take it like that. We thought we ought to tell you!"

"You did right, of course. If Madame Calvin is guilty, she must be punished the same as any other adulteress. But I am thinking of Anthony and the children, especially the children."

Just then one of them—David, Anthony's youngest—came tearing in. His yellow hair was tousled, his blue eyes grave as he rushed to John and tugged on the sleeve of his gown.

"Uncle Grumpy! Come home. Dr. Tertor sent me to find you. Auntie is very sick."

John did not even pause to excuse himself. In a panic he ran after the little boy all the way down the hill to the house.

The bed curtains were drawn when he entered the bedchamber, the room made sacred by intimate moments shared. But now people were crowding into it, prating inanities. And at Idelette's bedside stood the recently returned Francesca, reciting passages from the Scriptures! John's first impulse was to propel her out of the room with the toe of his shoe. But it is possible she has repented at last, he thought, for her tone was reverent, her eyes somber, her mien proper. Besides, he could not create a disturbance now. But when Francesca looked at him, he thought he saw a glitter of joy in her eyes. Fortunately at that moment Theodore de Beza appeared to take charge and he sent the visitors out.

As John bent in agony over the woman he loved, his heart beat slowly, painfully, and he forgot all human controversies, all irritations.

"John, dear," she whispered faintly. "Dr. Tertor says I am dying."

"There is no hope?"

She shook her head. "My heart is very bad."

He took her hand, and noticed how cold it was. "Ours has been a good marriage," he said. "Nine happy years. How can I go on without you?"

"You have your work, John. You'll lose yourself in that."

"I——" He paused, unable to continue.

"I commend Judith and Jacques to your care. My mother really needs Jacques with her in Liége. Let him go if you deem it wise, and care for Judith!"

"I will try. You know I will."

My beloved, he thought. If only I could have spent more time with you. If only I could keep you forever! His Idelette, who was so selfless, who had made life a joy, dispelling his loneliness, making his house a home.

She smiled gently. "God bless you, dear, dear John," she whispered.

I have never seen a sweeter peace on her face, he thought as she closed her eyes and took one last, long, shuddering breath.

John wept without shame, and for an instant he thought he was going to faint. He clung to the bedpost for support, despair engulfing him. Then slowly, without looking back, he left the bedside and went out into the evening.

Following the mountain street to the stately old church, he made his way through its monumental entrance. There were no worshipers inside as he walked down the long aisle to the tower stairs. He climbed to the top where he sat motionless upon the balustrade, looking down at the lights of the city. Behind him the old wooden steeple leaned bleakly against the moon. Above, the sky exploded with stars. Trouble. Trouble. Trouble. As soon as one of God's enemies was defeated another seemed to arise. His earthly refuge, his wife, was gone and his grief seemed unbearable. There is my work, he thought. Geneva is left. This old church must go on ministering to the needs of the people, calling them to righteousness. They need God today as much as the people who built it needed Him!

Suddenly through John's brain beat the words and music of the hymn that had haunted him for years: Martin Luther's Battle Hymn. Luther had been dead over three years, but his song of truth went on:

> A Mighty Fortress is our God
> A bulwark never failing. . . .

It sang through John's veins like a promise—a promise of ultimate victory. Reverently he bowed his head, and the familiar strength that came from communion with God coursed through him. There was still a great deal of work to do; he would lose himself in that as Idelette had suggested.

It wasn't long after the funeral that a man came to see John to ask for work. His long black locks, handsomely impudent face, and the slight hump on his back seemed familiar. It was Pierre Daquet, the thieving servant who had stolen the community purse years ago, so that Anthony, Louis, and John had had to beg their way to Strasbourg.

"I am a Christian now, a true Christian," Daquet vowed, folding his hands piously. "Have mercy. I need work!"

"What makes you think I would have mercy on a thief?"

"Surely you do not doubt the power of God's grace in the life of a thief?" Pierre was watching him closely.

Who am I to doubt the power of God in anyone's life? John reflected, and agreed to give the man a trial. He needed a servant badly, and if he had one, he could take in a few boarders.

Pierre moved his belongings in that afternoon and started at once to clean the house. While his work was less than immaculate, his efforts brought a certain order.

Absorbed in his purpose of making Geneva a godly city, John labored on with fierce determination. An endless stream of callers visited him, and letters from foreign lands arrived in great piles. He drove himself so relentlessly that his body sometimes was numb with tiredness, but his mind was always clear, and he did not forget to speak to Anthony concerning the gossip about his wife.

"Anne unfaithful?" Anthony scoffed. "An old wives' tale! That is what comes of belonging to the family of a world-famed man! Can't you see? Your enemies manufactured that lie to hurt you."

Maybe it is gossip, John thought. God's enemies continue to do everything to keep Him from having His way. Anne came often to visit. She and Judith were becoming good friends, and the girl declared that Anne was a fine woman.

As the months passed, John turned for help more and more to the Christian intelligence of Theodore de Beza. He didn't know what he would have done without the younger man's valuable assistance. A convert from Catholicism, Theodore had none of the bitterness of William Farel. He taught the doctrines of the Bible with joy, and had talent for poetry and for music. An excellent teacher, he was also a good administrator and a bulwark of faith, refusing to be frightened into any compromise.

Nerien had become a general helper at all the churches, since Matthew Cordier's poor health had demanded his retirement. John knew that it was by God's direct command that he had helped educate the foundling, that Nerien had been marked for special work in Geneva.

The years had brought many changes on the world scene. There had been deaths: Henry VIII and Francis I in 1547. In the same year, Emperor Charles V had turned his forces against the German Protestants and, with the cry that he would crush heresy, had crushed liberty. At Meaux, fourteen heretics had been burned in a single day, and thousands of the Waldensians in the Alpine valleys had been exterminated. In Guienne, a revolt against the salt tax had taken its toll of lives. In England, Archbishop Cranmer and young Edward's Protector, Lord Somerset, had just completed a revision of the Prayer Book, consulting by mail with John, with Martin Bucer, who was teaching at Cambridge, and with Peter Martyr, who was at Oxford. Martin and Peter were helping, also, to draw up articles of faith for the Church of England. Yes, John thought, the world was turning upside down, but God's hand could be seen moving through it.

Early in March, 1550, John, Theodore, and Nerien sat around the table in John's home study one night, discussing the problem of classrooms. So many students crowded into the auditorium and the chapels of St. Peter's that the need for a large building was desperate. Since the city had no money, John suggested that an appeal might be made to some individuals. As they conferred, a mail carrier arrived with a stack of letters, among them one bearing Lord Somerset's seal. He wrote:

There are those who urge a reunion with the Church of Rome. As long as Archbishop Cranmer and I have any influence there will be none. We can do nothing but renounce the doctrine of the Mass in which the body of Christ is literally eaten by the worshipper. We are indebted to you for your help with the new Prayer Book.

An act has been passed here permitting the clergy to marry. To forbid them to do so is against nature and, we believe, at the root of past immorality.

I am writing to ask a sacrifice. You are aware of the problem of securing teachers grounded in Biblical faith. Our need is desperate. Will you send us somebody who is qualified? There is an opening at Oxford.

John read the letter aloud, and when he had finished, Nerien said slowly, "As you read, I told myself: This is my call. You can get another to work here in Geneva. The field in England is plowed and somebody must sow. Master John, I want to go to Oxford."

John looked at him with the deep affection he had always felt for him. Nerien had heard a call and he would answer it. It would not be right to try to dissuade him. What if I never see him again? John thought, but he pushed that aside.

"Go with my blessings, Nerien," he said in a choked voice. "Go in the name of God. Help lay a strong foundation for His Church in England. And write often. I will be missing you."

Six weeks later John was sitting at his desk one morning putting the finishing touches on the manuscript of another commentary, one on Second Thessalonians. His secretary, Nicholas de la Fontaine, was waiting to take it to the printer's. There was a rustle of skirts, and for an instant John thought that it was Idelette. He looked up to see her daughter there, wearing a blue dress that set off her golden hair and stormy blue eyes. That is the way her mother must have looked at sixteen, he thought.

He leaned back and smiled at her. "Judith, hello. Have a seat. What can I do for you?"

But she did not sit down. She stood facing him, frowning. "I loathe Latin, Papa. Do I have to go on studying it?"

"Everyone should know Latin, Judith. A young lady should receive as good an education as her brother, and there are many scholarly books you will never be able to read if you fail to master that language." He stared at her gravely, wondering if he was doing the right thing. If only her mother were here! "If the good church fathers had not studied Latin and preserved so much of our culture, including the great literary masterpieces, the world would be poor indeed."

"Oh," she said. That was all, but her blue eyes were just as clouded as before.

After all, he thought when she had gone out, her question showed she was growing up. Women ought to think for themselves. . . . He soon forgot about her, however, and went back to another commentary—on Isaiah.

By the end of 1551 the commentaries had piled up, and early in 1552 a group came from Bern to ask him to write one on the Book of the Revelation.

"No," he replied promptly. "That is the one book of the New Testament I will never try to write about. It is filled with allegory and people are confused about it. I will not increase the confusion."

John felt so tired after the delegation had left that he knew he would have to rest a few minutes before keeping a supper engagement with Theodore. Nowadays, tormented by frequent headaches, a liver ailment, rheumatism in his knees, and even convulsions, there were many times when he longed to stay in bed. But he did so only when Dr. Tertor insisted on it, or when he was so ill that he could not get up. There was so much work to be done and he felt keenly the limitations of time.

He sank into a comfortable armchair in the drawing room and opened the Bible. Reading it and praying rested him more than anything else and brought new strength to his body as well as his soul. If only all men would feed their souls, he often thought, there would be more useful men. After Idelette had gone, the emptiness had been unbearable. But there had been his writing and his teaching, and he had Judith. He wondered where she was this afternoon, for she usually came home after classes. Perhaps she was with Anne.

He finished reading a portion of the Scriptures, and said his prayers, ending with one for Judith and Jacques, who lived with his grandmother in Liége. Then he leaned his head against the back of the chair and closed his eyes. . . . When he opened them someone was moving in the twilight which had gathered in the room. It wasn't Pierre Daquet. This man was tall.

"Anthony?" he asked.

"It's Theodore, Dr. Calvin. When you didn't arrive for supper, I came to see what was wrong. I was trying to move quietly so as to let you rest. You certainly need it."

John sat up straight. "That's an awful thing to do, to keep you waiting like that. I didn't intend to fall asleep. Just give me a moment——"

"There's no hurry about supper, but I have news that won't

wait. The Council has permitted Gaspard Favre to return, and he is vowing he will be a model citizen."

"I wonder." John was dubious. "Ami Perrin has asked to return, also. Geneva cannot stand any more unrest. And I am so tired!"

When Judith reached home that night, it was almost midnight. John had come in from Theodore's about ten and was waiting up for her. He went downstairs when he heard the door open. She came in alone.

"Where were you, Judith?" he asked, trying to make his voice sound casual. "I was a little worried."

"Don't worry about me. I can take care of myself. I was with a friend of Aunt Anne's. Do I have to answer to you for everything, Papa?"

"That was a rude question," he said sternly. "I have your best interests at heart. You know how fond I have always been of you."

"Then leave me alone. Don't quiz me as you do the councilmen!"

After she had gone to her room, John walked back and forth reflecting. Judith was not talking with him as she once had; she seemed to have turned to Anthony's wife. He remembered uneasily the gossip about Anne, and determined to try to be more of a companion to Judith, even if it meant slowing down on his writing.

The next morning he went to see Michael Sept in his blacksmith's shop to ask him to keep an eye on Gaspard and his constant companion, Philibert Berthelier. He found Michael with his sleeves rolled up, working his bellows.

"Master Calvin! I was just thinking of you. Gaspard and Philibert gave me an order to fashion a dozen daggers. The blades are to be thin and very sharp. I was wondering if I ought to ask you if I should deliver them. I hope those two don't start trouble again. I don't like the way they hang around the common room at the inn drinking with some of the most evil of the refugees. They get their heads too close together for my comfort."

"As far as strife in the city goes, the past two years have been comparatively quiet. I came to ask you to keep your eyes on Gaspard and Philibert. It would be tragic if rioting broke out again."

224

"What shall I do about these daggers? What do they want with a dozen of them?"

"I will place this matter in God's hands. It is as simple as that. They have a right to buy daggers if they wish to."

Michael stopped working the bellows and stood very still, frowning. "You know this scholar who hates you so? The man who wrote the damaging book about the Trinity?"

A new and terrible fear smote John. "You don't mean Michael Servetus? He's not here in Geneva?"

"No." Michael shook his shaggy head. "But I heard a hanger-on at the inn say he was headed this way."

"Father in Heaven, help us," John breathed a prayer, steadying himself by grabbing Michael's sturdy arm. Reassuring warmth radiated from it. John remembered having written Servetus, warning him not to dare come to Geneva. The hanger-on had probably heard the old rumor.

"I was shocked for a moment, Michael," he said calmly, "but I hardly think he will show his face here. It would be the worst thing that could happen to Geneva, now that we have had nearly two years of calm."

"I'll keep my eyes open, Master Calvin. You can count on me."

John dragged himself home, and by the time he had climbed the stairs to his study, the walls seemed to be reeling. With an effort he steadied himself and sat down. He realized that he was so dedicated to his dreams that he pushed himself too hard in trying to fulfill them. He should get into bed. Well, he would.

In a few minutes he was propped against the white-covered pillows, a sheaf of parchment, inkhorn, and quill at one elbow, the Bible and a pile of other books on the covers beside him. Lord Somerset had written that his valuable advice in building the Church of England was having good results, but that young King Edward and many others found the books of the Scriptures which were called Catholic books—James, First Peter, Second Peter, Jude, and First John—confusing. John agreed that there was a need for commentaries on this universal group, directed not to any individual but to the entire Church. He made up his mind to finish them for publication in a few months. The dedication would be to the young King. As he began work, he forgot his ailments, forgot all except the task he was engaged on. He didn't even hear the footsteps coming up to his room.

When he realized somebody was standing at the foot of his bed, he looked up with a start. It was Michael, his big features splattered with blood, a large bruise on the side of his chin. His brown hair was disheveled and one eye was black.

"What happened to you?" John demanded. He knew Michael did not drink too much, but he had the appearance of a man in his cups.

"Gaspard and Philibert attended a baptism this morning at St. Gervais, and drank for an hour afterward. By the time they reached my shop, they were staggering and truculent. I made the mistake of asking why they wanted a dozen daggers, and if they would be loyal to the city and to the Church now."

"I see they jumped you."

"They jumped me all right and both are able-bodied men. But I flattened them and dragged them one at a time to the Council. They will come to themselves in jail!"

John laughed in spite of his fury. But that night he tossed unable to sleep. Staring into the darkness, he pondered the new outbreak by his enemies. Gaspard and Philibert had a dozen new blades, and there could be only one conclusion. They were plotting another uprising. No wonder his nights were sleepless and his health ruined. . . . So hour after hour dragged into cheerless dawn.

Late that afternoon he went visiting with an elder and a deacon. This plan of calling, which he had initiated, was getting better results in consecrated lives than anything else he had tried. All the way home he thought how nice it was going to be to spend the evening with Judith. There was to be a concert in the auditorium of St. Peter's, and she had promised to go with him. But when he returned home and lit the candle on his bedside table, a piece of folded parchment lay there. It was a note from Judith, telling him she had run off to marry a French refugee!

In a mood of deep despair John took to his bed and spent another miserable night. Remorse struck at his heart. He regretted not having been a better father. He had really tried. There had been moments since Idelette's death when he and Judith had talked freely, been good companions, but many matters had intervened to keep them apart. It was dawn before he fell asleep.

He woke with a dreadful headache, so sick he couldn't get out of bed. The walls seemed to be crashing about him and he felt hot and cold at the same time. He sent Pierre for Dr. Tertor.

"The doctor is at Lausanne," the servant returned to report. "One of your boarders, the Sieur de Falais, has sent to Chalais for his physician. You must lie still until he arrives."

Several hours later, the physician came. John could not see his features clearly. But a big man moved like a monstrous cat to his bedside, and a voice that stirred unpleasant memories said he would mix a quieting potion.

"I prefer to wait until Dr. Tertor arrives," John said, for some vague reason he couldn't explain to himself.

"Proper patients do what they are told," the silky voice said.

"I am not your patient."

"In that case I shall leave you to your suffering."

The doctor gathered up his cloak and bag, and started for the door.

John's head throbbed so that he thought despairingly: I cannot wait for Dr. Tertor. "I will take the potion," he said aloud.

The irate man came back and threw down his cloak. There was a clanking and a rattling of bottles. A hairy hand held out a cup, which John took, gulping the contents quickly. The stuff smelled and tasted like filthy water with mud and acid in it. Benedict Tertor had given him a lot of awful medicine, but nothing like this.

John peered at the stranger towering above him, and gradually the doctor's face came into focus. It was an ugly face John had seen before in Ferrara. This man was the Carmelite monk, Hyeronymous Bolsec, the Inquisition's spy! What was he doing in Geneva posing as a physician? Had the scoundrel just given him poison? Was he to die at the hands of a quack physician in such a manner that nobody would suspect murder?

The devil read his mind and said with a laugh, "I see you remember me, Dr. Calvin. You fear poison? I have studied medicine, but I have no intention of using that knowledge to murder you, although the idea holds certain charm. How do you feel now?"

Half strangling, John gasped for breath. This is the way poison works, he thought in terror. It was a few minutes before he began to breathe freely again.

"I am glad my potion gave you a fright. You are so sure about everything, Dr. Calvin."

"Why should you hate me so?" John's voice was small, tired.

"Hate you? When you have written a book telling the rest of the world what to believe? A book that brutally declares God has destined some for salvation and consigned others to destruction?"

"You are talking about predestination. I have never given it the importance some people insist on giving it. I have defined predestination, as the Scriptures teach it, to be the free council of God, by which he governs the human race in all parts of the world, according to his immense wisdom and incomprehensible justice."

"Just what does that mean?"

"If he chooses some, the alternative is true. All cannot be elected."

"How could election extend to some and not others? Bah!"

John thought of Gaspard Favre. "What of the reprobate? If everyone were elected and patted on the head as an unwise father pats his disobedient children, an evildoer could well ask: Why bother leading a good life? That is where the Scriptures differ from the good Martin Luther and Philipp Melanchthon, whose emphasis was all love."

"To say that is to doubt God's power to save a man in spite of himself."

"That is not correct. The Scriptures clearly state that Grace, offered for salvation, is offered equally to all. The outcome hinges on free will, too. Some reject it. Others accept it. But no wind ever rises or blows but by the special command of God."

"Nonsense!"

John sat up, his suffering forgotten. "Bolsec, did you come to Geneva to tear down what the Presbytery has slaved to build here with God as Master Builder?"

"I am a convert to Protestantism. Does that surprise you? So I, too, use my intellect. And I will expose your ridiculous doctrine with my last breath!"

"My doctrine? God's doctrine." John pointed an accusing finger, and he noticed the seal on his ring—a heart held out to God, symbolizing complete submission to His will without counting the cost.

"There has been dissension enough in Geneva, Bolsec. As God's servant, I warn you we will not permit blasphemy against Him."

Three days later at five o'clock in the afternoon, John had a visitor more to his liking, William Farel, to whom he confessed his worries about the ex-Carmelite's threats. As John toyed with his supper—he had a poor appetite these days—William Farel strode up and down the kitchen. Lately Pierre seemed slow about picking things up. There were four boarders in the household now, the Sieur and Lady de Falais and two students, and today the cleaning had been neglected. Books were piled everywhere, even on the floor.

"It is difficult to give advice in this matter," he said at length, a look of frowning concentration on his square face. "Whatever you do, you are likely to have the devil's own time with this fellow. The result could be disastrous. Dissension here now will threaten the unity of the Church in all the other Swiss cantons, as well as the Geneva Church. You haven't won the battle in Geneva yet."

"I know." John pushed his food aside. "The Presbytery has asked Bolsec to respect its authority in matters of religion, but I fear he will not."

"I can understand why he's confused about election and predestination." William sighed and threw himself in the chair opposite John.

"People make it difficult," John said. "God is sovereign. He has a certain design. He is powerful enough to keep men within that design, if He so wills. Therefore, He is a part of all events."

"But there is free will? What's the difference between predestination and fatalism?" William asked with a puzzled frown.

"There is free will only within the giant framework of the design, according to God's will," John said firmly.

"That's a good answer. And you are fortunate to have Theodore de Beza to help you defend these truths. He is not only brilliant, but the students like him."

John nodded. "You should hear Theodore point out that the will of God is not subject to the will of men."

William spent the night and together they went to the Friday morning service at St. Peter's to hear a young preacher, John d'Andre. The custom at this service was to allow the people to discuss the sermon openly from the floor.

D'Andre expounded a text from John, pointing out that those who are not elected disobey God, but obedience is given to the elect.

When a monstrous man rose, John whispered to William, "Bolsec! He is losing no time."

"Men are not saved by election, but are elected because of their faith," Bolsec blustered. Then he began a tirade against the clergy of Geneva, declaring that they were false prophets and insisting that the city should find men who would preach the truth.

John's head had begun to ache, but he rose and walked shakily down the aisle. When he reached the front, he took a deep breath and faced the people. Augustine's words came into his mind and he quoted them: " 'What is commonly called fortune is regulated by a secret order, and what we call chance is only that, with the reason and cause of which we are not acquainted. . . . What we ought to say is "This was the will of God" and not "This was the will of fortune." ' "

"I suppose you think God's angels hover around, waiting to do God's will when he pulls the strings!" Bolsec sneered.

"Angels are ministering spirits, whose service God uses for the protection of His people. By them He dispenses His benefits among mankind and executes other works. It is written in the Scriptures: 'He shall give his angels charge over thee, to keep thee in all thy ways.' "

"Does each Christian have a special angel assigned to him?" asked a white-haired, eager-faced old lady.

"Whether or not each has a particular angel I cannot answer with certainty. But I know this: No wind ever rises or blows but by the command of God. In the words of Basil the Great: 'Fortune and Chance are words for the heathen.' "

To John's consternation Bolsec was waving his arms and shouting, "Dr. Calvin is always prating about the Scriptures. Have custom and tradition nothing to do with thinking? You may believe you are free in Geneva. Many doubt that. You are mental slaves to the ministers!"

He is forcing our hands, John thought in despair. He is defying law and order. Abel Poupin, taking charge of the situation, stalked toward the rear of the church. In a few minutes a trio of police arrested the infuriated Bolsec and marched him off to jail, struggling and swearing.

The Bolsec case dragged on for days and kept Geneva in turmoil. If we are too mild, John kept thinking, others also will be encouraged to undermine authority.

Two days before the Council was to meet to decide the case, the Sieur de Falais, wrapped in a heavy robe, came into the drawing room where John sat reading by the fire.

"Free Dr. Bolsec," he urged; "be merciful."

"But he shows no repentance. Anarchy results when people are allowed to defy laws!"

"Isn't his repentance between him and God?"

John thought for a moment. Maybe De Falais was right . . . perhaps the ex-monk should be given another chance.

When the Council met, on the recommendation of the Presbytery, Bolsec was granted his freedom temporarily, on condition that one of the councilmen accompany him at all times on his visits to the sick to ascertain that he did not undermine the Church or the State.

Abel Poupin, given the assignment for the first week, came on Saturday night to make his report to John. "Everywhere Bolsec visited he spoke ill of the Council and the Presbytery. You made a mistake in asking for his freedom!"

John's face set grimly. "With the prevalent unrest we cannot risk further mischief. The only thing the Council can do now is to make a public example of him!"

Five days later, on Thursday, the town crier went through the streets, blowing on a silver trumpet. "Hear ye! Citizens of Geneva, hear ye! And evildoers take note. The errant physician and ex-monk, Hyeronymous Bolsec, who has blasphemed the doctrines of the Church as contained in the Holy Scriptures and declared by the Presbytery, is herewith banished upon pain of being whipped, should he ever return to Geneva!"

John sat by the fire thinking with relief that the Bolsec affair was finally settled. The drawing room seemed unusually empty. He could hear his roomers moving around upstairs, the students' voices raised in argument. For an instant he closed his eyes, wishing that Idelette sat on the sofa beside him. He missed her most when problems were hammering at him. She had listened, advised and, on occasion, chided. Now he no longer even had Judith. Tonight he felt lonely. At least the cause of the dissension had been disposed of. The future of Geneva depended on peace.

He heard steps coming down the stairs, and presently the Sieur de Falais and his lady, a pretty woman in her thirties, stood in the doorway. He carried two leather traveling boxes, which he put down as he crossed the room to John.

"We are leaving for Bern, where you have forced my physician to go. Don't ever come there talking about a God who chooses to damn creatures made in his own image. You are the one who should be banished from decent society!"

Lady de Falais placed a gloved hand on her husband's arm. "Forgive my sire," she said in a gentle voice. "He is really ill and has need of the physician. I agree with you, Dr. Calvin. Dr. Bolsec had no right to come here and stir disunity!"

"Don't apologize for me, my Lady. Nobody else has such potions as Dr. Bolsec. Of course Dr. Calvin could never overlook opposition in any form. Come, my dear."

Lady de Falais shook her head at John, turned meekly, and followed her blustering husband out into the snowy street. My best-paying boarders, John thought in despair. And I believed he was my friend!

"Pastor Bullinger tells me that Dr. Bolsec is having his revenge," Theodore said with a grin two weeks later.

"He probably will."

"He's writing your biography, The Life of John Calvin. Seriously, he is at work."

"That should be quite a book before he gets through. About the only black deed I have not been charged with is immorality with a woman!" John said lightly.

But Theodore had something else to say: "Before Bolsec gets through with you, he might even think of that!"

On January 28, 1552, John was sitting in his study, looking out toward the Alps, clothed in winter ermine. The sun was shining and the air was clear except for the powdery snow, so that the peaks were plainly outlined against the blue. How lovely the mountains were in all seasons. He often thought of the psalmist who had written: "I will look unto the hills . . ." But this afternoon he knew he must concentrate on his new book, *On the Eternal Predestination of God.* He lifted his quill and began to write.

In an hour or so the door downstairs opened, and steps bounded up to his study. He looked up, expecting to see one of his student boarders, but it was Theodore who came in, shaking his head like a Hebrew prophet. His deep-set eyes were smoldering, there was a frown on his handsome face. Snow, melting over his cloak and hat, dripped to the floor.

"Pastor Fabri has just arrived from Bern to deliver his lectures. His journey over the icy roads was hair-raising. He brought news I find difficult to break to you."

"Come now, Theodore. It can't be that bad. Take off your wet cloak. Put it on the back of that chair and sit here beside me. I am used to bad news. I just hope it isn't that that scoundrel Michael Servetus is coming here. Geneva couldn't stand another Bolsec."

Theodore leaned forward. John thought he had never seen his face so grave. "Recently when we discussed the book Dr. Bolsec is writing about you, John, you said there was one charge your enemies had never made against you. You cannot say that now."

"Oh, Theodore," John said impatiently, "surely nobody has——"

"Bolsec is spreading it all over Bern that the Sieur de Falais left your house because you made improper advances to his lady."

John looked at Theodore uncomprehendingly. The younger minister continued to frown. This can't be true, John thought; not even my worst enemies would say I was unchaste!

"You are joking," he said in despair, for he knew his friend was not.

"John, I would never joke about anything like that!"

"Was Fabri certain?"

"Yes. He heard Bolsec tell Bullinger that when Lady de Falais refused to submit to you, you threatened to have her arrested on trumped-up charges. She was, so Bolsec said, so terrified that she urged her husband to flee from Geneva!"

"Did Fabri confront him with his lies?"

"Not only Fabri but another minister, Haller. Bolsec swore he had heard Lady de Falais say this in her husband's presence. Tongues are buzzing all over Bern!"

"Everything I have worked for is at stake!"

"If the news reaches Geneva, you may have to stop preaching."

Ami Perrin was back and he was again Captain of Police. His brother-in-law, Monsieur Tissot, was Judge of the Criminal Court. John wrung his hands. What could he do? Was Geneva to drop again into her old ways of licentiousness and greed?

"Let me go to Bern and expose Bolsec!" Theodore pleaded. "As soon as Fabri finishes his lectures, I will ride back with him."

John stared moodily at the mountains. "I will look unto the hills . . ." he murmured. God's mountains rising toward the bright blue sky for God's Glory. " 'If God be for us, who can be against us?' " Peace flowed through him, and suddenly his melancholy was gone.

"I appreciate your loyalty, my dear friend, but I am the one to go. Madame de Falais will never allow injustice. When Fabri departs, I will go with him."

"But your health. The Juras and the Alps are covered with deep snow. You are in no condition to make such a journey!"

"This is the kind of thing a man takes care of himself. If God intends me to protect my good name, I shall be safe."

As John entered the common room of the inn near the Kramgrasse at Bern, the bells in the top of the tall tower rang six times. The innkeeper, a tall polite man, who reminded John of Messire La Farge, said that the Sieur and Lady Falais were staying there but that the Sieur was away. He would send for his lady.

Her black brows arched when she came down the stairs and saw him. "Master Calvin, what are you doing here?"

He told her directly, watching her pretty face redden and her eyes snap. "We must confront Dr. Bolsec with his lie. I will go before the Council with you."

Early the next morning, February 17, when the Council of Bern convened, John and Lady de Falais asked to be heard. A beadle was sent to find Bolsec. When the beadle returned with the physician and he saw John, he turned white and then crimson.

The councilmen watched and listened as John cried in a thunderous voice: "I have come over the ice and snows of winter to confront you, Bolsec. Have you, or have you not, been circulating the damnable lie that I was a threat to Madame's chastity?"

The ex-monk stood with his mouth open. The accusing pastors, Fabri and Haller, stepped forward and Monsieur Fabri spoke.

"Dr. Bolsec said in my presence that when Lady de Falais refused to submit to Master Calvin, he threatened to trump up charges and have her arrested."

"He swore he had heard the lady say this in her husband's presence," Haller affirmed.

The Chief Syndic rose and looked sternly at the physician, who cast his eyes down. "Is there anything you wish to tell me about Dr. Calvin's character?"

Dr. Bolsec remained silent. He did not look up.

Lady de Falais stepped quietly toward the cowardly doctor. "If you made such a statement, I witness the fact that it is untrue. Dr. Calvin is a Christian gentleman!"

At last Dr. Bolsec raised his eyes. "What is everybody talking about? I never said anything against Dr. Calvin's character."

Pastor Fabri glowered. "In my presence and the presence of Pastor Haller and of other citizens of Bern you stated that you had heard Lady de Falais declare these things to her husband."

"Then, Lady de Falais, it is a lie that Dr. Calvin solicited your chastity?" asked the Chief Syndic.

"Yes. I affirm his innocence, gentlemen. Master Calvin is above reproach. I know. My husband and I lived in his house six months."

The Chief Syndic coughed and looked at the other syndics, who nodded meaningfully. "Master Calvin," said the Chief Syndic, "we find you absolved of the false charges this man has made against you. And we herewith admonish the physician Bolsec to guard his tongue and suggest that it would be wise if he finds another place to practice his art. We have no use in Bern for liars and especially for one who deliberately tries to blacken the character of an honest man!"

That is that, John thought gratefully. What next? *What next?*

16

1553-1558

That August morning John was dictating to Nicholas. There were at least twenty more pages of a manuscript to finish before the printer's messenger arrived. Four men who were out of work came asking him for help, and he paused to give them letters to possible employers. Within two hours fifteen callers had consulted him about personal or governmental matters.

Four important letters arrived, demanding immediate answers. One was from the young King of England's Protector, Lord Somerset, announcing that the frail king had died, that the Reformation in England was in danger, and the lives of the reformers were in jeopardy. It was rumored that Lady Jane Grey would be crowned queen, but if Mary Tudor succeeded in gaining control, heads would roll, for Mary hated anything that smacked of the Protestant faith. Another letter of urgency was from John Knox, the Scot who was trying to make his country Protestant. John had grown very fond of Knox when he had visited in Geneva and through their correspondence. Knox seemed determined to denounce Mary Stuart, but he sought advice as to whether or not he should stay in

Scotland or flee to the continent once more, should Mary Tudor come to power. A letter from Nerien requested a copy of John's Commentary on Hebrews, and remarked that he enjoyed his teaching in Oxford, but that it was not without danger. Since Dr. Bucer's death the year before, the animosity against those of the Reformed Faith had increased. The fourth letter was from Philipp Melanchthon, who continued to try in Germany to adjust the differences between the Church of Rome and the Lutherans. He wanted to know if John thought it would be wise, in the efforts toward unity, to offer to accept the Pope if he stopped claiming to rule by divine right.

When another knock came at the door and Theodore entered, John slapped the palm of his hand on the desk.

"Theodore! I have been interrupted constantly this morning. I can be frank with you. I must finish this commentary. Come back later. Please!"

Theodore shook his head. "You know me well enough, John, to know that I never interrupt your work unless it is necessary. Something serious has happened. It will not wait."

"All right," John said resignedly. "What is it?"

"Michael Servetus is here in Geneva plotting with Ami Perrin and Philibert Berthelier. He has been here four weeks!"

"Impossible. I would surely have seen him."

"He is staying out of your way. At the Inn of the Rose he has taken an assumed name."

John sprang to his feet, his whole body rigid. "I warned him. I told him not to dare set foot here!"

"A priest from Vienna recognized him and told Monsieur Bonivard that the Catholics had condemned him to be burned for blasphemy there and that he had escaped."

John stood tense and trembling. "Are you sure he is in some kind of a conspiracy with Perrin and Berthelier?"

"Yes. The priest told Bonivard they were plotting for Berthelier to create some situation in which the authority of the Presbytery can be defied. In that way the people would lose respect for your authority."

Nicholas, John's secretary, spoke: "Is this the man who wrote the blasphemous manuscript you let me read?"

237

John nodded. "We kept that manuscript. We still have it."

"Shall I send for some of the syndics?"

"Alert them, Nicholas. Ask them to have Servetus watched. Let us see just what he is up to, and what our best move is."

"Let me prefer charges against this man, Dr. Calvin. The law provides that the accuser in criminal cases be imprisoned, too. If you appear as accuser, you play right into Syndic Perrin's hands."

"What if he holds you? I need you."

"He won't consider me that important."

"Well, before any accusations are made, let us wait and see what happens. Maybe we can get evidence that he plots treason!"

Dressed in a brown doublet, white shirt, tight brown hose, and a hat without plumes, Michael Servetus appeared at St. Peter's the following Sunday. John Calvin was standing behind the lectern, reading the first passage of the Scriptures as Michael slipped into one of the few vacant seats. Once he thought Dr. Calvin's all-seeing black eyes looked in his direction, and his heart seemed to stop beating. Whatever prompted me to come here? he thought in terror. What if he recognizes me?

All through the Confession, the Psalm, the Collect for Illumination, the reading of the second portion of the Scriptures, and the short sermon, Michael kept his head lowered. It was almost as if he could feel doom suspended over him. Since it was not Communion Sunday, the service was concluded in less than an hour and a half. As the Aaronic blessing was being given, Michael started for the door.

A handsome man, probably ten years his junior, was standing just inside it. Michael thought the man's brown eyes sparked as he passed, and his feeling of unease persisted as he walked back to the Place Molard. Maybe I had better leave Geneva, he thought in panic. After Calvin's enemies rid the city of him, I can return. There will be need for men of intelligence, and I will have a place of power. I will make Geneva a city of intellect and rid it of this Biblical faith.

Hurriedly he stuffed his belongings into his saddlebags and was about to start down to the lake to hire a boat when there came the sound of marching feet on the square outside. He ran to the window and saw a dozen uniformed men crossing toward the inn.

A moment later a knock sounded on his door, and his heart stood still, as a voice cried, "Open in the name of the syndics of Geneva!"

Feeling like a trapped animal, he slid the bolt back.

"Michael Servetus, alias Villarovanus, we arrest you in the name of our Council. You are to come with us."

"Where am I to be taken? And with what am I charged?"

"To the jail, where you will be held until you appear before the Little Council to answer charges which will be read to you."

"I suppose Dr. Calvin is my accuser."

"No. The complaint is signed by one Nicholas de la Fontaine. Will you come now?"

Syndic Perrin has influence, Michael thought as he marched along between the men. I will call loudly for liberty. Feeling will rise against those who persecute me. . . . In imagination he could see himself standing tall before the Council of Two Hundred, denouncing Dr. Calvin's severity, his unsound theology, waving the flag of liberty, making such a speech before the Council that Dr. Calvin recoiled before him. He sobered for an instant. Did Dr. Calvin ever recoil before anyone? With the minister's powerful enemies on the Council he might!

With a swagger Michael stepped through the gates of the old prison, crossed the immaculate courtyard, and moved along the dustless corridor. He understood that Dr. Calvin insisted on keeping the jail clean. Buoyed up by his dreams, he walked on air. He had long suspected that Dr. Calvin might have been the one who betrayed him to the Papists of Vienna. Anyway Michael hated Calvin's arrogance.

Before the soldiers left they hammered on his chains. Then they confiscated his purse with ninety-seven gold crowns, six gold rings, and a double gold chain worth twenty crowns. He made no protest. His friends on the Council would see that he got everything back.

The next morning the soldiers took him before the Little Council. Ami sat in the middle of the row of solemn syndics. In his pudgy hand was the baton of office of Chief Syndic. Relief swept Michael; he had nothing to fear.

"You have been brought here to be told that the indictment will

239

charge you with treason against the state and blasphemy against God," Ami said sternly.

"I would like a lawyer your Worships," the prisoner said quietly.

Ami coughed and looked at his colleagues, who shook their heads.

"The Ordinance of 1543 denies counsel to one accused of heresy," Ami said, just as if he and Servetus had not spent evening after evening together at the Inn of the Rose, drinking and planning Dr. Calvin's downfall. "You will be brought back on Thursday, at which time the indictment will be read."

When Thursday arrived and the charges were read, there were twenty-three counts. John Calvin was there, and Michael looked at him defiantly, lifting his chin and voicing his belief in pantheism, denying the doctrines of infant baptism, and predestination. When Dr. Calvin began to question the prisoner about his belief concerning the sovereignty of God, something seemed to snap inside Michael.

"Thou liest! Thou liest! Thou miserable wretch!" he exploded, shaking his fists. "Thou art jealous because of my great mind."

Dr. Calvin's full lips thinned, but he held himself with dignity.

The trial dragged on and on, and Michael could not sleep at night for wondering what Dr. Calvin would ask him next.

"Is it true that you attacked my explanation of salvation, grace, and the divinity of Christ?" Calvin asked blandly one afternoon when Michael's head was aching and he was so tired he could not think.

"I did not," Michael lied.

Ice touched his spine as Dr. Calvin picked up a book from the long table in front of the syndics, saying, "This is evidence that shows who the liar is, for it is one of my books with the prisoner's handwriting on the margin, tearing these Christian beliefs apart."

The syndics moved in their stalls, and arched their eyebrows at one another as the damning evidence passed from hand to hand. Michael threw his shoulders back, striding forward until he stood in front of the appalled judges.

"Everything is God and God is everything. The Devil *is* part of the substance of God!" he said, watching Dr. Calvin's eyes light like torches.

The moment was spoiled by the entry of three men into the chamber. They were commissioners from Vienna and Michael felt sudden fear, as they asked that he be delivered to them, since he was under a previous sentence there.

"Is this your wish?" Ami asked him.

Quickly Michael shook his head. There would be no chance of a second escape from Vienna. Here, in Geneva, his powerful friends would get him free.

After the commissioners had left, Michael ventured to look at Dr. Calvin once more. His eyes were still full of fire, and fear again struck at Michael's heart. Perhaps he might not be released! Ami Perrin and Philibert Berthelier would be afraid of the fire in those eyes, too. Nobody could defy Dr. Calvin and win!

On the twenty-sixth of October, 1553, Michael Servetus, led by two guards, appeared at the Town Hall. No concern showed in Ami Perrin's eyes or in his froglike voice as he pronounced sentence:

"We condemn thee, Michael Servetus, to be bound and led to the Place of Champel, to be fastened to the stake and burned alive, together with thy book on the *Errors of the Trinity* as well as another written by thy hand, even till thy body be reduced to ashes. Thus thou wilt finish thy life as an example to others to deter crime!"

The Libertines just used me as a tool, Michael Servetus thought in disbelief and terror as he threw himself to his knees. "In mercy, the sword! *Not fire!*"

Ami sank his jowl into his ruff and threw the words out carelessly, "The Imperial Law demands burning. Note the statute books."

John Calvin's heart beat painfully as he watched the procession wind its way from the prison, led by Chief Syndic Ami Perrin and the city herald. A group of men-at-arms followed, in steel helmets, shining breastplates, and closed breeches. Next came the prisoner in mourning cloth, surrounded by soldiers. At his side strode Master Farel in his somber black gown, carrying a Bible. His face was full of compassion as he watched Michael Servetus stumble up the hill, dragging his heavy chains.

As the procession neared the stake, etched starkly against the sky,

John felt something of the same pity he had felt so long ago for another prisoner, the hermit of Livry. He wished the Council had granted the request he had made for mercy, for death by the sword instead of fire, for this obstinate, conceited anarchist. Fire was so horrible. Despite Servetus' efforts to undermine God's work and the dishonor he had brought to His name, he was a human being. When John had written his old friend Farel, asking him to come from Neufchâtel to try to persuade Michael to show some repentance in order to save his life, he had hoped this would accomplish the impossible. William had pleaded to no avail. Michael was a traitor. Worse than that he had blasphemed God; and he continued to blaspheme Him.

A terrible quiet prevailed. There were only the sounds of footsteps and chains clanking. Not even a bird sang. Doom seemed suspended over the hilltop, and men shuddered. Then Master Farel paused beside the piled leaves and faggots and lifted a heavy hand for silence as he prayed for the soul of Michael Servetus.

When the prayer came to an end, Ami Perrin signaled the executioner. The soldiers thrust the prisoner against the stake and fastened him by his chains. They piled brush, leaves, and faggots around his feet. Ami Perrin strutted up and pressed a wreath of sulphur and leaves down upon his head, pointing a pious finger at the heretical books tied to Michael's side.

"Set fire! Burn the heretic!"

The dry wood and leaves ignited as the torch was touched. The flames crackled upward, until the executioner poured water from a row of huge urns on them, making them sputter. Smoke rolled up from the sodden leaves and wood. Then again the fire blazed, its sputtering alternated with the shrieks of the dying man.

"Jesus Christ! Thou Son of the Eternal God, have mercy upon me!"

Theodore de Beza moved to John's side. "What a stubborn wretch!" he whispered. "He has been known as a sower of great heresy throughout Christendom. Even as he faces his Creator he will not say: 'Thou *Eternal Son of God.*'"

Conspiracies and quarrels continued to beset Geneva. What bothered John most was that men like Philibert Berthelier drank, gambled, made illicit love, and then came boldly to church with no signs of repentance. Warning after warning of the Presbytery was ignored. John's reputation had been irreparably harmed by those who blamed him for the burning of Servetus.

In the midst of that affair John had forbidden Berthelier to sit at the Lord's table unless he repented of his sins. In defiance of the authority of the Presbytery, and John's own ban, the Council of Two Hundred granted Berthelier permission to take the Lord's Supper. With excitement still running high over the Servetus case, this fresh controversy endangered everything that had been accomplished in Geneva.

That Sunday John walked up the hill to St. Peter's in the fitful wind that blew dust into his eyes and flapped his worn furred robe around his bony knees. His temples were throbbing and his hands felt like ice. Ami Perrin passed him, strutting across St. Peter's Square. His glance was truculent, and he held his neck stiff, nodding curtly.

The church was full, as it usually was, but there was an unusual air of expectancy, for word had gone out through the city that the Lord's Supper was to be denied Philibert Berthelier, the son of the patriot and statesman, although the Council had ordered that he be allowed to take it.

When John and his assistant took their places behind the Lord's Table, facing the congregation, John directed the people to rise. " 'Our help is in the name of the Lord who made heaven and earth. . . .' " The voices joined reverently with his, and the Confession of Sin followed:

"And as thou dost blot out our sins and stains, enlarge and increase in us each day the gifts of the Holy Spirit; that as we acknowledge our unrighteousness with all our heart, we may be moved by that sorrow which shall bring forth true repentance in us, mortifying all our sins, and producing in us the fruits of righteousness and innocence which are pleasing unto thee; through Jesus Christ our Lord, Amen."

As John led the congregation in the Old Hundredth Psalm from the Psalter of 1551, he looked for Philibert's arrogant face, but he could not find it.

There followed the Proclamation of the Word, the Great Prayer, ending with the Lord's Prayer, and another used when the Lord's Supper was celebrated. After the Confession of Faith and a second Psalm, John waited quietly beside his colleague while the elders brought the elements to the Lord's Table.

After the bread and the wine had been passed to the ministers first, according to the custom, since they were the Christian leaders at His Supper, John prayed silently for strength to do what he had to do. He stood quietly looking at the people who had come to be renewed with Christ's promises and His Word. Then in a voice charged with power he said:

"I will die before this hand shall stretch forth the sacred things of the Lord to those who have been judged despisers! This sacrament is a feeding in the heart. I invite all—including any members of the Church of Rome—who are sincerely sorry for their sins to partake of the Lord's Supper. But the unrepentant shall not profane it!"

The silence that followed was awful, as if men expected God to reach out his hand and touch them. Quietly, reverently, John began passing the elements while his assistant read passages from the Holy Bible. And when the repentant had been served, John's heart exulted. Once again he had obeyed God. He had refused to serve the elements to the unrepentant, the plotters, the hardened sinners. The Lord's Table was undefiled. And thank Him, too, that Philibert Berthelier had not made a public issue of his rejection.

That afternoon as John preached what he believed was his farewell sermon, one thought buoyed him: he had done God's will. His Scripture lesson was from the Acts of the Apostles in which Paul said good-by to the Church at Ephesus. He told the congregation that he was not a man who taught others to fight against the magistrates, but that the civil government had no right to interfere in the Lord's business. "Since these things are so, allow me, also, brethren, to use the words of the Apostle: 'I commend you to the Lord and the Word of His Grace.'"

Theodore came up jubilantly afterward, Ablard Corne waddling behind him. "John, you have won! You have won this bout in the battle for God!"

"I don't understand, Theodore. I defied the Council of Two Hundred!"

"Philibert Berthelier did not dare show himself. He and the other Libertines knew they were beaten. Men who have been luke-warm to your laws are clustered out there on the square now talking about how heroic you were. The citizens are behind you. The Council will have to concede!"

John could not speak. The lump in his throat would not let him. Now, with peace surrounding him, he would have time for a final revision of his *Institutes*. There was so much more he wanted to make clear. First he would take a trip to see John Knox, who had left Scotland and was with some refugees at Frankfort. He would try to bring peace between two factions in Germany, and invite Knox and the refugees to Geneva. Then he would return to the serenity of a life where he did not have to fight hour after hour, day after day, month after month, and year after year.

As John rode back into Geneva in November, 1555, behind the herald who had accompanied him for his protection, he was very tired, but he had accomplished his mission. John Knox was com-ing to Geneva. The quarrelsome refugees from London were com-ing, too. The Scot was a stirring preacher and he could help in the churches. Perhaps Geneva could, in turn, temper Knox, so that when God opened the way again in Scotland, he would not be so violent.

The driver helped John down in front of his house and carried his traveling box into the hall. Home at last! How restful it would be to lie down on his own comfortable bed. How quiet the house was! He had closed the door and started up the stairs when he heard voices, a man's and a woman's. They seemed to be coming from his bed-chamber. There was giggling, too, as shrill as a peacock's scream.

John would never forget the sight that met his eyes as he pushed open the door. Anthony's wife, Anne, and John's own servant, Pierre Daquet! Animal puppets on the devil's strings, he thought in hor-ror. Anne's eyes met his and widened in terror. Her face went as white as the bare flesh of her body. John, thinking immediately of the four young Calvins, whirled and ran down the stairs.

The Christian yardstick? he thought in anguish. What I would like to employ now is a two-thonged leather whip! He beat upon the table. Then alarmed at the violence of his feelings, he sat with his head in his hands. He prayed. How could he tell Anthony? What words would he use?

In a few minutes Pierre came down with a traveling box and ran from the house. Then Anne, fully clothed now, appeared in the doorway, her face stained with tears.

"Don't tell Anthony, John. Be merciful!"

He shook his head, feeling as if all this must be a nightmare and he would wake up. "You are guilty, Anne. The laws of Geneva have a penalty."

"Think of the children. Think of Anthony!" She threw herself at his feet, grabbing him around the knees, sobbing.

He stood erect. "I am thinking of them."

Her eyes narrowed. "Think of what this will do to you. For the first time you are a power in Geneva. You are respected at last, looked up to. If your enemies learn of this, they will say you are a failure, that you cannot even control the members of your own family."

John helped her to her feet. "Do not kneel to me. Kneel to God, if you are truly repentant. But, Anne, you must be accused before the Council."

Her face contorted. Her eyes became narrow slits. "All right, Master Holiness, we shall see! I will inform the Council that I am not the only member of your family to indulge in this crime. . . . Ask anybody at Vaud about your precious Judith!"

John felt as if she had dug a dagger into his heart. He believed her. Judith wrote on occasion. She came to visit. But she seemed to find it difficult to look him in the eyes. Anne and Judith had been seeing a lot of each other. Oh, Idelette, I have failed you! he thought. I have been so busy saving Geneva and the world that I have lost Judith.

"What you say, if true, grieves me. You knew it would. But Geneva is becoming a city of righteousness, prayer, faith, decency, and law. Don't you see, Anne? The law must be for all!"

John's heart sank when he saw Anthony coming in to take Anne home, as he usually did when she was in the city. Although he broke the news as gently as he knew how, he saw his brother's face age, his eyes widen with horror and incredulity.

"But it can't be true! It can't be!"

Anne turned her face to the wall.

"You are to bring your children here to my house," John told his brother after Anne's banishment. "Together we can love them, lead them. David especially needs direction."

Anthony stood in the study doorway, frowning. "John, I know how you love the young, but mine are healthy, normal children, and they are noisy, especially David. What about your work?"

John smiled. "I could make a very fine revision of *The Institutes of the Christian Religion* to the music of children playing and chattering. Those are not irritating sounds but happy ones. I can imagine . . ."

He paused, unable to continue as he remembered Judith. The pain in his throat choked him. He vowed he would have more time for the young Calvins. When spring came again, they must have some picnics in the mountains. There was one spot to which he had always intended to go with Idelette, Judith, and Jacques, where you could look across to Mont Blanc and France. But he had never gone. There had always been Geneva and the Church. Anthony patted his shoulder comfortingly. Anthony understood.

"Memories are painful but sweet, too. My children are very fond of you. David may call you 'Uncle Grumpy,' but notice how ready he is to climb on your lap! We'll move in at once."

Theodore appeared in John's tower study one Saturday night. "The large majority of Geneva's people have learned to love you, John," he announced happily. "Everywhere the citizens are saying that you are one of the brave to insist that justice is justice, whether the offender be a Calvin or a Berthelier. They realize that you could have hushed up your sister-in-law's offense, but that you refused to compromise. Now that they understand how much you have done for them and Geneva, their hearts overflow. Francis Bonivard came to see me today. He has decided to contribute a substantial sum to build an academy. Others will make donations, too. John, the Academy can be built!"

So another battle was won for God. Years before the Council had set aside the Chapel of Notre Dame la Neuve at St. Peter's for the classes of the school, but this auditorium had soon been full to overflowing. A proper system of education with adequate space for classes had long been the primary need. A fierce joy swept John. "Oh, Theodore, Theodore. Our work for God will survive!"

There was a light in the eyes of the former dandy who now lived a truly selfless life. "You are Geneva's greatest citizen!" he said jubilantly.

Citizen? John thought. I have never been a citizen. How I wish I were. Citizen of Geneva, the jewel of the Alps.

"Oh, Theodore," he said with a sigh, "I am so happy but so weary!"

He had not told Theodore that morning of the longing that had beset his years. If he had, Theodore might have taken a hand in bringing about the fulfillment of that personal dream. But on this wintry morning, on this blessed Christmas Day of 1559, the citizens of their own volition were making him a citizen. John Calvin, *citizen*. His cup was overflowing.

This year had been remarkable for the peace in Geneva and in the whole world. There was some unrest of course, and there were always the scoffers. When the Infant Jesus had come on that first Christmas Day, there had been scoffers and unrest, too. John sighed. All the days of his life the world had been in convulsion. Three years ago, after a struggle of thirty-five years, Emperor Charles V had abdicated, giving the Netherlands, Spain, and Italy to his son, Phillip II. With Henry II of France, Phillip had planned a march to Geneva to exterminate the Protestants. Geneva had been in an uproar when Henry, struck in the eye by the broken lance of the Count of Montgomery, his own Captain of the Guard, had died eleven days later.

It had been forty-two years since Martin Luther had nailed his Ninety-five Theses to the door of the Wittenberg Church, and the Protestant cause was spreading throughout France with an estimated half million Protestants there, including the powerful Admiral Coligny, the Prince of Condé, and the King of Navarre.

In England, Mary Tudor's bloody reign had ended. With the

248

crowning of her half sister, Elizabeth, at the end of 1558, strength had come to the Reformation, though happily the Catholics were not actively persecuted. Calvin thought of John Knox with a smile. He had tried to teach the unruly Scot statesmanship, but word had recently come from Scotland that he had told Mary of Guise she was God's enemy, and he had attacked Cranmer for his failure to erase all evidences of Catholicism from the Church.

John Calvin remembered the letter he, himself, had written to the leaders in England that he would cross ten seas, if it would help to bring unity to the body of Christians. And he had meant it. For he still longed for a proper union of all Christians. What a power a church united for Christ could be in the world!

Philipp Melanchthon, now sixty-three years old, was giving his last years to this cause. Still more pliable than Martin Luther had been, he worked on a plan for accepting the customs and practices of the Church of Rome along with, and modified by, the truths of the Bible. He persisted in suggesting that the reformers accept the Pope on the condition that he no longer claim to rule by divine right.

The Catholic Counter-Reformation continued, too. The Council of Trent still met, and many external and some internal reforms had been adopted. Nepotism, extravagance, injustice were being abolished. Immorality was suppressed as John was trying to crush it in Geneva. The consecrated Ignatius Loyola, who had died three years before, and his Society of Jesus had accomplished many reforms, bringing strength to the old Church. The writings of the late Cardinals Sadolet and Contarini lent strength to internal reform, but there was need for more internal reform, a return to the authority of the Bible where the doctrines of the Sovereignty of God, the priesthood of every believer, the forgiveness of sins, and salvation by faith through His grace were shown forth in all their life-giving power. Men, learning of them, making them a part of their lives, would know the GREAT SECRET—that when they were doing God's will, His miraculous power flowed through them and they were invincible!

But the worldly-wise will never share this secret. The Son of God, the Mediator, had united himself to his children in such a way that they need never doubt themselves to be sharers both of His life and His riches. He brought with Himself everything required for their salvation. The worldly-wise, so inflated with pride and presumption, will scarcely condescend to the scholars, or to unlearned men of faith, to poor shepherds in the field.

It is wisdom that we learn from these shepherds to come to our Lord Jesus Christ, John thought. For although we may have all the sciences of the world stuffed in our heads, of what use will that be when life fails us? Wise men came from the East on that first Christmas Day to pay homage. But the shepherds had to come first, in order that all presumption might be abolished.

John looked at the faces of the vast crowd assembled before him in St. Peter's. These people, or many of them, had seen the darkness lift. Fanatics reject everything contrary to their thinking, he reflected. Some forget that our Lord was a Hebrew and that Christianity has a great inheritance from the sacred body of Hebrew literature. How can men scoff at the very race God chose as an instrument of his great gift? Shame on such! There were still in Geneva mockers who had never been touched by awareness of their sins. But the Angels of Paradise, Ministers of His Truth, had been sent. The peace which the angels preached carried with it the joy which the first angel foretold: "I announce to you a great joy, that is, the salvation you will find in Jesus Christ."

"Oh that the message of the angels might ever be a burning lamp, to show the way of faith, *that men may know!*" he prayed silently. The Bibles, which were now available to the people, God's special revelation, would one day be in every house. Peter Robert's Bible was read everywhere. A complete English Bible was in the making, too. William Whittingham, consulting with Theodore de Beza, John Knox, Miles Coverdale, and himself, had translated the New Testament, using William Tyndale's 1534 edition, Theodore's Commentary of 1556, and John's Latin text. A group of Jewish scholars, acquainted with the originals, had translated a complete Old Testament. They would soon be published together as a new Geneva Bible, in which the chapters would be divided into verses for easier reading. Of a popular quarto size, it would be sold inexpensively, since an Englishman named John Bodley had contributed a great deal of money to the work.

John's years of struggle in Geneva had taught him many things.

The worldly may triumph, though only for a time, since they can never be happy without fighting God, but the true joy of His children is to serve Him in all fear and humility and to give themselves to His obedience.

A tired man of forty-nine, it was cheering to know that when he died the work would go on, for there was Theodore. In addition, churches all over the world were seeking ministers trained in Geneva. The Reformation had given man the Holy Scriptures, which taught him that he was heir to the promises of God. It had given him a new conception of his dignity—a man who belonged to God was the equal of kings and even popes. Henceforth in Geneva men would walk as Sons of God, heir to His promises.

The hermit's song echoed in John's ears, as if he had heard it only an hour ago. The words burned in his brain, repeating themselves over and over:

> A mighty fortress is our God,
> A bulwark never failing; . . .
>
> By our own strength is nothing won
> We court at once disaster.
> There fights for us the champion
> Whom God has named our Master.
> Would you know his name?
> Jesus Christ, the same. . . .
>
> The body they may kill:
> God's Truth abideth still.
> His Kingdom is forever!

Martin Luther's Battle Hymn. The hermit's. The hymn of all the long line of reformers—the Peter Roberts, the Clement Marots, all who "stood not mute." John Calvin's hymn, too. The words sang through his veins exultantly as joy swelled within him. He could feel the love, the warmth of the people surrounding him. Their faces mirrored it. Human love was almost divine. It wrapped around a man and kept him strong. His friends were waiting for some word on this occasion when his heart was so full he could hardly speak.

Slowly he rose. His knees shook a little. With tears of gratitude filling his eyes he moved to his accustomed place directly behind the communion table, that table which he had refused to desecrate by administering the Lord's Supper to the unrepentant.

His heart continued to swell until he was afraid it would burst, but his voice was firm and joyous as he said: *" 'If God be for us, who can be against us?' "*